Nikki noticed immediately how his wet shirt clung to his flat stomach, his muscled arms...

The second his brown eyes met hers, she felt a jolt, a zinging connection—as though she knew this man. Intimately.

She couldn't move. Her blood ran hot through her veins. Instinctively she knew he was a man of fiery emotions. Everything would be extreme. His temper. His lovemaking...

His hand touched her shoulder. Her skin burned, and a shivery chill swept through her. He seemed as rattled as she felt. He asked, "Who *are* you?"

"Nikki Navarro." She tried to turn away, to be free of this disturbing stranger. He wouldn't let go. He led her to the master bedroom suite and pointed to the painting hanging over the mantel.

Nikki gasped. She might have been the twin of the bride in the portrait.

He demanded again, "Who are you, *really?*"

Dear Reader,

Hi, all. As far back as I can remember, my mother was an avid reader of mystery, and her tastes in books helped shape my own. So I think it is only fitting I now have her reading and enjoying Harlequin's wonderful Intrigue line. Thanks, Mom.

I wish you all a happy, carefree summer, with just a sweet pinch of mystery to keep it interesting. I love hearing from readers. You can reach me at: P.O. Box 3835, Sequim, WA 98382. Please enclose a SASE for response.

Adrianne Lee

Adrianne Lee

The Bride's Secret
Adrianne Lee

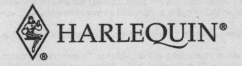

HARLEQUIN®

TORONTO • NEW YORK • LONDON
AMSTERDAM • PARIS • SYDNEY • HAMBURG
STOCKHOLM • ATHENS • TOKYO • MILAN • MADRID
PRAGUE • WARSAW • BUDAPEST • AUCKLAND

To Larry, who is always my hero. To Kim, Karin and Krissa, and to Brandi and Savannah—you are my heart.

THANKS

Fred Yilek, for giving me the Guide '98; Denise Royal; Susan Abraham; and always, Anne Martin, Kelly McKillip, Susan Skaggs and Gayle Webster

ISBN 0-373-22524-5

THE BRIDE'S SECRET

Copyright © 1999 by Adrianne Lee Undsderfer

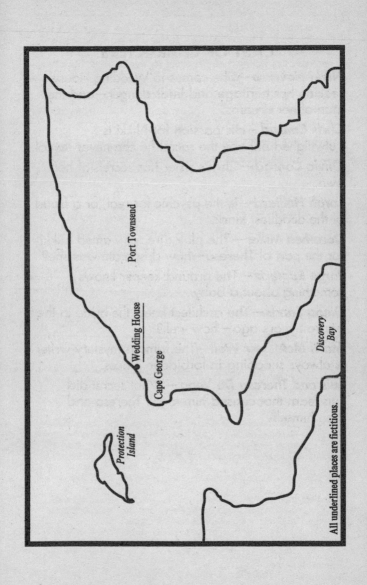

Port Townsend

Wedding House

Cape George

Discovery
Bay

Protection
Island

All underlined places are fictitious.

CAST OF CHARACTERS

Nikki Navarro — She comes to Wedding House seeking her heritage and finds danger — and the man of her dreams.

Chris Conrad — His passion for Nikki is outweighed only by the secret he can never reveal.

Olivia Conrad — Chris's sister has secrets of her own.

Lorah Halliard — Is the psychic for real, or a fraud of the deadliest kind?

Dorothea Miller — The play director wanted Nikki for the part of Theresa — how desperate was she?

Jorge Rameriz — The groundskeeper knows something about a baby.

Diego Sands — The architect knew the bride in the portrait years ago — how well?

Marti McAllister Wolf — The famous mystery writer is always snooping in forbidden places.

Luis and Theresa De Vega — What secret did Luis learn that caused him to kill Theresa and then himself?

Chapter One

It might have been a ransom note, the irregular letters cut from various printed material. But her father had not been kidnapped. Nikki Navarro stared at the note she'd received last month and shivered. "The answers you seek can be found in Wedding House." Hope stirred in her chest, sped her heartbeat.

Hope...and a skittering, inexplicable fear.

She lifted her gaze from the note to the wrought-iron gates. The huge black barricades connected white stucco walls that seemed to heave from Discovery Bay below like mammoth icebergs, stretching the length of the road in both directions, solid barriers that blocked all view of the grounds and the house.

Wedding House—the infamous mansion Luis De Vega had built as a gift for his bride, Theresa. Nikki could not imagine eliciting such love from a man that he'd bestow gifts as lavish as this incredible estate upon her.

Theresa De Vega must have been a special woman. A shiver traced down Nikki's spine. So special Luis had murdered her and two servants then killed himself two years after the wedding. Why? What sin had Theresa committed?

"And what does that tragedy have to do with my father?" Nikki murmured to herself, the words lost in the purr of the idling taxi engine. Her driver stood near the gates, conversing with a man on the other side of the fence. She could see next to nothing of the man. Nor, although her window was ajar, could she make out what was being said. Edgy, restless, she shifted her attention to the sky.

The sun hovered low at the edge of the horizon, tainting the skyline the ochre and purple of a fresh bruise. It would soon be dark. Nikki glanced at her driver again, silently willing him to hurry. Now that she was here, she was anxious to get inside.

From the information she'd managed to garner, she knew Wedding House had sat empty, a groundskeeper the only resident, for the past twenty-five years. But eighteen months ago it had been claimed by Luis's relatives, who were turning it into an exclusive bed and breakfast.

For the rich and famous.

And for the ghoulish minded—anyone wanting to believe the place was haunted by the tragic Theresa.

Nikki fit neither category. Her reasons for coming here were two-fold: business and personal.

The cab driver scrambled back inside and plopped onto the seat. "That groundskeeper is one spooky man...like something out of the Addams family."

"Oh?" Nikki glanced at the gate. The man had disappeared, and the gates were gliding apart. "I didn't see him."

"Consider yourself lucky."

The hair on her nape prickled. Had the groundskeeper sent her the note? The note about her father? Spooky or not, he was one person she intended to speak with during her visit here. She tried catching a glimpse of him as the taxi lurched forward. But he'd vanished as though he'd never existed.

The driveway, made of brick, wound downward through twin rows of enormous maples, their branches twined into a natural overhead arch. Nikki felt as though she were descending into a tunnel. Hating the tension swirling inside her, she forced her gaze to what she could see of the grounds, catching glimpses of wild-looking rose and lilac bushes, and clumps of rhododendrons.

Beautiful, and yet shadows leaped off the tree trunks, eerie and startling as ghosts in a graveyard, giving the impression of evil in the Garden of Eden. She jerked her gaze to the roadway. Ahead light beckoned—glistening blue light.

They emerged onto a flat, open area laid in brick and looking like some tatty red quilt spread on the ground at a picnic for giants. Her breath caught.

The blues and greens and golds of the rolling hillside, sparkling bay and velvet sky, washed and blended by the dying sun, reminded her of a life-size watercolor. And in the center, as startling as a pop-up picture in a child's book—the De Vega mansion, all white stucco, black wrought-iron and crimson roof tiles.

Wedding House.

Nikki hugged herself against an unexpected chill.

The cabby let out a low whistle. ''Man, I heard this place was something else.''

Nikki tore her gaze from the house. In the dimming light she spotted tennis courts, an Olympic-sized pool, a huge dock and boat house, and what appeared to be a private beach.

Again she had the impression of evil lurking just beyond the beauty. She imagined photographing the buildings in the dying light. It would make for an interesting set of photos, but not for use in her latest project. Not unless she wanted to drive people away from the bed and breakfasts she would include in the new coffee table book.

She exited the cab and inhaled deeply. Salt air slammed into her nostrils, refreshing and sobering, but it did nothing to ease the tension that clutched her. Just the opposite. Did this unsettled feeling arise from her personal concerns? Or her overactive imagination?

Or was there something terribly wrong with Wedding House?

She hoisted the straps to the bags containing her precious camera equipment and her laptop over each shoulder, then clutched the handle of her wheeled carry-on and headed toward the portico.

The double front doors swung open and a brunette slightly older than Nikki stood framed in the archway. She might have been Morticia Addams herself, with her pasty complexion and flowing black gown. "At last," the woman gushed. "The *final* guest."

Nikki swallowed hard. It sounded as though "Morticia" were about to close Wedding House for good, instead of launching its grand opening. "I'm Nikki Navarro."

"Yes, of course. I'm Olivia Conrad." A tight chignon held her ebony hair off a face more striking than pretty. Her black eyes flashed, and her smile seemed too bright, too forced.

She began to sweep down the wide step, then froze. She blinked, frowned, her features arrested, startled.

"What?" Nikki's hackles rose and her heart dropped to her toes. "What is it?"

"WHAT THE HELL?" Chris Conrad swore as he wrenched the pipe tighter and another gush of water sprayed him in the eyes. This grand opening was starting out as more of a grand headache. One disaster after another. *Doomed.* For the millionth time the word slammed his mind. Nerves. That was all. Control, Chris. He drew a deep breath, closed his eyes and welcomed the calm that came slowly, predictably. He'd hate to think he'd given up a lucrative contracting business to restore this lovely old structure if it were doomed.

Another shot of water wet his shirtfront. Chris flinched and swore again. He'd turned off the water, why was it still spitting from this joint? He wrenched on the pipe again. The spurting stream slowed to a trickle, dribbling from the shower head, down the long brass tubing into the drain of the old claw-footed tub.

He detested plumbing. But the plumber couldn't come until next week. Neither this bathroom, nor Chris, could wait that long. *Impatient. Short-tempered.* He ground his teeth, hating the traits he shared with Uncle Luis. His *crazy* uncle Luis. All his life he had striven to suppress these traits, but this past year he'd felt his grasp on them slipping, bit by bit, month by month.

No, he wouldn't think of that. This leak was a minor annoyance—as had been most of the restorations to the mansion. Despite the length of time it had sat unoccupied, except for rebuilding the fire-damaged dining room, surprisingly few repairs had been required to bring it up to code.

So, why were these problems cropping up now? It was as though someone or something were sabotaging the house on purpose. As though someone or something didn't want the house lived in again.

The ridiculous thought made him grin. Lord, he was

starting to sound like Lorah Halliard. He shook himself. Next he'd be believing in crystals and karma and ghosts.

The portrait flashed through his mind, dissolving his grin. He swore again and gave the pipe a final twist. The leak stopped. Holding his breath, he reached beneath the sink and turned the water back on, then checked the connection. Drip free. Satisfied, he dried the pipe, shone the length of it with a polish rag, then swabbed out the tub. He stood back to admire his handiwork.

To Chris, houses were like living beings, absorbing the essences of those who inhabited them. This one had a sad, melancholy feel to it. He supposed *that* would be its attraction to the overly rich and bored.

But he wasn't sure he approved of Olivia launching their grand opening with a reenactment of their uncle's murderous rampage. She swore it was her idea, but he suspected she'd let herself be talked into it by that Miller woman, who headed up the local theater group.

Probably drive people away in droves. Not that he cared particularly—except that it would matter to Liv. And that would be the biggest disaster of all. He tucked his polish rag into his tool chest and closed the lid.

If she weren't so fragile, he'd have kiboshed the whole idea—sent the theater troupe scurrying off his property like a herd of unwanted rats.

In fact, if he'd had a choice, this mansion was the last place he'd be calling home. But Liv needed his support. And the truth was, she might be his only hope of holding on to his sanity.

"WHAT *IS* THE MATTER?" Nikki asked, wondering if the woman had lost her sanity.

Olivia Conrad blinked and slapped her hand to her chest. "Oh, my, please forgive my rudeness. It's just that you seem very like...someone."

Someone? Nikki wondered, her pulse lurching a beat faster. Like her father, maybe? Perhaps Olivia Conrad had sent the note. She stifled the urge to ask her. Before this week was out, she would have the answer to that and several other questions. But she had to handle her investigation with cunning and tact. The straightforward approach had already resulted in the note and an inexplicable sense of danger.

"Please, let me help with your luggage," Olivia offered in a solicitous tone. Seeming flustered, she reached for the wheeled carry-on. "Wedding House doesn't have an elevator, I'm afraid, and your room is on the third floor."

"That's okay." Nikki hadn't expected the mansion to be this huge, but she intended to inspect every inch of it, if necessary, before leaving. She relinquished the carry-on bag, then followed Olivia Conrad inside.

The foyer was as massive as one of the rings in a three-ring circus, but there was nothing transient or bohemian about the cool Italian marble floor or the Ming vase perched dead center on a Louis XIV table.

"This way," Olivia said, heading for a sweeping, open-railed staircase set against the back wall. The broad steps curved graciously to the landing above, circled the second floor, then continued to the third.

Moving beside her hostess, Nikki lifted her gaze, taking in the spacious view of both upper stories, feeling as though she were seeing it from some bottomless pit. She shook off the ugly thought.

But as they ascended side by side, she barely listened to Olivia, who chattered on about the decor in a flat monotone that reminded Nikki of a tour guide. Her attention spun across her surroundings, her photographer's eye automatically noting details.

A multifloral runner, in a pattern of alternating shades of forest green and wine-red, hugged the middle of the oak stairs. Its deep nap swallowed every footfall. A delicate, pin-striped wallpaper tracked from floor to ceiling, broken only by wine-red crown molding. Swags of velvet cloth, in the same pattern as the carpet, framed the row of leaded-glass windows at each landing.

The intense hues, obviously chosen for their beauty, left her chilled inside. The green seemed too cool, the wine-red too much the shade of spilled blood. Was the mansion's tragic history coloring her perception of it? Perhaps with the sun spilling through these windows, she'd feel differently.

Right now, however, night pressed their panes and cast the landing in gloomy shadows. The dim, sporadic lighting encouraged her sense of something amiss.

As they circled the second-floor landing, passing six closed doors, Olivia said, "These bedrooms have their own bathrooms. There are only two bedrooms on the third floor, and I'm afraid they share a bathroom."

"That's all right." Nikki adjusted the weighty strap of her laptop bag. "I'm just grateful you could squeeze me in at the last minute."

"To be honest, I'd have given up my own room to have Wedding House included in a coffee table book that is already sold. That kind of free advertising might make us a real success story."

Which was precisely why Olivia Conrad had offered the room free, Nikki mused. But *she* wouldn't be party to taking what amounted to a bribe. Of the twenty bed and breakfasts on her list for reviewing, only ten would make the book. "Like I said, I'm not guaranteeing Wedding House will make the final cut."

"I understand. But I appreciate the opportunity nonetheless."

Doors to the last two rooms before the staircase to the third floor stood open. Olivia pointed to the first. "This is our TV room."

Nikki peeked inside. "Small, but elegant."

"A necessary evil." Olivia led on, gesturing with her free hand toward the second much larger room. "This is our ballroom. At the moment it's being used as a costume-design and dressing room for the play we're putting on later in the week."

"You mean—" a female voice like that of a small girl issued from the ballroom "—if that replacement for Anna Jo arrives."

"Dorothea?" Olivia asked. "What are you doing here so late? It's nearly 10:00 p.m."

"Waiting for that new actress to arrive." Surprisingly, the little-girl voice belonged to a middle-aged woman. She stepped into the hall. She had the lean body of an athlete and wore a form-fitting turquoise jumpsuit that complemented her flame-red hair. Her large brown eyes veered toward Nikki. "Oh, there you are."

Before she could step backward, Nikki found her chin caught in Dorothea's hand. She twisted it to one side, then the other. "Well, you certainly do 'look' the part. Now if you can act, we're back in business. I'm Dorothea Miller. Did you bring your credentials?"

"Oh, no, Dorothea." Twin dots of color leaped onto Olivia's cheeks. "No one sent Ms. Navarro. She's a guest."

Dorothea blinked and stepped back. "Oh. *Mea*

culpa. But, it is a pity. She'd be perfect for the lead. Wouldn't she, Liv?''

"Well, I—"

"I'm sorry, Ms. Miller," Nikki interrupted, sparing Olivia further embarrassment. "I'm a photographer and writer, but I've never aspired to acting."

"Maybe you should. If only for this week. You would be perfect."

Perfect? Nikki wanted to ask why, but Olivia spoke first.

"You're only saying that, Dorothea, because you're desperate. No one else is going to arrive tonight. You'd best call it a day." Olivia gestured for the stairs. "Let me show you to your room, Ms. Navarro. I'm sure you'd like to get settled."

"Yes," Nikki said. "Nice to meet you, Ms. Miller."

Dorothea nodded, but something serious churned behind her shrewd eyes, and Nikki feared she might try again to recruit her into her play—if the wayward actress didn't show up. Nikki felt Dorothea's gaze drilling into her back as she continued up the last few steps and gained the landing above.

On this floor the first door stood open. "This is our library. As you can see, it is extensive and comfortable. Feel free to borrow any book you'd like during your stay."

The double doors of the next room hung open, the entrance barred by a velveteen rope. Gold and turquoise tapestry covered chairs, walls, windows and bed. The massive cherry wood suite of furniture was fit for a king and queen and, Nikki estimated, was straight out of the early 1800s.

Olivia beamed. "This is where the notorious Luis and Theresa slept. In that very bed. On that very mattress.

We're considering only using it for special guests like the president and first lady. If we get lucky enough to have them visit.

"And this is your room." Olivia opened the first of the last three doors. "The bathroom is between this room and the last."

As she pointed to the door it swung open. A man emerged, a workman in blue denim shirt and jeans, carrying a tool chest. His ebony hair was brushed off his high forehead in thick waves. Nikki noticed immediately how sexily his wet shirt cleaved his flat stomach, his muscled arms.

But it was his face that arrested her. All planes and angles, his skin a deep golden tan, his nose bold, his mouth wide in a sensuous way that intrigued her almost as much as his crooked smile. He'd make a great subject.

"It's fixed good as new, Liv." He grinned at Olivia, then turned his attention to Nikki.

The second his warm brown eyes met hers, she felt a jolt, a zinging connection as though she'd stuck her finger in a live socket—as though she knew this man. Intimately. If not in this life, then some other. So acute was the shock she wanted to run. She couldn't move.

Her blood ran hot through her veins at the look in his eyes. Instinctively she knew this was a man of fiery emotions. No halfway measures for him. Everything would be extreme. His control. His temper. His lovemaking.

The realization shook her hard. She hadn't come to Wedding House for a sexual encounter with a plumber. She turned toward her room and heard his tool chest hit the floor with a loud thudding clatter.

His hand landed on her shoulder. Her skin felt burned

beneath his touch, and a shivery chill swept through her. Swallowing hard, she steeled her nerves, reined in her wild emotions and glanced back and up at him.

He was gaping at her, his face pale beneath his tan. He seemed as rattled as she felt. "Wh-who are you?"

"Nikki Navarro." She wrenched free of this disturbing stranger and plunged into her room, hitting the light switch on her way to the bed. She plunked her heavy bags onto the comforter without really looking at the room. The man still stood in her doorway.

She strode toward him and signaled to Olivia to hand her the carry-on. Nikki gave the man an indulgent smile. "This is my room, you'll have to speak with Ms. Conrad about getting one of your own."

Again Nikki signaled to Olivia for her bag. But Olivia made no attempt to comply. She stared at the two of them as though at a loss. Her eyes looked glazed. Nikki wondered if she was on medication of some kind.

"I already have a room of my own," the man said, bracing his hip against her door so she couldn't close him out. "The one at the end of the hall."

Nikki's mouth fell open. She'd be sharing a bathroom with this rude plumber? She felt like laughing, but the way he continued to stare at her sent the urge fleeing. "Why are you gawking at me?"

"Who are you?" he asked again, his tone more demanding.

Her temper shortened. "I told you already. Nikki Navarro!"

"Who are you *really?*" He ground the words between clenched teeth as though she were torturing him.

But he was the one torturing her. *Who are you really?* That question was the bane of her existence. Who was she, *really?* The daughter of Carmella Navarro, deceased. Father, unknown. Maternal and paternal relatives, unknown. She had no more roots than that. A family of one. Unless Wedding House held a clue to her father, she would remain an enigma even to herself. But she could hardly tell these two that. "I don't know what you mean."

"Don't you?" His tone, his look held sarcasm. He motioned toward the hallway. "Come here and I'll show you."

"Oh, I don't think that's a good idea," Olivia protested.

The plumber ignored her. "Come on."

Reluctant, yet curious, Nikki followed him, stepping over the velvet cord into the De Vega bedroom suite, and up to the fireplace. He pointed to an oil painting hanging over the mantel.

Nikki gasped.

Behind her Olivia moaned, murmuring something unintelligible.

Nikki paid her no heed, her gaze riveted on the painting. It was the portrait of a bride, caught for posterity in her wedding finery. Her golden blond hair peeked from beneath a snowy, bejeweled veil, the white lace pristine against a face as rich with natural color and beauty as a summer sunset. The artist had been skillful, for the bride's aquamarine eyes shone with pride, defiance and a touch of some secret sadness.

A loud roaring started in Nikki's ears. Although she would never describe herself as a natural beauty, she could not deny the resemblance between herself and the bride in the portrait. They might be twins.

The plumber demanded again, "Who are you really?"

Nikki's knees wobbled. *Who was she really?* Excitement tangled with confusion inside her, spurring a million questions and one tiny germ of hope that at long last she'd found a clue to her true self. She didn't know how, but it was impossible she and this woman weren't related. "Who is the bride in the portrait?"

But she knew even before the plumber said the name. "Theresa De Vega."

Chapter Two

"Is this your idea of a joke, Liv?" The plumber growled. "Or did Dorothea put you up to hiring her?"

Nikki swallowed her shock over the portrait. She resented his tone and the way he kept poking his index finger at her. She stepped to within a quarter inch of his touch, her hands planted squarely on her hips. "Excuse me, Mr...plumber...no one hired me for anything. I'm a guest at this establishment."

His raven eyebrows arched like devil wings as he spun fully toward her. "Are you saying it's only a weird coincidence that you look like Theresa De Vega's long-lost twin?"

Coincidence? No, she wouldn't say that. But what the relationship *was* needed investigating. "I have never seen a photograph of Theresa De Vega. I certainly didn't know we resembled each other and I can't explain it."

He looked as though he thought she *could* explain but wouldn't. The scowl on his captivating face darkened to something akin to a thundercloud. He shifted again toward Olivia Conrad. "Come on, Liv. What gives?"

Crimson blotches appeared on Olivia's pasty cheeks.

She seemed terrified of something. "I...I have no explanation. I was as surprised as you when I saw her." She glanced at Nikki, looking as though she'd just remembered something vitally important to her. "Good grief, Christopher. I would appreciate it if you would cease embarrassing me and our guest."

Our guest? Nikki started. Her gaze darted to the plumber. She'd shared an intense, unnameable energy with this disturbing man from the first moment their glances met. Was he married to Olivia Conrad? The possibility caught her breath.

"I do apologize." Olivia fluttered, looking as though she feared Nikki would not accept the apology and as though she could throttle the plumber. "In his other life, my rude brother bossed around a rowdy crew of carpenters. Apparently he misses that life."

"Your brother?" Nikki released the air trapped in her lungs as she now saw the slight family resemblance between brother and sister that had eluded her earlier. She supposed she hadn't noticed immediately because Christopher was healthily tanned while Olivia had the sallow skin of someone recovering from a long illness.

"Chris, this is Nikki Navarro." Despite Olivia's continuing distress, her voice held a reprimand. "The writer I told you about? The one who is considering putting Wedding House in her new coffee table book?"

Chris Conrad's arresting features twitched as if he was a man with a rock-solid mind-set, a man who didn't like anyone chipping away at the notions he'd formed. But there was something so tender in the look he now sent his sister, Nikki knew he had a soft side. How she'd love to have a sibling. Siblings.

But she felt nothing sisterly toward Chris Conrad.

He shoved a lock of his wavy ebony hair from his

forehead. His damp shirt clung to his muscled belly, his formidable arms; sexuality wafting from him like a heady fragrance.

Nikki grappled with the effect it kept having on her: the heating of her blood, the sweet tingling deep in her belly, the urge to sink into his arms. The compulsion was so powerful it threatened to engulf her. He took a step toward her. She wanted to move back, but she might as well have been standing in ankle-high sand.

His smoldering brown eyes bored into her. "I'm sorry, Ms. Navarro. I didn't mean to..." Words seemed to fail Chris. He appeared more embarrassed than contrite. His neck grew red. Finally he extended his hand. "I'm sorry. Of course we're both glad to have you as our guest."

But neither looked particularly glad, Nikki thought, studying their faces. Chris still had his hand out to her. She eyed it warily. Recalling the sensation of that hand on her shoulder, she wasn't sure she wanted to touch him again. But why should *she* be rude? Hesitantly she offered her own hand. And immediately wished she hadn't.

The contact once again felt electric. Her mouth dried. "You're forgiven, Mr. Conrad."

"It's Chris," Olivia said, seeming a bit more nervous than she'd been earlier. Nikki couldn't decide if the woman was worried about Wedding House's inclusion in her new book, or about what her resemblance to the bride in the portrait might mean. Olivia's smile faltered. "We needn't be formal, need we?"

"Of course not," Nikki said, trying to ease the woman's distress, though she couldn't ease her own. In ten short minutes, everything she'd known about herself had been shattered into a million tiny pieces.

Olivia sighed noisily. "Well then, I'm sure Nikki would like to get settled in her room, now that the bathroom is fixed. It *is* fixed, right, Chris?"

"Right."

"Good. I've got to see that everything is ready for breakfast. Oh, it's served between seven and eight-thirty in the morning, Nikki. In the dining room. Just follow your nose."

Nikki and Chris trailed Olivia into the hallway. As Nikki retrieved her carry-on and turned toward her room, she felt Chris watching her. She glanced over her shoulder, expecting to so discomfit him, that he would quickly look away. Apparently Chris Conrad didn't play those games. He stared at her with bold curiosity. And with a flicker in the depths of his eyes that she would swear was fear.

"Chris?" Olivia beckoned from the top of the stairs. "Are you coming? I really need to speak to you."

"I'll be right there." He gathered his toolbox and moved away, muttering beneath his breath, "I swear this opening is one disaster after another."

Nikki shivered and glanced after him as he descended to the floor below, wondering if he meant *she* was the latest in a string of disasters. Or had her first impression of Wedding House—that it held both beauty and evil— been more on the mark than she knew? Was there malice afoot? Was someone sabotaging the Conrads' grand opening?

"What's the matter this time?" The softly asked question jolted Nikki. She jerked toward the first room along the hallway. The library, if she recalled correctly. A woman of about thirty-five, tall and lean with a shock of white-blond hair the color and texture of a scoop of

French-vanilla ice cream, was eyeing her curiously. "Another tragedy?"

A shiver scurried down Nikki's spine. "Another?"

"Seems like one thing after the other is vexing that sexy man." She started toward Nikki.

"He does seem to have a temper," Nikki said, recalling the trouble Chris Conrad had had apologizing. As the woman neared, Nikki thought she looked familiar, but was unable to say why.

"I'm Marti McAllister Wolf."

Nikki blinked, recognition flashing into her brain. "The mystery writer?"

"In the flesh."

Nikki laughed. *In The Flesh* was the title of Marti's third book, the one that had lifted her from literary obscurity onto the *New York Times* Bestseller List. "I'm a big fan of yours. I've read all ten of your Bambi and Bruno mysteries."

"How wonderful." Marti's intense hazel eyes narrowed on Nikki like twin microscopes. But since Nikki stood in the shadow of her doorway, she doubted Marti had seen her fully yet, not enough to realize she was speaking to a clone of the woman in the portrait. "And does my newly discovered fan have a name?"

Nikki introduced herself. Her name hadn't the same effect on the mystery author as Marti's had had on Nikki. Nikki gripped the handle of her carry-on tighter. "Actually I'm a writer, too, though I guess photojournalist might be more appropriate. My present project is *Bed and Breakfasts of the Northwest*. A coffee table book."

"Really? How interesting. I considered doing a bed and breakfast series once. You know, Bambi and Bruno do the B and B circuit, but I didn't want to cut in on

Mary Dahiem's territory. Besides, my mysteries are considerably darker than Mary's. In fact, for my work-in-progress I'm borrowing some of the elements of the De Vega tragedy."

Nikki stepped into the light.

Marti gasped. Her eyes rounded. "Holy Joe, has anyone ever mentioned that you—"

"Resemble Theresa De Vega?" Nikki finished for her. "I've only just discovered it myself."

Marti shook her head. Her thick vanilla hair bobbed slightly. "You could be her daughter."

"Oh, no. I'm sure I'm not." *But am I?* For the second time in twenty minutes, the riveting thought stole through Nikki's mind like a dank and clammy fog. Carmella's hair had been black, her eyes coffee-brown. All of her life Nikki had thought she'd gotten her blue eyes and blond hair from her father. Now she didn't know what to think.

She wasn't, however, ready to embrace the alien notion of being Theresa's daughter, couldn't countenance such disloyalty to the woman who'd raised her, the only mother she'd ever known. And yet, there had to be some familial connection between herself and the woman in the portrait. Would it lead her to her father?

Maybe. Just maybe. For this actually gave her the first ever solid lead. A place to start. "I have to admit, though, that I am curious about the resemblance. Since you're writing a book on the tragedy, I assume you've done some research on the De Vegas?"

"As much as I could. There is very little known about them, actually."

Nikki's hope wobbled. *Please, God, not another dead end.* "Would you know Theresa's maiden name?"

"Ah, an easy one." Marti grinned. "Aznar."

"Aznar." No, it meant nothing to Nikki. She'd never heard her mother mention anyone named Aznar. But it was the one thing she'd never had. A name. A solid lead. Excitement licked through her. If only she could get on the Internet now. But she hadn't even lifted her computer from its case. She gestured toward her bag. "I hope you won't think me rude, but I need to unpack...."

"No, of course not. I only came up to...to donate a couple of my mysteries to the Conrads' collection." Marti pointed along to the library, stepping back as she spoke, retreating. "I'll see you tomorrow. I suspect you aren't through asking questions about Theresa De Vega."

Before Nikki could respond, Marti spun on her heel and hurried to the stairs. Nikki stared after her for a long moment. Then the silence of the third floor began settling around her, the quiet somehow rife with tension as though the house held its breath.

Shuddering at the creepy sensation, she quickly wheeled the carry-on into her room and shut the door, locking it behind her. She inhaled shakily, her gaze flying over the room as though she expected demons to leap from every corner. But other than the gloomy decor—blues, whites and grays, like the waves of an ocean in turmoil—it seemed a safe, if compact, harbor.

The furniture, as eclectic a grouping of antiques as any other B & B fare, were expensive, well-preserved and well-cared-for pieces. As though each item—an oak headboard, a maple dresser, a walnut rocker, and a pine desk—had been hand-picked, rescued, like puppies from a dog pound. And were just as beloved.

This couldn't be a regular guest room. It must be Olivia's room. After all, her brother had the only other usable bedroom on this floor. Nikki sighed and shook her head. The woman was so desperate to have Wedding House in the new coffee table book, she had given up her own room.

Not that that would ensure it would get in.

Nikki searched the walls, noting with a mixture of disappointment and frustration that there was no phone outlet in the room. She'd have to wait until tomorrow to go on-line—providing there was an outlet she could use somewhere in the mansion. She lifted the carry-on onto the bed and began unpacking.

As she hung the last of her clothing in the closet, she heard water running in the bathroom. Chris? Visions of him flooded her mind, and she found her knees going weak. She sank onto the bed and drew a deep breath. What was this overwhelming attraction she felt toward the man? The very thought of him set her heart pounding, her pulse racing like a teenager with a crush. She was too practical and too old for such foolishness.

And yet she'd never reacted to any man like she'd reacted to Chris Conrad the first second she'd laid eyes on him. Her whole body, her whole mind, seemed to know him instantly. Intimately. She shook her head, trying to make sense of it. She couldn't blame it on her shock over the portrait, because she'd met Chris *before* she'd seen it. Then what was this unbalancing ache to be with a man she'd known less than two hours?

Nikki rose from the bed and placed the bag containing her computer and disks on the desk. Whatever it was, she didn't have room for it in her life. Didn't have room for a man in her life. Any man. Except her father. An old bitterness reared inside her.

All of her life she'd known her father had abandoned her mother and her before she was born. From the time she'd been old enough to understand what that meant she'd felt as though part of her were missing, something vital to her very identity. Over the years it had produced a cold spot in the center of her heart.

But every time she brought up the subject of her father, her mother reprimanded her. Carmella refused to tell her one thing about him, even his name. This had led Nikki to ask if he were in jail. Carmella's face had blanched at the suggestion—as though it might be true—and she'd insisted Nikki forget him.

But Nikki couldn't.

The more stubborn her mother grew, the more curious Nikki became. The more determined. She learned genealogy, made contacts on the Internet with others seeking parents, with organizations that specialized in finding lost relatives, even searched newspaper morgues.

Then she'd met Gary. And eventually they'd gotten engaged. He wanted her to forget finding her father. He claimed she was preoccupied with it. Obsessed, even. Giving more time to a man she'd never met than she gave to him. The suggestion still riled her.

Nikki pulled the laptop from the bag and set it on the desk. She wasn't obsessed. It was just that chasing leads took time. If Gary had really loved her, he'd have understood that. Wouldn't he? Instead, he'd sought solace in the arms of her roommate. Her best friend, Linda. They'd eloped.

She squelched the aging hurt. Her need to find her father had doubled then. Her need to know why she wasn't lovable. Was it something she'd inherited from him—a man so awful her mother wouldn't even speak his name?

But even this argument hadn't convinced Carmella to

tell her one thing about him. If anything, the question had frightened her. Why? The cold spot in Nikki's heart ached like a sore that wouldn't heal.

She placed the hard plastic case containing her disks to one side, zipped the bag and set it on the floor. Carmella was dead now. She could no longer object to Nikki finding her father. And he, Nikki thought, was the only man she could deal with at the moment. Maybe forever.

The running water shut off, startling her out of her dark musings. She spun toward the wall that divided her room from the bathroom. It might as well not have been there for the clear vision of Chris that filled her mind's eye. She pictured him at the sink. With his shirt off. Washing. Shaving. Yearning feathered through her.

She shook herself. This was insane. She would not act on these feelings. Would not encourage any kind of physical relationship between herself and Chris Conrad.

But sleep would be impossible if she couldn't get her mind off this attraction and the million unanswered questions about her connection to Theresa De Vega. Even though it meant braving the eerie hallway, maybe she should find a book to occupy her overactive imagination. She remembered the two mysteries Marti had just donated to the mansion library. She'd quickly snatch one up and hurry back to her room.

As she opened her door and stepped out, Chris emerged from the bathroom. His unbuttoned shirt gaped over his faded jeans. Ebony hair sparsely sprinkled his broad chest, his flat belly. Nikki's mouth watered. She hadn't meant to look, hadn't meant to notice, hadn't been able to stop herself.

She pointed toward the library. "I'm just going to get something...to read."

"Sure. To read." His voice was husky, and he seemed unable to pull his gaze from her mouth. Her body tingled with unbidden sensations that were so tempting, so intense that in that moment, she'd gladly have given the advance money from the new book to act on them. Instead, she forced herself to turn away, slowly moving one leaden foot then the other toward the library. The trek seemed to take an hour. All the while she felt his gaze on her. But she dared not look around for fear of getting swept up in a sea of emotions she didn't fully understand and would not encourage.

Once in the library she sank into the nearest chair and stared at the floor-to-ceiling shelves of books without registering so much as one title. Chris's door closing was like the snap of a hypnotist's fingers, releasing her from his spell.

Cursing herself and the power he seemed to wield over her senses, she rose from the chair and crossed to the bookshelves. Books were categorized by author. She found the *W*s and scanned the row. "Wochek, Woden, Woods. Nothing by Marti MacAllister Wolf. Hmm. Maybe Marti had misfiled the books. She started at the beginning of the *W*s. Nothing. She glanced at the tables beside the reading chairs. Not there either. Nikki frowned. Had someone visited the library while she unpacked and taken the two books Marti had just donated?

Or had Marti lied to her about the books? She thought for a second, recalling the way the woman had stumbled over the reason she'd been in the library, and decided Marti *had* been lying. But why? What had the mystery author really been doing in this room?

Puzzling that, she hurried back to her room, spent a few brief moments in the bathroom, then crawled into bed. The mattress was firm, the pillow soft, and her mind faded from too much new information. She snuggled into the covers, imagined Chris nuzzled into his own pillow just down the hall and fell asleep in seconds.

But she didn't sleep well.

Her dreams began with portraits of brides and one elusive groom, who looked exactly like Chris Conrad. Too soon the groom changed into an older man with blond hair and blue eyes, whose features she couldn't quite see. She spent the night chasing the man down one dark corridor after another, trying to catch a glimpse of his face.

She awoke exhausted. Needing coffee. Unfortunately they offered no such accommodation in her room. She'd have to make an appearance at breakfast.

The bathroom showed signs that Chris had already showered: a towel tossed carelessly into the laundry chute, droplets of water in the tub. She could smell the warm, soapy scent of him on the steamy air. But she didn't want to think about him. She locked the door, hung her robe on the hook, stepped into the tub and pulled the shower curtain around her. As the warm water beat down on her she could fill her mind with nothing except Chris Conrad standing beneath the same spigot a short while earlier.

Curse the man. He was a distraction. She had to keep her attention on business. Not on him. She lathered her hair and rubbed her scalp hard, as though she could massage him from her thoughts. Nothing worked.

Finally she gave up in self-disgust. She slid back the curtain. The fan whirred overhead but had little effect on the steam lingering like an unwelcome mist. Nikki dried herself, donned her robe, then wrapped the towel, turban style, around her hair. As she lifted her head to gaze into the mirror, she froze.

Someone had left a message on the steamed-over glass. A warning. "Leave Wedding House or die."

Chapter Three

Nikki's heart leaped with surprise. With terror. She scooted back. Bumped the wall. Her gaze flew to every corner of the oversize bathroom. She was alone. The door was still locked. Then how...?

She forced down several deep breaths. She had to think. Had to reason this out. Calmer, she stared at the handwritten message. She couldn't tell whether a man or a woman had printed it. But only she and Chris shared this bathroom. Had Chris written this—after his own bath—knowing when she showered the steam would make the lettering visible again?

It was the most likely scenario. But why? He hadn't struck her as a man who'd deliberately scare women—and certainly not in such a cowardly way. She'd have thought he'd come right out and tell her to leave, if that was how he felt.

If not Chris, then who? Olivia? Marti? Dorothea? She didn't know. Couldn't guess. She dried her hair, anger blowing away her initial fright. Little might be known about the De Vegas, but there had to be something to hide, or someone wouldn't be trying to frighten her off.

Deciding to use a bit of shock therapy herself, she donned a weddinglike, lacy white summer dress, fixed her hair about her face as much like the woman in the portrait as possible, then started down to breakfast. Maybe her appearance would startle someone enough to tip their hand.

Sunlight stole in through the windows at the second-level landing, dappling the dark carpet with splotches of light. But even the golden rays couldn't warm the chill from the house, nor erase the tension poking between her shoulder blades.

Nikki hurried down to the second floor. Voices inside the ballroom slowed her steps. A man and a woman. She craned to hear, caught the unmistakable tones of Chris Conrad, and her feet ground to a halt. The hysterical note of the woman belonged to Olivia. Nikki would recognize it anywhere.

She glanced up and down the hall. Deserted. She retreated a step toward the open doorway and brazenly eavesdropped, hearing Olivia say, "But what if she is?"

Chris sighed. "She's not…but if she is, I promise, I'll take care of any problems. Now, don't worry."

Ice glazed Nikki's heart. Were they speaking about her? Did Chris's promise to take care of any problems mean he'd actually do something underhanded to her? *Had* he scrawled the threat on the bathroom mirror after all? The cold spot inside her began to spread. Footsteps. They were coming toward her.

With her heart leaping to her throat, she ducked into the TV room and hid behind the door. The buzz of their voices reached her as they strode the length of the hall and descended. Shaken, Nikki emerged from her hiding place and sank onto one of the chairs facing the television. The black screen reflected her image. The woman staring back at her looked as pale as her dress, her eyes too wide, her expression too distressed.

The fact revived her anger. They were wrong if they thought they could chase her away. She wasn't leaving until she knew what her connection was to Theresa. She took a full five minutes to calm down, to regain her composure, then she hurried to the stairs and started down.

Fresh roses adorned the entryway table, the scent sweet and rich, but not strong enough to eclipse the alluring aromas of hot coffee and warm cinnamon rolls wafting to her from beyond the large parlor.

"Ah, good morning, Ms. Navarro." Dorothea Miller strode through the front door, as spry as Nikki recalled from last night. She wore another jumpsuit, this one hot pink, as much in contrast with her flame-red hair as her little-girl voice was with her shrewd brown eyes. She studied Nikki's appearance with raised eyebrows, then nodded toward the dining room. "Good, I'm in time for breakfast. Smells delicious, doesn't it?"

"Yes," Nikki answered with false enthusiasm. Food wasn't her objective at the moment. And no matter how friendly this woman seemed, she worked in theater, around actors, was probably an actor herself. She could be playing a carefully staged role.

"Olivia's cook is a gem," Dorothea gushed. "Dining room's this way." She pointed in the direction Nikki had been intending to go.

Across the parlor Nikki spotted a pair of French doors. Through the glass she saw three people seated at an oblong, claw-footed oak table. None of them was Chris Conrad. A tangle of disappointment and relief swept through Nikki. She wasn't sure which she dreaded more, seeing the man or not seeing him.

Muted conversation grew loud as Dorothea thrust open the doors. All heads turned toward them. Alert for reaction, Nikki could have sworn Olivia sucked in a sharp breath. Or was it one of the others? She couldn't be certain.

She didn't recognize either of the people seated beside Olivia. But both were obviously acquainted with Theresa De Vega and had been told of her resemblance to the ill-fated bride. She'd planned on having the upper hand. But under their collective curiosity, she felt self-conscious, as if she'd committed some faux pas.

Apparently Dorothea had already met these guests, for she wished all a cheery good-morning, then headed straight for the sideboard hugging the wall behind Olivia. Silver servers were spread across its surface, and Dorothea began lifting lids and filling a plate.

Olivia, again dressed in solid black with her ebony hair swept into a tight chignon, introduced Nikki, gesturing first to the man on her right. "This is Diego Sands. The architect?"

She said the last questioningly, as though Nikki might have heard of him. She hadn't. Nor did she like the way he studied her. Nearing fifty, Diego had jet-black hair, graying at the temples. His face was more interesting than handsome, his nose large, his black eyes intense yet warm. He seemed someone who would conquer whatever he set his sights on, and that he'd do it without his target knowing what had hit them.

Right now *she* felt targeted.

"And this—" Olivia swept her hand toward the woman "—is Lorah Halliard. The psychic."

Nikki flinched. She'd been wrong. She did recognize this woman. She had not only heard of Lorah Halliard, she had seen her once or twice on a local Seattle TV show.

Lorah, swathed in loden silk, her dramatic brown

eyebrows drawn downward toward her small nose, stared at Nikki with narrowed, eerie eyes of such a pale green as to be almost translucent. Her makeup seemed applied with an artist's brush, in fine, deliberate strokes. Nothing by mistake. She had to be close to sixty, but could pass easily for forty.

Lorah specialized in helping people locate family members who'd mysteriously disappeared. For the first time in hours, Nikki's hope stirred. If she could speak to Ms. Halliard alone, maybe the woman could answer some of her questions about her father. About her mother.

Nikki acknowledged the introductions, then helped herself to coffee and a small amount of scrambled eggs and bacon. She sat next to Diego, across from Lorah and Dorothea. Diego hadn't stopped watching her since she'd walked into the room, and she felt less like a bug under inspection beside him than she would have sitting across from him.

Oddly, Olivia, reed thin, was rapidly devouring a meal fit for a man twice her size. Between bites she said, "I hope you slept well, Nikki."

"The ghost didn't disturb you, did she?" Lorah asked before Nikki could swallow her own mouthful of egg and respond to Olivia.

Nikki choked over her food. "Ghost?"

"Yes." Diego sighed. "Before you and Ms. Miller arrived, Ms. Halliard was telling us she believes Theresa De Vega's spirit haunts Wedding House."

Nikki eyed the psychic. Maybe she wouldn't help her after all, once she learned they held opposing tenets. "I don't believe in ghosts."

"Ah, another skeptic." Lorah gave a dismissive wave of her hand. The charm bracelet on her left wrist tinkled loudly, reminding Nikki of a belled cat. "But I didn't say I 'believe' she haunts this house, I said she *does*. I've seen her."

"Phooey." Diego dropped his napkin onto his plate. "You probably just saw Ms. Navarro, here."

"I assure you, Mr. Sands, the specter I saw was not Ms. Navarro."

"Specter, smecter." Diego shoved his chair back and stood. "Excuse me, ladies, I want to explore this wondrous estate, and I don't expect to encounter any phantoms."

"You don't have to believe me, Mr. Sands." Lorah also excused herself and stood, placing her napkin beside her empty plate. She strode to the door with Diego. "But ignore my warnings at your own risk."

Warnings? Nikki blanched. What warnings?

As the door shut, Dorothea leaned toward Olivia. "I've had the best idea, Liv. We could use this ghost angle to enhance the opening festivities." Dorothea stuffed the last wedge of a sticky cinnamon roll into her mouth. "Maybe get Madame Halliard to hold a séance."

"Oh, no, Dorothea. Chris wouldn't stand for it." Olivia glanced nervously at Nikki, as though she'd rather this conversation were kept private, as though she'd have leaped at the séance idea if Nikki hadn't been privy to it and would know it was nothing more than a publicity stunt.

Nikki concentrated on her food, pretending to ignore the two women. The general public was attracted to the notion of bed and breakfasts being haunted. It could well be a draw to a place like Wedding House. But Nikki had a feeling that Olivia didn't believe in ghosts any more than she did. That Olivia *knew* Theresa didn't haunt this mansion.

Dorothea insisted, "If we set it up before he finds out about it, then his objections would be moot."

"Please, Dorothea." Olivia gave her a stern look. "We have more important things to settle today. Perhaps we'd better talk in the ballroom."

Dorothea frowned, her brightness dimming with the soft reprimand. "Of course. I'm ready, if you are. I'll take some coffee with me, though. Need my java today."

The two women excused themselves and moments later were gone. Through the glass of the French doors, Nikki saw their heads lean together, as if they were discussing something in earnest. She recalled Lorah Halliard's mention of "warnings" and wondered if impending disaster were being orchestrated even as she watched—by these two diametrically different women, one as colorful as a carnival, the other as dark as the shadows in her own gardens.

The door beside the sideboard swung open, and a young woman came through with a tray. She began gathering the used dishes. Nikki helped herself to a second cup of coffee, then studied the girl. A teenager, she realized on closer observation. "Good morning."

"'Morning. We keep the coffee fresh all day, if you want refills. All we ask is that you return the cups to the sideboard when you're done."

"I'll keep that in mind." Nikki sipped her coffee and watched the girl work. "Do you know anything about Wedding House?"

"Some. I've lived in Port Townsend all my life." The girl lifted her head. "What do you want to know?"

She'd been studying this room and, unlike the rest of

the house, there was something inauthentic about it—as though it had been recreated, instead of restored. "Would you know if this is the section of the house that was damaged in the fire?"

"The fire 'mad Luis' started, you mean?"

"Yes."

"Couldn't say. I only started working here this week. It's a summer job, you know."

"I see. I just thought there might have been rumors over the years, something that indicated—"

"Isn't that information in the brochure Ms. Conrad puts out?"

Nikki smiled. "I hadn't thought of that. It probably is. I'll have to look."

"Should be some on that table in the entrance. If it's not mentioned there, you could always ask Mr. Conrad. He did the restoration work on the mansion. He's in the kitchen right now."

In the kitchen. Nikki's pulse leaped, evoking the tangle of opposing emotions. Did she want to see him? Yes, she decided, more than she wanted to avoid him. But what if he didn't like her hunting him down in the far reaches of the mansion? She supposed she could say if she was going to include Wedding House in her book she needed to see the kitchen, as well as every other nook and cranny about this place. It was the truth.

She topped off her coffee, then followed the girl through a swinging door, down a short hall and into an old-fashioned farmhouse-size kitchen with lots of work space and modern appliances. The scent of baking bread permeated the air.

Chris Conrad sat on a stool pulled up to a butcher block table, reading a newspaper. Intent on whatever article held his focus, he paid no attention to the girl who carried the dishes to the sink. Or to the woman—presumably the gem of a cook—who was cleaning vegetables at a second sink near the stove.

Intermittent sun shone in through a wall of garden windows that gave a breathtaking view of the cloud-clotted sky and the sparkling bay. Gentle light touched Chris's raven hair, giving it a bluish hue. His expression seemed less fierce than usual in this relaxed state. But Nikki couldn't disregard the conversation she'd overheard. How would he handle her if she was "the problem" he and Olivia had been discussing? Was he capable of violence? She remembered his quick temper and decided she didn't want to find out firsthand. "Good morning, Chris."

He jerked as though she'd slapped him, rustling the paper. His brown eyes settled on her, then opened wider than usual at her look. His jaw dropped. His surprise lasted a whole second, then a cloud shifted across his face, darkening his expression much as the clouds in the sky outside blotted the sun. "Ms. Navarro."

"Oh, I thought we weren't going to be formal. It's Nikki, remember?"

He shifted against the back of the stool and stroked her from head to toe with an assessing gaze, this time like a man aware of his sexuality, aware of the silent attraction bouncing between them. Nikki steeled her nerves against the sensuous onslaught that his glance pulled through her traitorous body. Damn her. Damn him.

He said, "Is something wrong?"

The question startled her. Was he asking about his effect on her? Or fishing to see whether or not she'd seen the message on the mirror? "Why would you assume something was wrong?"

He shrugged. "Our guests don't usually come into the kitchen."

She tipped her head to one side and tried to read him. She found it impossible. Maybe she should just tell him about the message and be done with it. But her nerves felt as raw as the vegetables the cook was peeling. She waved a hand. "I need to see the whole house if I'm going to include it in my book."

"*Are* you going to include it?" He looked disinterested.

Was he? "I won't know that until I've visited all the others on my list. Do you care?"

"Personally, no. But my sister does, and anything that makes Liv happy...well, let's say I won't object."

"I shouldn't think you would."

"Would what?"

"Object to free advertising."

"Wouldn't make me much of a businessman, would it?" Although he said it with conviction, she had the distinct impression being a businessman was not a priority with Chris Conrad. But his sister was another matter. There was no mistaking the determination to make and keep his sibling on an even, happy keel. Nikki couldn't help liking him for that. Or keep from wondering if such a man could harm any woman.

She glanced at the two women in the kitchen with them. "There *is* something I'd like to discuss with you. Alone."

His dark eyebrows slipped into a frown. "Okay."

He suggested the dining room. It was still deserted. She started to ask him about the writing on the bathroom mirror, then lost her nerve. "Chris, this room—it doesn't seem as old as the rest of the house."

"It's not. This room and part of the parlor were destroyed in the fire my...uncle set.'' As he spoke of his uncle, his hands clenched into fists. But as his gaze shifted over the workmanship, his eyes lightened, the tension at his mouth softened, and his fingers uncurled. ''It turned out damned well, considering what had to be done.''

He launched into a description of the necessary shoring up of the frame of the house in this area—speaking as though she understood and shared his interest. She admired the joy he took in his craft, envying the fulfillment he seemed to receive from working with his hands.

Such strong hands.

He spun to her, smiling. The sexy, unconscious grin turned her knees to mush. Conjured images of those hands on her body. Those fingers writing threats on steamy glass. She blurted, ''Did you leave me the warning on the bathroom mirror?''

''What?'' He appeared genuinely surprised.

''Someone wants me out of this house. I wondered if that someone was you.''

The suggestion seemed to hit a nerve. But he didn't deny it. Couldn't? Or wouldn't? She wished she knew. ''Was it you?''

''I don't write on bathroom mirrors,'' he said tightly. He stalked to her, halting a hair's-breadth away. His eyes were as dark as chips of tar. ''If I want someone to leave my house, I ask them politely. If they resist—'' his gaze traveled up and down her, not seductively this time, but as though he were sizing her up ''—and if they're too big to remove bodily, I call the police.''

Nikki blushed. Ire flared through her. ''Well, I didn't imagine the threat. You can see it for yourself.''

''Show me.'' He gestured for the door.

Side by side they ascended to the third floor. She moved fast, anxious to prove to him that she wasn't a liar. Anxious to see his reaction to the message. Anxious to know whether or not she could trust him.

By the time they reached the bathroom, the food in her stomach felt congealed—as heavy as the tension between them. She flung open the door. He walked in first. She hung back, pointing. "There."

He squinted at the mirror.

"You might have to look closely." She started toward him. "It was very clear with the glass steamed."

He shook his head. Nikki's pulse wobbled. She stepped beside him, eyeing the mirror. All she saw was Chris's and her reflections framed like some family photograph, the images clear, undistorted in the gleaming glass. She leaned forward to fog the mirror with her breath. Not a smudge in sight.

She sucked in a gulp of air. "Someone wiped it clean."

He looked skeptical. "Are you sure you didn't imagine it?"

"Positive."

"I mean, you've had a shock, what with your resemblance to Theresa and all," he continued, as though he hadn't heard her. "Maybe your imagination is working overtime."

"I said it was here." She glared at him. "Now it's not. Someone wiped it clean."

She expected another argument. Instead he grew thoughtful. Then conspiratorial. "Someone is trying to sabotage this opening. Maybe even scare Liv. And what better way to distress her than by frightening you, by ensuring Wedding House won't be in your book?"

"You think someone would go to those lengths?"

He shrugged. "If I knew *who* was behind it, I'd have a better idea why they were doing it. And how far they'd go."

She hugged herself.

"Watch your step," he spoke quietly, as though not wanting anyone else to hear. "Cut this visit as short as you can."

"Are you saying I'm in danger?" She felt chilled to the bone at the suggestion.

"I honestly don't know." He reached a hand as if to touch her cheek, then let it fall. "But I wouldn't want anything to happen to you."

For a charged second they stared at each other. Nikki thought he might kiss her. Instead, he brushed past her and hurried out. She stood staring after him. His tenderness and his warning had her reeling. What was going on in Wedding House? Was she in real danger? Could she find out her connection to Theresa before something awful happened?

She had a terrible sense of urgency. She needed to get in touch with her Internet contacts and see what she could find out about Theresa Aznar.

As she exited the bathroom, she spied a flash of purple coming out of the library. Marti beamed at her. "Nikki, just the person I wanted to see."

Marti hurried along the hallway to join her. This time the mystery author carried a purple-covered book, something that looked like a journal.

Nikki nodded toward it. "Taking notes for the work-in-progress?"

"Trying to." Marti pursed her lips. "I was hoping to find something in the library relating to Wedding House."

Nikki frowned, recalling that this woman had lied to

her about what she'd been doing in the library last night. Maybe she was lying still. "Isn't all that information in the brochures?"

"Only what they want you to know," she said cryptically. "I'm after something else."

"Like what?"

"Don't know. Call it intuition. But something about this tragedy is upside down." She arched an eyebrow. "Maybe I'll find a clue in that room down the hall."

"The master bedroom?"

"Yeah. Want to help me look?"

"Sure." Nikki wanted another look at the portrait, too. Wanted to tear that bedroom apart looking for clues about her relationship to Theresa. She'd do her e-mailing immediately afterward.

As they came abreast of the master suite, Marti leaned over the railing and grinned ghoulishly. "Supposedly, Luis De Vega shoved Theresa over this railing at this exact spot."

Nikki shuddered, then scowled. "That's history I could do without knowing."

"Holy Joe, I didn't mean to shake you up." Marti grimaced, lurching away from the railing and hugging her journal. "I'm always forgetting others don't share my love for the morbid. Please, forgive my bad manners."

"No problem."

They stepped over the velvet cord and into the bedroom. Marti turned toward her, her vanilla hair shifting. "Have you heard the rumors of Theresa haunting this house?"

"With my breakfast, and I'm warning you, I don't believe in ghosts."

"Really? Well, I'm keeping an open mind." Marti

laughed as though at herself. "Can't think of a better place to haunt. Wait till you see this bathroom...it's unbelievable." She disappeared through a large door at the end of the room.

Nikki had seen all the bathrooms she cared to for one day. She spun toward the portrait and again her gaze snagged the picture holding her spellbound. She truly could have posed for this painting. What did that mean? She stepped to the hearth, studying the canvas carefully, wondering how to discover the bride's secret.

The sheer curtains at the French doors that led to the balcony spread as if by a sudden breeze. Nikki lurched toward the movement, her pulse sputtering.

A man rushed through the opening and into the room. Fear flashed through her.

He was stooped, yet tall. His leathery flesh and tan work clothes were streaked with dirt as if he'd been rooting in soil. A cloth hat was pulled low on his forehead, half hiding a face that seemed melted, the skin puckered and hideous. His black eyes flared with fright, or...madness.

The groundskeeper? Nikki gasped.

In Spanish he cried, "For the love of God!" His voice, a pained wail, wrapped around her like a coil of barbed wire. He leaped toward her, brandishing a pointed weapon.

Nikki yelped and reared backward, slamming hard against the fireplace. The breath rammed from her lungs.

"Why do you torment me?" the man cried. He clutched one hand to his chest and flailed the air between them with the pointed weapon—a chisel, she realized with horror. He was going to stab her.

"Leave this house, Theresa!" he shrieked. "Or *I* must send you back to hell!"

Chapter Four

Nikki shook her head. "I'm not—"

"Holy Joe!" Marti's book hit the carpeted floor with a muted thud.

The man jerked toward her, then back to Nikki. Confusion and fright stole the madness from his eyes. He stammered, "L-leave me alone."

Clutching the chisel to his chest, he ducked past Nikki and hurried from the room.

"What in the world?" Marti's eyes were rounded, her face overly pink. "Who was that frightful creature?"

Nikki's heart raced. Her knees wobbled. "The groundskeeper, I think."

"Jorge Rameriz?" Marti retrieved her book. "He looked about to stab you with that chisel. Why, for goodness' sake?"

Nikki drew a steadying breath, then laughed nervously. "He seemed to think I was Theresa. He said if I didn't leave here, he'd personally dispatch me to hell."

Instead of being appalled, Marti seemed elated. Her eyes gleamed with excitement. "Ooh, maybe he thought you were the ghost. Perhaps he's had encounters with her.''

"There is no ghost in this house, Marti." Nikki felt her composure returning at the ludicrous idea, at the lack of sympathy from this woman. "If anything, he was reacting to my resemblance to the portrait. He's definitely a sandwich short of a picnic.''

Nikki could almost see the wheels turning in Marti's mystery-conjuring mind, as if she suspected this episode was a vital clue in her investigation of the De Vegas. She said, "Maybe I'll have a little chat with him. He was here, you know, at the time of the murders. And servants are often the best sources of information.''

Nikki recalled her conversation with the kitchen helper. That young woman hadn't been of much assistance. But Jorge Rameriz was a different matter. She'd meant to speak with him since coming here. Of course, she'd envisioned the encounter being an enlightening one, not a frightening one.

She supposed she'd still have to speak with him, but not immediately. "I intend to talk with him, too. But not right now. Let him calm down. Regain some of his sense. Next time I meet that man, I want to look as little like Theresa De Vega as I can manage.''

"Good luck with that, my dear. I'd say you've set yourself an impossible task.''

Nikki prayed that wasn't so. Chris's caution to watch her step, Jorge's threat, the psychic's presages, the message on the mirror—someone was determined to chase her off. Or worse. She shivered. Damn it all. She would not give in to this mass intimidation. She would, however, find out what she could, as quickly as she could, about Theresa. "Speaking of tasks, would you know where I could find a phone outlet? I have to send some e-mail.''

''The TV room.''

NIKKI SPENT the next hour and a half composing, sending and reading incoming e-mail. One of the missives was from her editor, checking on her progress on the book. She lied, stating that she'd already begun compiling information, photographs. She sent out several e-mails with questions about Theresa Aznar.

She actually felt hopeful as she unplugged her laptop. Though she knew not to expect answers with lightning speed. The Internet and e-mail were only as fast as the person at the other end of the communication.

The waiting would drive her mad. She'd be checking anxiously, over the next day. This was the first time she had a name, a solid starting place. Something for her contacts to work with. Perhaps Aznar family members would come out of the woodwork. Someone who knew Theresa. Maybe someone who knew something about her.

Meanwhile she'd better start making good on the promise to her editor. She returned her laptop to her room, changed into jeans and a T-shirt, donned a baseball cap and gathered her camera equipment.

Her first stop: the master suite. She snapped several shots of the painting. Wait until her publisher saw this. Wedding House was a shoo-in for the book, but she wasn't about to mention that to anyone. Not even the Conrads.

She spun away from the portrait and finished the roll of film with photos of the room. No one intruded on her, but she felt as though she was not alone, as though someone watched her. She sneaked several glances at the painting, half expecting to see Theresa's gaze following her, but all she saw in those aquamarine eyes, so like her own, was the same pride, defiance and touch of sadness she'd seen the first time.

She was alone in the room—with her overactive imagination. And yet the odd sensation of being watched stayed with her. Needing to shake off the dark feeling, she headed downstairs.

On the second floor, she encountered Dorothea standing in the doorway of the ballroom, sipping from a coffee cup. Her normal exuberance was missing. She seemed upset, worried. Nikki tensed. "Is something wrong?"

"Only everything. The actress I hired to play Theresa can't be found. Seems she skipped with the airfare Olivia put out for her at my behest."

"That's too bad." Nikki relaxed a modicum.

"I don't suppose you'd save my bacon and fill in? Please."

Nikki shook her head, hating to deflate the hopeful look in the older woman's eyes. "I'm no act—"

"Oh, the role doesn't require acting, only reacting."

"Sorry, I'm much too busy with my own work."

Dorothea sighed and nodded toward the camera dangling from Nikki's neck. "So I see. Would you like a shot of me? Then you can take another after Olivia kills me." She struck a pose, inadvertently splashing some of the liquid from the cup onto the hip of her jumpsuit. Dorothea swore and brushed at it. "Now there's a waste of good Russian vodka."

Nikki couldn't help thinking this woman's high voice made her sound too young to be drinking alcohol, and that she must really be upset, drinking before noon. "Surely, there are other actresses. Seattle has to be a great resource and you wouldn't have the outlay of more airfare.''

"Yes, I know. But the actress we were flying in from California looked like Theresa. Not as much as you, of course.'' She gave her a regretful half smile. ''Authenticity is very important to this play.''

Inexplicably her words chilled Nikki. Dorothea retreated into the ballroom, and Nikki hurried for the stairs. Her mind whirled to the publicity stunt Dorothea had planned a few hours earlier, and she realized the woman wasn't merely presenting an enactment of the De Vega tragedy, she was exploiting it. Why? In order to titillate an audience of prospective guests? Or to ensure Wedding House had no future?

Nikki glanced at the open ballroom door. What was Dorothea getting out of her part in this? A huge salary? Or something less obvious? Perhaps some personal satisfaction that no one suspected? How well did Olivia know this woman? Could *she* be the one sabotaging the mansion? Was she crying "poor me" about the actress and the airfare to throw suspicion from herself?

Or was Nikki on the wrong track altogether?

Frowning, she stepped outside. The clouds had gone and the sun shone like a heat lamp, warming the morning with brilliant rays of golden light. The air tasted briny, yet fresh, and rang with the clamor of a pair of squabbling seagulls. Nikki felt her dark mood lifting with the soft breeze from the bay. She pulled her camera from its case, removed the lens cap and peered through the viewfinder, first at the gulls, then at the pleasure craft knifing through the glittering waters.

She snapped a couple of shots, then pivoted, swinging the lens over the landscaping and redbrick driveway. Two cars were parked there, one a rental, the other licensed locally. Probably belonged to Dorothea. Again, she wondered about the woman. Should she mention her misgivings to Chris? At least mention the séance?

She had no idea where to find him. Had no proof, just suspicions—that might well be unfounded. She forced her attention to the house. Her practiced eye swept from roof to portico, from turret to turret, her inner focus on camera angles. Within moments, she'd plotted how best to visually capture the aura that would most appeal to travelers, and she set about committing the images to film.

"It's interesting, don't you think?"

Nikki swung her camera toward the speaker. Diego Sands. The architect. Her mouth dried. She lowered the camera and forced a smile. "And very beautiful. But I suppose you're talking from a structural angle, while I'm referring to the visual."

"Sadness." Diego Sands's dark eyes bored into her like beacons searching her soul. He lifted his hand as though he might touch her hair.

The thought sent a cold shiver down her spine. She shifted a step away from him.

He dropped his hand and smiled at her. "I've always been sensitive to the pervasive influences of happiness and sadness. Like this house, you seem to have some deep sadness in your heart."

Nikki flinched as though he'd struck her, as though he'd touched that icy spot inside her. But she didn't answer him. The secrets of her heart were none of his business. She raised her camera again and snapped his photo. "You find the house sad, then?"

He laughed, looked away, then back at Nikki. "So, are you related to Theresa Aznar?"

Nikki's throat seemed to close. She straightened and

peered over the camera at him. Was she Theresa's daughter? Or perhaps Theresa was her aunt? Her father's sister? With difficulty she said, "I didn't even know I looked like her until I saw the portrait last night."

"That's not an answer."

"I have no reason to believe so," she lied. She disliked his questioning, suspected it was more than curiosity. But why? He'd called Theresa by her maiden name. Had he known her? Known Luis? Could he answer any of her questions?

"The resemblance suggests a connection." He looked hopeful in a way that echoed something deep inside Nikki. That disturbed her. "Perhaps a blood tie."

"Did you—"

"Yoo-hoo, Mr. Sands." Lorah Halliard was emerging from the gardens.

Diego grimaced, then with a resigned smile, excused himself and trudged toward the psychic as though fearing she might see something dreadful in his future.

"We aren't finished with this conversation, Mr. Sands," Nikki whispered. "Especially if you have information about my relatives."

She forced herself to finish the shots she wanted of the house, then decided to inspect the pool. She hoped to be able to use it during her visit here. In high school, she'd been a champion swimmer, and laps were still her favorite form of exercise. Considering the tension in her muscles, she should use it now.

As though a cloud had crossed the sun, Nikki felt the flesh rising on her neck, that eerie sense of being watched...again. She glanced back at the house. She couldn't see anyone, but the sensation loomed with a life of its own, clinging to her like an itchy robe. She was beginning to hate this mansion. She thought of the secret sadness in Theresa De Vega's eyes. Had she, also, come to hate Wedding House?

The ground leveled suddenly as Nikki approached the six-foot-high white wrought-iron fence surrounding the pool. The water gleamed a brilliant false shade of aqua, reflecting off the glass doors of the cabana.

She scanned the building. It seemed to have a basement or second story below, accessed by the path leading to the beach. The boathouse maybe? She raised her camera and began snapping photos. Through the viewfinder, the cabana had an old-fashioned elegance like something out of a Lana Turner movie. Lana had been her mother's favorite actress.

Or was that a lie? Had Carmella Navarro actually been her mother? Would she discover that everything she knew about the woman who'd raised her was false? The cold spot in her heart was spreading like ice on a winter pond.

A man walked across her vision. Her pulse jumped, and her finger came down automatically on the shutter. Chris Conrad. He seemed to fill the viewfinder, to crawl into her head like an unwanted virus blasting her nervous system, robbing her of logic and resolve, leaving her vulnerable to the mysterious and compelling attraction that seemed to grow between them with each encounter.

She would not respond. Would not let her feelings for him mature into anything more than mutual respect. And, after this morning, she did respect him.

He looked slightly taken aback, slightly amused. "Changed clothes, huh?"

"Yes." But *he* hadn't. He wore faded jeans and a faded blue denim shirt with the sleeves rolled to midforearm—glorious forearms with dense ebony hair emphasizing his tanned skin. Her pulse skipped pleasantly, and she lowered the camera. Their gazes met and held.

Chris felt as though the air had been sucked from his lungs. She was as breathtaking in those jeans and T-shirt as she'd been in that sexy dress earlier. And that hat, hell, it made her look like a kid. Almost. He inhaled raggedly, clutching the metal No Lifeguard On Duty sign he'd been about to hang, until the edge dug into his palm.

He didn't want to notice the way the sun danced off the golden tendrils of hair peeking from her cap, the way it kissed her bronzed skin, warmed her aquamarine eyes. Didn't want to acknowledge his body's reaction to her, the ache to pull her into his arms and ravage her lush mouth.

She gestured toward the cabana. "Did you restore this, too?"

"A coat of paint inside, some new furniture." He glanced at the building. "The outside was a mess, though. In places the stucco was chipped off completely, exposing the chicken wire mesh. Gulls can do a lot of damage."

She nodded toward the sign he held. "Does that mean the pool is available at all hours?"

"I suppose it does. Are you a swimmer?" She had a swimmer's body—long, lean and firm in all the right places.

"Actually, yes. It's my favorite way to unwind and I'm feeling in real need of unwinding."

"Oh? Anything 'new' I should know about?"

She seemed to want to tell him something, then changed her mind. His curiosity was piqued, but from what he'd learned about her thus far, he doubted pushing was the way to get her to open up. He spun on his heel and strode past her. Plucking a screwdriver from his back jeans pocket, he began bolting the sign to the gate.

"Let me help." She lifted one corner of the sign.

He gazed down at her, and something warm and erotic reached into him. His throat seemed to shrink. He pulled his gaze from hers and concentrated on the sign, but their fingers brushed and his blood felt hot in his veins.

His gaze dropped to a spot of patched concrete near his left foot. It reminded him of the rift he'd felt inside himself this past year, a sense that he was splitting in two and nothing could patch him together again. He feared the self he knew, wanted to be, would break off and fall away, leaving him as insane as his uncle.

For some reason this woman made his grip on his emotions slip with breakneck speed.

"There we go." He tightened the last bolt and stepped away from her. The best thing he could do was keep a safe distance between this enticing woman and himself. Starting right now. He'd just retrieve his toolbox and head back to the mansion.

Instead, he heard himself say, "Would you like to take some photos inside the cabana?"

"Yes, actually."

He slid open the glass door, the only window in the large room. Wicker furniture stood grouped for conversation on a tile floor. The fluffy seat cushions bore bright flowers in rainbow colors and smelled new. A liberally stocked wet bar hugged the left corner wall.

"How about a drink?"

"Mineral water, please."

He stepped behind the bar, gathered two plastic disposable glasses and a bottle of mineral water, then turned toward Nikki. Her inviting gaze landed on him, and Chris felt as though he'd been kicked in the gut. He pulled air into his constricted lungs. What was it about her that had him wanting to run like hell for the nearest desert island one minute, and fantasizing about swimming with her in his pool the next?

She'd bewitched him. From the moment they'd met, the first second he'd laid eyes on her, she'd latched on to his heart, his emotions, his thoughts. Why? Why this woman who so resembled the woman who'd driven his uncle insane? What had brought her to Wedding House? Something about her was eerie and irresistible. As though his blood connection to his uncle had drawn her to him. As though they would have met no matter what. Was that possible? Did things like that really happen?

Terror grabbed him—not because the universe could set events in motion, but at the thought that history might repeat itself. That he might be a threat to Nikki. That he might destroy her as Luis had destroyed the bride she resembled.

Cold fear settled at the base of his spine. No. If Nikki had secrets, they could mean nothing to him. Couldn't make him violent. He didn't know this woman as Luis had known Theresa. Didn't love her. Dared not get involved with her.

Damn, he wanted to get away from here. If not for Liv, he'd leave today. This minute.

"How well do you know Jorge?" she asked.

The question rescued him from his dangerous musings. He frowned. "Jorge? My groundskeeper?"

Nikki nodded and reached for her drink. "I had a rather unsettling encounter with him upstairs a while ago."

"Oh?" Chris felt something odd twist inside him as she related the incident. Something deeper than a proprietor taking offense for a guest. Something akin to outrage. How dare Rameriz? How dare anyone threaten one hair on her precious head?

Heat climbed his neck, and his hand fisted so tightly around the plastic glass it popped, slicing into his palm. Icy mineral water oozed through his fingers. Along with blood.

He swore.

"Oh, my. You've cut yourself." Nikki rounded the counter. Snatching up a dish towel, she grasped his hand in hers and wrapped the towel around it.

"It's okay," he protested, trying to pull free, totally embarrassed by the attention. She gripped him harder. She was stronger than she looked. Smelled better than anything he'd been close to in a long while. Her delicate scent filled his nostrils and zinged straight to his heart.

His throat felt too thick, his tongue knotted. *Say something, idiot. Anything.* "Jorge's usually quiet. Keeps to himself. Tends the flowerbeds. Keeps the yard workers operating on schedule."

Why the hell was he defending the groundskeeper? He'd like to ring the man's neck. "I'll speak to him. Make certain he stays away from you."

"Don't be too hard on him. I suppose I startled him—looking like the portrait and all."

Yes, he could understand how that might startle Rameriz. Her resemblance to Theresa *was* startling. Especially to him. But he was impressed with her request for fair treatment of someone who'd attacked her. As he'd feared, Nikki Navarro wasn't just another pretty face. This woman had compassion. And depth. What would he find if he began peeling back the layers? The question filled him with the urge to run again.

His body resisted. A force he could neither name nor ignore brought his uninjured hand to her face, and he cupped her cheek in his palm, her skin silken and warm against his. She didn't pull back, but closed her eyes, sighed. His pulse twanged with a note that was clear and sweet, and he lowered his lips to hers. Gently, as though sipping from a honeyed urn, he tasted her lush mouth, the flavor something he'd waited his whole life to savor.

Her response was so delicate, so giving, a wildfire exploded through his veins. He pulled back, shaken by the intensity threatening to overwhelm him and push him beyond the walls of good judgment. He saw the look of wonder in her eyes, the same amazement and questioning he was feeling. His breath, quick and shallow, seemed to tangle with hers like delicate, unbreakable threads pulling them together for another kiss.

"Chris? Are you here?" Olivia called.

Chris and Nikki lurched apart. He answered, "Yes, Liv."

He tossed the towel into the sink and hurried out to meet his sister.

Nikki slumped against the bar, listening to the Conrads. Olivia said, "I need you in the ballroom. Dorothea must have left a window open when she went home last night."

"What happened?" Chris sounded as though he couldn't care less. "Did her costumes get damp or something?"

"Worse. A bird flew into the room. We can't get it

out or catch it. Dorothea is hysterical. She's sure it will soil the costumes or peck her eyes out.''

He cursed. "I swear, Liv, these incident can't be random.''

Chris's voice grew less distinct and Nikki stepped from the cabana in time to see that the Conrads were halfway to the house. She couldn't believe she'd allowed herself to be swept into a kiss with Chris. She didn't have time for a relationship. Couldn't make room for one in her life. She had the book assignment, and her family to find. Both would occupy every waking minute.

But she couldn't forget the protective glint she'd seen at the back of his warm eyes, the outrage as she'd related the incident with Jorge. Couldn't deny her reaction to his kiss. Her desire that he kiss her again.

God, she didn't need this complication. Didn't want to get to know Chris Conrad any better. Her nerves felt frayed. Maybe a walk on the beach would blunt some of her edginess. As she reached the next terraced level, she peeked into the boathouse.

The inside smelled of oil and creosote and rotting seaweed. Life preservers and an old pair of water skis hung from the walls, ready for use. There were three boat slips, empty, each fitted with slinglike straps which she assumed held boats suspended when the tide was out as it was now. She gazed down into one of the seemingly endless pits and realized a person could break his or her neck if unfortunate enough to fall through one of these openings.

Or were pushed.

The terrifying thought brought her jerking around. But she was alone. No one lurked in the inky shadows waiting to attack her.

Shivering, she hurried out into the warm sun and scurried down to the beach. It was deserted. And suddenly, a walk by herself no longer appealed. She turned back up the path.

Maybe one of her contacts had e-mailed her already. It was early, but she wanted to check.

She scooted past the boathouse, half expecting Jorge to leap out at her. Her pulse boomed in her ears. The warm air did nothing to still the goose bumps rising on her bare arms, nothing to dispel the feeling someone was still watching her. Spying on her. She scanned the grounds, but saw no one. In fact, no one seemed to be outdoors.

Suppressing a shudder and the urge to run, she picked up her pace and climbed the path. She glanced at the house. Her gaze darted from window to window. All she could see was the sun reflecting back at her.

As she neared the pool the hair at her nape prickled. She cast a nervous glimpse through the wrought-iron fence. Deserted. Still, her nerves jarred with every step.

She was breathless when she gained the redbrick drive. She slowed her pace, edging close to the house. Her gaze was riveted to the rhododendron bushes that hid the main gardens beyond the portico.

Would Jorge come scurrying out with his chisel again? Stab her this time?

Fear coiled in Nikki's belly and stopped her cold. What was she doing? This was silly. She was acting like the heroine in some gothic novel. Definitely not like herself. Enough!

How could she allow an unsettling encounter with an old man, whom she could easily best in any physical bout, fill her head with flights of fancy? A self-deprecating smile twitched at her mouth.

She tugged off her cap, tilted her head back and wiped her arm across her brow.

A glint of light flashed from overhead. Something solid flew straight toward her.

Nikki yelped. She stumbled, lurching slightly to her left. Something zipped past her shoulder and stabbed the redbrick at her feet.

A chisel.

Exactly where she'd been standing a millisecond earlier.

Chapter Five

Nikki stood frozen, staring at the chisel as though it were a poisonous snake about to strike. She wanted to run. To duck and hide lest something else fall from the sky. But her feet were cemented in place. Trembling began in her toes and climbed her limbs, rattling through her like a minor earthquake. What if that chisel—now sticking out of the mortar between two bricks—had hit her head?

The horrid thought released her arrested limbs. She forced her gaze to the windows overhead. The chisel had either been dropped from the second or third floor. Her pulse bucked. A window on the third floor stood ajar. The library window.

Was Jorge still there? Furious, she sprinted up the porch steps and inside. As loud as her pulse thumped in her ears, the house oozed quiet—a stillness so alive it brought goose bumps to her flesh.

She rushed for the stairs and scrambled to the second floor. The air here seemed even more charged, as though everything and everyone, except her, had been frozen in some bizarre game of statues. She considered knocking on closed doors—summoning whomever she could to help. But she hadn't time. Didn't want Jorge to get away. She circled the hall at a flat-out run. The TV room was deserted. The doors to the ballroom, closed.

The camera banged against her breastbone as she clambered up the next level. Her chest felt tight at the exertion, at the trepidation of coming face-to-face with that crazy old man.

She hit the third-floor landing breathless and slowed, approaching the library with caution. Her nerves twitched. Her flesh felt clammy. Swallowing hard, she stepped into the doorway. She couldn't believe what she saw. It was empty. The window, shut. "No-o-o."

Her hands fisted, and a silent scream resounded in her head. The window had been ajar only a moment ago.

Where had he gone?

She jerked around, her skin crawling now at the idea of finding him behind her. But he wasn't there. Her gaze winged along the hallway to the master bedroom. Was he there? Or in her room? Chris's room? The bathroom?

Her mouth went so dry she couldn't swallow. She considered heading back downstairs. But what if Jorge had managed to make it to the second floor without her spotting him? What if he was hiding in the ballroom? Or behind the door in the TV room, as she'd done earlier?

The fury and outrage that had gotten her up the stairs collapsed. She could hardly pull a breath into her restricted lungs. She grappled for courage and made a quick decision, opting for the safety of her room. Her locked room. Digging the key from her pocket, she staggered along the hallway, silently willing the other guests to emerge from wherever they seemed to be hiding.

But no one came.

She wanted to run. Ached to run. Screamed to run. But her feet felt weighted in concrete, as stuck as the chisel in the mortar, each step a struggle, each creak of the old house sure to alert Jorge of her approach. She pressed her lips tight, terrified of crying out. She couldn't pull in a speck of oxygen.

As she crept past the corded-off master suite, a chill shimmered across her flesh. Was the groundskeeper hiding in there?

A noise beyond her room jammed like a steel rod down her spine. Her pulse galloped. Someone was in the bathroom. Coming out of the bathroom. Nikki's stomach plummeted to her feet. She rushed to her door, key in hand. With her gaze riveted on the turning knob, she thrust the key at her lock. But she was too clumsy. Too frightened. She couldn't make it go in.

The bathroom door inched open. A scream climbed her throat. She spun her gaze to the lock on her own door and drove the key home.

"Nikki?" Chris stepped out of the bathroom.

She jerked toward him. Her breath flew from her lungs. Her knees buckled. She slumped against the wall.

He rushed to her, catching her gently, saving her from sliding to the floor. "Dear God, what's wrong?"

"Nothing, I—" But she couldn't speak. Couldn't explain.

He lifted her like a groom carrying his bride across the threshold, easily, as though she weighed nothing, and pushed her door open. Even through her shock, she felt safe in his arms. He carried her to the bed and placed her on the coverlet with such care she might be an injured child.

Worry darkened his chocolate eyes as he gripped her

wrist. "You're snow-white and your pulse is racing. What happened? Not Rameriz again?"

"Yes." But it was all she could manage as the full impact of her near miss sank in with sharp teeth. She trembled anew, shaking as if with cold. Chris pulled the coverlet up and wrapped it around her, but she kept shivering. He pulled her into his arms then, and began stroking her hair, whispering to her, the words unintelligible, the tone calming.

When the trembling ceased, he eased her onto her pillow. "I'll be right back."

Chris hurried from the room, returning a second later with a paper cup of water. He helped her into a sitting position, his strong arm reassuring and warm against her shoulder blades, and made her drink. His gentle actions, reassuring touches and solicitous concern salvaged her composure, chased off the last of her fright.

She set the paper cup on the bedside table. "Thank you. I'm okay now."

"Okay enough to tell me what Rameriz did that upset you so badly?"

"Yes." She sat straight against the headboard as she related the incident.

Chris swore, his handsome features twisted into a mask of fury. He seemed angry enough to hit something. Or someone. Presumably Jorge Rameriz. He swore again, then shut his eyes, his thick lashes like ebony brush tips against his tanned cheeks, as he inhaled and exhaled. His tensed facial muscles began easing, and soon his expression showed no sign of rage.

He opened his eyes. The anger remained there, simmering way at the back, almost out of sight, almost hidden, but there. He'd gotten a grip on it, reined it in as though he'd explode otherwise—as though his very life depended on controlling his temper. In a voice without a trace of ire, he said, "Your color's better."

She felt her cheeks heat. "I feel fine now. Thanks to you."

He rose from the bed, seeming embarrassed by her gratitude. She didn't want him to leave. Didn't want to be alone. "Where are you going?"

"To get that chisel, then to talk to Rameriz."

She threw off the coverlet. Stood. Her legs no longer wobbled. "Come on. I'll show you where it is."

"You sure?"

"Yes." She grabbed her cap and stuffed her hair into it. Up close and personal, she didn't want Jorge imagining she was Theresa. "Aside from the past fifteen minutes, I'm usually a brave woman."

His mouth quirked at that, something between a grin and a grimace. Again she had the sense he was controlling whatever he was feeling about the attack on her. "You didn't come to Wedding House to test your bravery."

"For women of the nineties every day can test our bravery."

One of his raven brows arched at that, a look of admiration flitting across his face. A pleasant heat wrapped her heart, but the feel-good sensation lasted mere seconds. She had to quit responding to this man. Her attitude didn't deserve his or anyone else's respect. The only reason she approached life head-on was her upbringing. She'd been taught from an early age to rely on herself, was independent because her mother had made sure Nikki understood she couldn't count on any man to see to her security in this world.

Not the way Olivia could rely on Chris. Lean on him.

Was that why Nikki found him so attractive? Because he was a man who could be relied on? And was her self-reliance what attracted him to her? Did Chris sometimes consider the role of big brother a burden? It wasn't a question she knew him well enough to ask. And in spite of the heat he stirred in her, she had no intention of ever knowing him *that* well.

She followed him from her room, but once in the hall, she caught Chris's arm. He glanced down at her as though she'd touched him somewhere intimate. His flesh seemed to pulse beneath her grip, his eyes blazed into her, warming the rest of her body as well as her heart. "What is it?"

That's what *she* wondered. What was this pull between them that caused her mouth to dry, her pulse to thrum, her body to ache with need? She ran her tongue across her lips and watched his gaze follow as though he were mesmerized by the action. The notion sobered her. She cleared her throat, released her hold on his arm. "Jorge might be hiding in the master suite."

Chris frowned, appeared to shake himself mentally, then nodded. "Okay. Wait by the library for me."

He stepped over the velvet cord.

"I'm coming with you," she insisted, and joined him. But she held back as he searched the bathroom, the closet, under the bed and out on the balcony. Like every other time she'd come into this suite, Nikki found herself drawn to the portrait, pulled as if by some invisible magnetic field to stand near the fireplace and gaze at the woman she so resembled.

That spot inside her, that tiny cold ache she'd had since childhood, reached gelid tendrils through her, stripping the warmth she'd felt only minutes ago. She hugged herself and whispered to the painting, "Who am I to you?"

Not knowing threatened to consume Nikki. Would her contacts have any information for her yet?

Probably too soon.

Her stomach twisted. Patience had long been her motto. She'd had no choice. From the beginning she'd known finding her father would be an odyssey, would take years, and she'd schooled her tolerance with that in mind. But now the prize could be within her grasp, and her patience had flown off like the gulls she'd heard squabbling this morning.

"He's not here," Chris said, scattering her thoughts. She pivoted toward him. He closed and locked the balcony door. His gaze shifted from Nikki to the painting, then back again. Was he also wondering about her relationship to Theresa? Or had he accepted that the resemblance was coincidental? The knot in her stomach tightened.

"What are you thinking?" he asked.

It was exactly what she'd been wondering about him. She pressed her lips together, unwilling to pursue her line of thought. "I was trying to figure out why Jorge said he'd send Theresa 'back to hell.'"

"What do you mean?" Chris tucked his shirt into the back of his jeans, pulling it taut across his flat belly as he stepped over the velvet cord. He spun toward her and offered her his hand. She stared at it a moment too long, becoming self-conscious.

Voices rose from the floors below, soft conversational tones. Nikki tensed. The guests she'd prayed would come to her rescue half an hour ago had appeared—all the statues unfrozen, moving and breathing and chatting, all unaware of the attempt on her life.

Waving his help aside, she joined Chris in the hall. She kept her voice hushed. "Jorge said Theresa belonged in hell. If she were a victim in this tragedy, why would he think she deserved that fate?"

Chris frowned, mulling this over. He leaned his head toward her. His aftershave wafted to her, teased her with images of the kiss they'd shared. *No.* She didn't want to remember. To dream of another kiss.

He spoke softly, with skepticism. "You think Rameriz was implying she was something other than a victim?"

Nikki struggled to force her attention from Chris to the matter at hand. She shrugged, recalling Marti McAllister Wolf's notion that there was more to this tragedy than met the eye. That something was backward or upside down. "Well, he was on the De Vega staff from the time Theresa came to Wedding House as a bride. Maybe he knows something about her, or about that night, that he's never told."

"And maybe trying to save my uncle's victims cost Jorge his sanity as well as half of his face," Chris stated flatly. His expression was bland, but not disinterested. *Controlled* would best describe it, as though he didn't dare tap into what he really felt about the twenty-five-year-old tragedy.

Why? She studied his handsome face, but could find no answer. The bride wasn't the only one with secrets, she realized as they started downstairs.

Olivia and Dorothea were emerging from the ballroom. Chris's sister smiled up at them. Dorothea gave a theatrical shudder. "Ooh, don't they look just like Theresa and Luis?"

The heat drained from Nikki's face, and beside her, she felt Chris stiffen.

Olivia was instantly flustered, her pale cheeks flashing with swaths of color. "Lunchtime. Will you be joining us, Chris?"

"Later. We have something to see to first."

"Oh?" Olivia's eyebrows twitched, her expression displaying a mix of hope and worry. Perhaps she was recalling Chris's rude treatment of Nikki the first night here. Perhaps she feared he'd do or say something that would ensure Wedding House's exclusion from her book.

Nikki would like to tell Olivia not to worry, but letting any of the proprietors know that their bed and breakfast had been selected or rejected for her book before she'd visited all twenty would hardly be fair.

"We'll be in soon," Chris said.

"But—"

Ignoring his sister's protest, he caught Nikki's elbow in his firm, warm grip and guided her away from the two women and toward the next staircase.

Marti came out of her room as they passed. She stepped back, seeming surprised to encounter them, almost as though she'd been caught doing something wrong. She recovered instantly and asked the same question Olivia had about lunch.

Chris gave her the same answer, then hastened Nikki down the stairs and out the front door. Clouds were creeping across the edges of the horizon and the gentle breeze was stronger now, blowing in cool gusts.

Nikki swallowed against the nerves in her throat. "It's this way." She pointed to the edge of the house. "Directly below the library."

They scrambled to the spot. She froze. Her gaze darted across the bricks. Her throat tightened. The chisel was gone. Recalling Chris's first reaction to the missing message on the bathroom mirror, she leaped to defend herself. "It was there. I swear. I didn't imagine it."

Chris glanced at the library window, then at the brick walk. He squatted and smoothed his fingertips over the mortar. He gazed up at Nikki. "I believe you. But even if I doubted your story, there's a hole in the mortar to confirm it."

She exhaled sharply. "I should have realized—"

"Don't apologize." He raised to his full height and caught her gently by both upper arms. His touch was brotherly, concerned, but the look in his eyes was anything but that of a sibling. Mixed with worry and passion, the rage deep within those brown orbs burned slightly higher. "Go on in and have lunch. I'll see what Rameriz has to say and let you know the outcome later."

"No way." She shook her head. "I couldn't eat a thing. I want to hear what Rameriz has to say, too."

"Are you sure?"

She flashed him a hard smile. "Oh, yeah."

They crossed the redbrick driveway and climbed the steps that led between two towering rhododendron bushes. It was like stepping into another world. The manicured gardens spread like a football field between the house and the stucco fences. The air was hushed and dappled and shadowed, and smelled of sweet blossoms and green vegetation.

"Rameriz lives in the gatehouse." Chris pointed toward the right. "It's at the back of the gardens, near the front gates—in those trees."

For all her brave words to Chris about courage, she couldn't still the nerves in her stomach. "The gardens are beautiful. Jorge obviously loves plants."

"Yes. My uncle must have trusted that he would

watch over these grounds, keeping the plants alive, nurturing them as long as he was physically able. He had a provision in his will that Rameriz retain the cottage as his home until death."

Apparently, Nikki thought, gazing at the well-tended plants, it was only human life Jorge didn't seem to respect. "Were he and your uncle close?"

"Not that I know of." Chris rubbed his palms together and peered down at her, his handsome face so earnest, she wished for a moment she did have room in her life for this man. That she could make room. But she couldn't.

He said, "Mother saw to it that Rameriz kept the place up. She hoped Olivia and I would eventually take an interest in the estate and bring it back to life."

Something about the way he said this struck a sour note, as though he regretted his part in the restoration of Wedding House. And yet, he'd done the work beautifully, even described the work to her in words rich with joy. What did he regret?

Again, it was a question she doubted she'd ever ask. "Your mother didn't want to live here herself?"

He laughed, but there was no mirth in the sound. "God, no. To my mother her brother, Luis, was a saint. She wouldn't hear anything against him, not even after he killed three people."

"Then why wouldn't she live here?"

"It was Theresa. Mother blamed her for driving Luis to act as he did."

Nikki grazed a rosebush, and a thorn pricked the back of her hand. She winced, then sucked on the wound. The salty taste of blood in her mouth reminded her that danger and evil lurked among the beauty here, that she must always be on her guard. "And did your mother ever say *why* she blamed Theresa?"

He exhaled noisily. "Only that she was a temptress. I suspect it was pure jealousy—that Mother would have resented any woman Luis married."

"Maybe." Nikki had heard of sibling relationships where a sister so adored her brother, she couldn't bear any woman in his life but herself. Was that why Chris's mother had disliked Theresa? It was one possibility, but was it the only one? "Or maybe there's some reason your mother felt the same way about Theresa as Jorge does."

"I wonder if he'll tell us. There's his place ahead." Chris pointed to the right again. This time she saw it: a stucco cottage nestled beneath a stand of maple trees.

A row of rosebushes stood like a natural fence separating them from the front yard. The cloying scent of the blossoms reminded Nikki of her mother's funeral. Her chest squeezed with sadness. She tried shoving the memory back, but it refused to retreat, as though it were a warning of dangers ahead, as though the American Beauties were a boundary between lucidity and insanity, as if stepping beyond this barrier would be to lose her mind.

Chris seemed to have no such qualms. He charged on. She swallowed her misgivings and trudged after him. Jorge Rameriz might have information that could lead to her finding her father. To finding her family. She had to talk to him.

But would he be rational?

Chris knocked on the door. "Rameriz, you in there?"

Nikki stepped up beside Chris. Her pulse beat too fast, and her palms were damp, but she wasn't sure whether she looked forward to or dreaded this confrontation. She was more glad than she would admit that Chris was with her.

The door swung open. Nikki's heart leaped. The old man she'd seen in the master bedroom suite that morning stood framed in the archway, a dim light at his back. He smelled of sweat and fresh earth and fried bacon. But other than his frightful face, he might be some kindly neighborhood grandfather.

He gazed at Chris, giving her only a cursory glance. "Señor Conrad, come in, come in. I am eating my lunch. You and the miss are hungry?"

"No, Jorge." Chris cleared his throat. "We're here about another matter."

Jorge frowned. "*¿Sí?*"

Chris leaned toward the old man. "Ms. Navarro says you threatened her this morning."

Jorge blinked as though Chris had struck him. "What?" He turned his full gaze on Nikki now, narrowing his dark eyes. "Why you say such things? I never seen you before."

Nikki couldn't believe this. He seemed genuinely not to recognize her.

Chris wasn't about to give up. "Could we see your chisel?"

"My chisel? *Sí*, I have it." He pulled a chisel from his back pocket. The tip was as pointed as it had been when he'd wielded it at her that morning.

"Is this the only chisel you have?"

"*Sí*. I have it many years. I keep it sharp myself."

"Where were you forty minutes ago?"

Jorge shifted his weight from one leg to the other. "Weeding along the back fence." He pointed to the dirt stains on his knees. "I will finish this afternoon."

Nikki sighed. They were getting nowhere. This man

wasn't going to admit to anything. Hoping to shock him into a confession, she whipped off her cap and shook her hair, letting it fall about her face.

The groundskeeper reared back as he might if a spider had suddenly appeared next to him.

"*Dios*. She look like...Theresa." He lifted a gnarled brown finger and pointed at her. "Is she the baby?"

Chapter Six

Is she the baby? Nikki's heart stopped then started with a thump so loud she could hear it. Her breath lodged in her lungs and her head reeled. Was it possible? Had she been here as a baby? Did this deranged old man actually know the answers to all of her questions? Sweet, awful hope reared inside her.

"What baby?" Chris asked, his face scrunched in disbelief.

He'd obviously never heard about a baby in connection with Theresa. That didn't mean anything. His mother might not have told Chris and Olivia about a baby, Nikki supposed, but misgivings snatched at her budding hope.

Jorge's eyes seemed to glaze, and he stumbled back a step into his cottage. He shook his head. "I know of no baby."

Nikki stiffened in shock. "But you just—"

"Why you say these things, *señorita?*" He eyed her suspiciously. "You loco?"

He implored of Chris. "She loco?"

"Listen, Rameriz!" Chris stepped closer. "Tell us about this so-called baby."

"I can't...I don't..." His eyes swam with denial. He

lifted his shaking, weathered finger at Nikki again. *"Sepa. Sepa."*

She knows. She knows.

Chris jerked toward Nikki, confusion stark in his narrowing eyes. "What do you know?"

"Nothing." Nikki shook her head, feeling as befuddled as he looked. The cold spot inside her throbbed like the wound from the rose thorn. She didn't know anything, but it seemed there *was* something to know. Her impatience to get to her computer and check her e-mail galloped out of control.

Jorge slammed the door.

Chris jolted, then glared at the glossy red portal for two whole seconds, obviously stunned. He lifted his hand to bang on it—perhaps bang it down from the fury on his face.

"No." Nikki caught his arm. "Please."

She couldn't get the strange look in Jorge's eyes out of her head. Had he endured tiny strokes? Was he in the early stages of Alzheimer's? Suffering from posttraumatic stress disorder? Her stomach knotted. Would the truth about Theresa Aznar De Vega be forever locked in his elusive memory? "This was a waste of time."

"Not really." Chris rubbed his hands up his forehead and through his hair. "I'd no idea Rameriz could be so irrational."

Chris glanced at the door again, worry spreading through him like a spilled drink. He'd never known Rameriz to be violent. Or to act in such an erratic manner as he'd just witnessed. He could understand the old man thinking Theresa had returned from the dead when he saw Nikki—the resemblance *was* eerie—but attacking her? Putting her life in jeopardy? He couldn't afford to dismiss this as nothing.

Couldn't risk it.

"Come on." Wanting Nikki safe from potential harm, he caught her by the elbow and guided her away from the cottage, past the rosebush fence and into the denser gardens. "I want to get back to the mansion and call the police."

"About Jorge?" Nikki wrenched free of his grip, gawking up at him with a look of shock—as though calling the police weren't the most natural next course of action.

Chris scowled. "Certainly about Jorge."

"But why?"

"Why?" Chris couldn't believe this. "Because he attacked you. Twice."

"But it's my word against his." She lowered her head, her shiny golden hair falling forward, distracting Chris. Despite his worry about Jorge, he recalled the feel of those silken strands in his fingertips, recalled holding her trembling body, recalled the passion and warmth of her mouth. No! He mustn't remember, mustn't act on the yearning she roused in him. She didn't know it, but she should be more afraid of *him* than Rameriz.

She raised her head. Her teeth snagged the corner of her lower lip, drawing his attention to her mouth—her sweet, eager mouth.

His heart skipped a beat. He swore silently and stepped away from her, fighting the desire to pull her against him, to taste her lips again. "That Wolf woman, the mystery writer, was there when he accosted you in the master suite. She'll corroborate your story."

"Yes, but I was alone outside." Her voice rose a

notch. Her aquamarine eyes were earnest and dark, her voice breathy. "Just because he wielded a chisel at me earlier doesn't prove he dropped one from that window. The police will want proof. We have none. Not even the chisel. Plus, I didn't actually *see* him drop it."

Why was she protesting so much? Chris shifted his body back, warding off the ache to drag her into his arms. Just the thought threatened to be his undoing. He shoved his hands into his pockets. "What *did* you see?"

She blew out a noisy breath and hugged herself, as he yearned to hug her, the incident apparently still able to rattle her. "Just the chisel falling toward me...and afterward, an open window."

Itching to move, to put some distance between them, he started forward again, finding the path to the front drive. She fell into step beside him, bumped against him as they walked—the way strolling lovers might. The accidental contact teemed with awareness. And promise. Chris slammed the thought away. He would never be Nikki's lover. If anything, these wayward longings were proof that he was losing control of his emotions.

With difficulty, he forced his mind to Rameriz. "There might be fingerprints on the window latch. The police could check that out."

"Maybe." She sounded uncertain.

Chris glanced down at her, tried reading her expression, but trees and shrubs cast shadows across her eyes, and he could only guess at her thoughts. If he didn't know better, he'd think she was trying to protect the old guy. But that made no sense. So, what the hell was behind her hesitation?

Before he could ask, she said, "Are you sure you want the police here right before your grand opening? I mean, what would the other guests think?"

He hadn't considered that. He shook his head. "Not to mention the gossip it would stir in town. Liv would be horrified."

"Exactly." Oddly, Nikki seemed relieved.

She leaned closer to him, snagging him with her perfume, a fish on the hook—and, Lord, a part of him wanted her to reel him in. He cleared his tightening throat. "But I can't have Rameriz on the loose if he's a threat to others."

"I don't think he's a threat to anyone but me."

"Because you look like Theresa," he grumbled. Her strange behavior had him wondering if her resemblance to the murdered bride was all there was to it. Was Nikki hiding something from him? Had she chosen Wedding House randomly as a candidate for her new book? Or did she have some secret reason to be here? Something to do with the baby Jorge mentioned? "It takes us back to the question of why Rameriz thinks Theresa belongs in hell."

As though she'd heard his thoughts, she said, "What if there was a baby here at the time of the tragedy? It's something we could check out." She gave him a hopeful glance. "Maybe your mother has some information about this?"

The mansion loomed ahead. Chris longed to run to it. "Can't ask her. She's on a cruise in the Bahamas."

Nikki waved the hand holding the cap. "Well, there have to be other ways to check it out. Town or county records. Newspaper reports. If a baby was born here, then—"

"Born here?" Chris rammed to a stop.

"It's just a thought." She shrugged.

Nikki gnawed her lower lip again, diverting his attention to her enticing mouth. With every ounce of will he possessed, he lifted his gaze to hers. "I'm afraid Rameriz's question about the baby was nothing more than the rambling of an old man whose mental faculties are failing."

"He doesn't seem that old to me. Maybe Jorge's distress stems from his not being able to save Theresa from Luis's rampage. I've studied a little about PTSD, post-traumatic stress disorder, and I know that sufferers often endure episodes of reenacting the original incident. Usually the occasions are incited by some new trigger or other. The person's subconscious wants to change the outcome of the initial event. Perhaps my resemblance to Theresa is causing Jorge to experience such episodes."

Chris considered, but quickly shook his head. "Given that theory, wouldn't he do all he could not to harm you?"

She frowned thoughtfully. "He didn't actually attack me in the master suite, just threatened me. What if his guilt at being unable to save Theresa made him hate her over the years? Maybe he wants her where she can't make him feel guilty."

"But why would he think she was in hell?"

"Because he hates her now?"

"I don't know. Sounds weird to me." He struck out ahead of her.

She caught his arm, tugged him around. "Do you have a better guess?"

The heat in her eyes sent a tickle of desire feathering along his nerves. "As a matter of fact I do. You didn't see Rameriz at the window."

"I didn't see anyone," she snapped. "So?"

"You definitely startled Jorge, but that didn't drive him to violence a moment ago. If anything, it drove him into hiding. Seems like he'd duck if he saw you instead of striking out, or dropping a chisel from the third floor.''

Like bleach poured over a rainbow, the color drained from her face. "Are you suggesting someone else dropped the chisel?''

"Yes, but not with the intention of actually harming you.'' He stared at her hand on his arm and his throat grew tight. "But I wouldn't put it past Dorothea Miller.''

"What?'' Nikki gave a sharp laugh.

Her sweet breath fanned across his face, inviting him. God, how he wanted to accept that invitation, to kiss that lush mouth until it was as swollen as a ripe plum. No. He peeled her fingers from his arm. He couldn't allow this...this...whatever this was between them to capsize his shaky equilibrium.

Nikki stepped away from him. "Dorothea didn't know about my encounter with Jorge and his chisel in the master suite.''

Chris blew out a taut breath. "She could have heard about both from Marti Wolf. And then when she saw you coming up from the beach, she took advantage of the situation and dropped the chisel.''

"Where would she have gotten a chisel?''

"From my toolbox. I had it with me when I went to get the bird out of the ballroom.''

"My God, she could have. And she'd have had time to retrieve it while you and I were in my room.'' Nikki made a face. "But why would she do that?''

"Publicity.''

The color rushed back into Nikki's cheeks as pink as the rhododendron blooms behind her. "Publicity?''

"Yes. The police hauling Rameriz off for a mental

examination, perhaps keeping him, the rumors of a second man going insane at Wedding House." Maybe a third man, he thought, feeling his private demons closing in. "The grand opening. Stories in the newspapers. Maybe TV."

"Adopting the premise that all publicity is good?"

"Especially—in the case of Wedding House—if it's bad."

She stiffened as though she'd been struck in the spine with a poker. Fire flared in her eyes. "We need to talk to that woman."

Nikki pivoted and stalked away from him.

"She'll deny it," Chris warned, catching her arm. He brought her around with such force, she lost her footing and fell against him. Her full breasts pressed against his chest and he lost control of his resolve, felt his resistance slipping, was only aware of her and the need that coursed through his blood like a jet stream, heated and vaporous and omnipotent.

A tiny part of him cried out that this was dangerous, that she was dangerous, and yet he could not stop. He had to possess Nikki, if only for a moment, if only here and now.

His mouth came down on hers like a spark to a pile of dried wood, and flames flared to life within him, tiny tongues of burning warmth that licked through his veins, his nerves, his pores, until hunger ignited his loins. Food couldn't sate this craving, only she could. He clasped her backside, clamping her body along the length of his, searing her with his mouth, his touch, his throbbing need for her.

Nikki could no more stop this sensuous onslaught than she could stop the drive to look for her father. She lifted her arms around Chris's neck, returning his kiss, opening her lips, welcoming his probing tongue, urging him on to this breathless pleasure consuming her.

The cold spot in her heart filled with firewater, the chill fled, and delicious warmth spread through her, provoking a feeling of being loved that she'd dreamed of since childhood. How was it possible for this man, this stranger, to give her a sense of family, of belonging, a glimpse into what it would feel like to be whole?

Would loving Chris make her whole? Or would she end up in love, lost and brokenhearted...again? The possibility drained the heat from her, all passion fizzling like so much flat soda pop. She struggled against Chris's chest, breaking off the kiss.

He released her and stepped back, his breath hard and fast. The anger was back in the far reaches of his dark eyes. Nikki's mouth dried. She'd seen a man go ballistic when denied sex, had dealt with his angry frustration, felt lucky to have escaped his wrath. But Chris looked...relieved? As though he'd just missed being killed. As though kissing her was repulsive.

She blinked, hurt, her temper rising. She hadn't initiated this kiss. Or the other one.

"I—" she started, but couldn't find the words. "This—"

"Don't." He stepped back. His chest heaved, his breath shallow now. He jammed his hand through his black hair. For a long moment they stared at each other, neither speaking, the silence as loud as a scream.

Chris glanced away first, then his gaze settled on her anew. But she could see he'd regained control of himself. "I won't call the police on Rameriz, but I will keep an eye on him for now."

Nikki nodded. Part of her prayed Jorge wouldn't prove the only source she'd have regarding Theresa

Aznar De Vega, but if he was, she wanted him accessible.

They started along the path again. She struggled to catch her breath, to ignore the tingling need and the aching hurt wrangling inside her. For the rest of her visit she would avoid this man at all costs. Just do her digging, find what she needed to know about her family, and go on to the next bed and breakfast.

Chris Conrad could give his insulting kisses to someone else.

As they stepped onto the redbrick drive, she said, "You're right about Dorothea denying she attacked me. But if she did toss that chisel out the window, I'll find a way to worm it out of her."

"If I can help you, I will." He looked as though helping her were the last thing he wanted to do, as though he were as determined to avoid her as she was to avoid him. The knowledge should have cheered her. To her horror, it made her heart ache, made her feel more unloved and unlovable than ever.

Chris started up the porch steps. "Just how do you expect to get close enough to Dorothea to make her confess?"

"I'm not sure." What did he care? "Hopefully, an opportunity will present itself."

He held the mansion door open for her. Nikki wanted nothing more than to head straight upstairs, grab her laptop and collect her e-mail. The sooner she had her information on Theresa, the sooner she could find her father, or her family. The sooner Chris Conrad would be out of her life. Forever.

Olivia stepped out of the shadows of the foyer as though she'd been waiting for them. Nikki reared back.

Chris swore. "Jeeze, Liv, you'll give someone heart failure."

Olivia glanced from one to the other, apparently trying to ascertain what had happened between them. Given what *had* transpired between them in the last two minutes, Nikki figured his sister probably didn't like what she saw on either of their faces.

Olivia asked, "Is everything okay?"

"Fine." Nikki assured her.

"Good. Then come along, you two. Lunch is getting cold."

Looking disinclined, Chris scowled. "I thought it was cold cuts."

"Mrs. Grissom made clam chowder and fresh bread just for you, Chris. The least you can do is eat it while it's hot from the kitchen."

He rolled his eyes. However, as though they were small children being herded to lunch, Chris and Nikki accompanied Olivia to the dining room. Even the delicious-smelling bread didn't stir Nikki's appetite. The thing she hungered to devour was her e-mail.

The three guests she'd already met, Diego Sands, Lorah Halliard, and Marti McAllister Wolf, remained seated as Nikki and the Conrads joined them. To her disappointment, Dorothea Miller was not present.

Full bowls of a thick white soup resided at each place setting, and two baskets heaped with steaming bread stood within easy reach of both ends of the table. Despite the mouth-watering aromas, Nikki doubted she could eat a thing.

Chris and Olivia took the chairs at each end of the table, leaving the only other spot to Chris's left. Her resolve to avoid him was not getting off to a great start. She took the seat, which was directly opposite Diego.

"Good afternoon." The architect eyed her with reproach. Nikki wondered about it for a second, then realized she must look a mess in her T-shirt and jeans, her hair needing to be combed. She supposed he preferred women to wear dresses and heels. If so, she was bound to be a continuous disappointment to him. Her clothes ran from functional to comfortable.

She concentrated on her food, but felt Diego's gaze on her. Wishing he'd quit scrutinizing her, Nikki squirmed inside.

She glanced up sharply, her gaze meeting his, as a notion dawned. Was it, perhaps, the puzzle of her he found intriguing? The incidents with Jorge, then Chris, had driven from her mind the questions she wanted to ask this man. She might not need the information hidden in the groundskeeper's memory...not if Diego had known Theresa.

"Did you two get your errand handled?" Marti asked, curiosity gleaming in her hazel eyes.

"Yes." Chris's tone suggested she should change the subject; this one was none of her business. Seeming not to notice or care that he was being rude, he dug into his soup and bread with a renewed fervor.

Olivia's pale cheeks reddened, and Marti gave Nikki an inquisitive half smile that clearly showed she intended to pursue this issue later.

"Something bad happened," Lorah stated.

"What?" Chris, about to take a bite of bread, stopped and gaped at the psychic.

Nikki blushed.

Lorah said, "Mark my words, it is only the beginning."

A knot started twisting in Nikki's belly.

Chris shook his head and grinned lopsidedly. "I really wish you'd stop portending doom and gloom, Lorah. It's tiresome."

He returned his attention to his soup, apparently immune to the bristling egos and injured feelings surrounding him. But the uncomfortable silence that followed his outburst was as thick as the chowder.

"Skeptics beware." Lorah's throaty voice broke through the heavy quiet like a pickax through ice. "All will be revealed in the séance."

Chris's head snapped up, and his narrowed gaze landed hard on his sister. "What séance?"

"Well, er, Christopher." Olivia's face waxed as pale as milk. "I was going to tell you later. Privately. But I, well, I guess my little surprise is out of the bag."

"Is there a problem?" Lorah asked. She was poised to take a nibble of the tiny piece of sourdough bread that she held between her thumb and index finger.

Nikki swallowed a nervous laugh at the absurdity of the psychic's question. A child could have seen they'd pushed Chris's hot button. Lorah knew she had, too, but she seemed intent on stirring his already whirling temper.

"Only if you think you're doing this séance here." Chris's dark eyes flashed.

"Of course I'm doing it here, dear man. Here is where the ghost walks."

"The hell she does!" Chris lurched to his feet, all but knocking the chair over. He slammed down his spoon, staining the crisp, white tablecloth. "I won't have this, Liv."

"Chris, please." Olivia flushed to her roots as she tried signaling to him that he was humiliating not only her, but their guests, as well.

He paid no heed. He slapped his napkin onto the chair and stormed out.

"Holy Joe, that man does have a fire raging in him." Marti observed with a sigh of admiration. She glanced pointedly at Nikki. "The woman who lands him will be in for a life of passionate tangles."

Whoever that unlucky woman was, she could have him, Nikki thought, still smarting from the aftermath of Chris's kiss. Passionate tangles, indeed. He was downright unpredictable—like a volcano struggling not to erupt. The idea startled her. How bad was Chris Conrad's temper?

Just where did he draw the line? Could Chris be as violent as his uncle? Was that the reason he seemed to fight to control his emotions? The thought tightened the knot in her stomach. Made her sick. And sorry for him. But he was not her concern. Would never be her concern.

Olivia apologized to everyone, but most particularly to Lorah Halliard.

"Don't worry, Olivia, dear. I'm not offended by cynics. Your brother isn't the only skeptic I've encountered here." The psychic glanced at Diego, then Nikki. "But in time all will realize they should have listened to me."

Chapter Seven

Nikki left the dining room with her head as full as her stomach and equally as unsettled. She refused to worry about Chris, but he cruised the edges of her thoughts like a mosquito she could hear and not see.

She trudged for the stairs, forcing her mind to the psychic's warning. Truth or fiction? Lorah had been reticent, refusing to explain the dire-sounding portent. She hadn't seemed to care that she'd singlehandedly disrupted lunch. In fact, Nikki suspected she was pleased with Chris's outburst, delighted to have distressed the other diners.

Lorah understood human nature, had an insight into people that few could rival, knew which buttons to push with whom. She wanted all in attendance at her séance and was merely ensuring her audience. Nikki, however, planned to be gone before any table levitating and spiritual contacts took place.

Diego left the dining room as disgusted as Chris, but without the show of temper. Anxious to question him, Nikki nearly followed, then realized Marti would likely tag along. Nikki wanted to speak to Diego alone. So she dawdled over her meal until Marti finally announced she had pages to write.

Nikki gave the mystery writer enough time to reach her room and be safely occupied before making her own excuses and leaving Olivia and Lorah to partake of the delectable-looking strawberry shortcake Mrs. Grissom offered for dessert.

To her disappointment, Diego was not in the parlor or foyer. No one was. She hurried up to the second floor. The whir of a sewing machine came from within the ballroom. Dorothea? She hesitated, then decided she wanted her e-mail more than she wanted a confrontation at the moment. She made it to her room without encountering anyone, collected her laptop and dashed back to the second floor. No e-mail. Disappointment carried her back to her room.

It was a bit early, she told herself, grappling with the alien impatience that seemed to be driving her today. It took a concerted effort to settle down at her desk and start the preliminary work on her book, but she soon became engrossed in describing Wedding House and the portrait, her fingers flying across the keyboard as she processed her initial feelings about this bed and breakfast. She was surprised to discover four hours had passed when she closed the laptop. Surely by now there would be some response to her earlier e-mails.

She went down to the TV room. There was one e-mail. From her editor. Nothing from any of her sources about Theresa Aznar. Nikki blew out a disappointed breath. Damn. She hated the impatience that kept nipping at her. From the beginning she'd known it would take years to find her father. *If she found him.* A search with few leads couldn't be rushed. But now that it might be a matter of days, perhaps hours, until she had the information she'd long sought, she was as jittery as an espresso junkie.

Chris Conrad. This was his fault. His presence undermined her, made her want to cut and run, not stick this out to its natural conclusion. Damn it all. She would not be driven from the only place she'd ever been that promised a clue to her family. She closed her laptop and disconnected from the phone outlet. For the first time in her life, waiting was the hardest thing she'd ever done, but nothing worth having, she reminded herself, came easily. And this was everything she'd ever wanted. Everything she would ever need.

Chris would not drive her from it—not one aspect of it. She wouldn't allow him. She'd keep her distance and survive her visit here with her heart intact.

"I know, Liv, it's a mess." Dorothea's voice issued from the hall. "*Both* actors' agents said I called and canceled. I don't know what's going on. I swear I didn't do any such thing."

"Of course not, but who would have?" Olivia sounded anxious.

"I don't know. It's very odd."

It was strange, Nikki silently agreed. Someone seemed bent on destroying the Conrads' grand opening. She wondered fleetingly whether or not Chris's theory about Dorothea and the chisel was wrong. Whether someone else, someone neither of them suspected, had dropped the tool from the library window. The thought raised goose bumps on her limbs.

"The actors aren't coming, then?" Olivia asked, her voice reedy.

"I managed to straighten it out, and they may make

it after all. But meanwhile Tomas made a commitment and can't be here until next week and Victoria took a commercial and won't be free until then, either.''

"So, it's not a total disaster?"

"Yes and no. We can't hold things up until then. I need someone to fill in for rehearsals, in case they don't get here. If only I could get Nikki and your brother to play the roles of Luis and Theresa...but they're both opposed to the idea.''

Nikki froze. She'd wanted some way to get close to Dorothea, hoped an opportunity would present itself, but acting in her distasteful skit? God, she couldn't believe she was even considering it. But...what if it were the only chance she had? After all, it was probably just a rehearsal or two.

And Chris wouldn't be involved. He'd never agree to stand in for the actor playing Luis. If anything, he was disgusted by his uncle. Nothing and no one could talk him into taking on the role, even for a few rehearsals. Especially opposite Nikki.

And making Dorothea happy would stop her attempts at sensationalistic publicity. Would keep Nikki safe. Nikki had nothing against promotion, but she wanted Wedding House in her new book, a book about reputable bed and breakfasts, not establishments and proprietors who were hungry for notoriety at any price. So, keeping the scandals controlled suited her purposes as well.

With her mind made up, Nikki gathered her laptop and stepped into the hall. Olivia and Dorothea stood on opposite sides of the gaping ballroom doors. Dorothea faced Nikki. Her brown eyes were bloodshot, either, Nikki guessed, from too much vodka, or too many hours at the sewing machine. "I couldn't help overhearing you a moment ago. About the actors being delayed?"

Olivia lurched toward her, looking more pale than normal, seeming as much a ghost as the one Lorah claimed haunted this mansion.

Dorothea squinted at Nikki and sighed. "Yes. It's a disaster."

Olivia knotted her hands together. "I wanted this launch to be something people would talk about for years to come. Dot and I have worked months and months trying to get everything perfect, but secret forces are against us."

Nikki didn't want to, but couldn't help feeling sorry for Olivia Conrad. The last of her doubts scattered. "I'd be willing to fill in for the actor playing Theresa...until she arrives."

"Are you serious?" Olivia's features twitched. "Would you really?"

"Yes. Provided you don't actually expect me to 'act.'"

"Of course not. Why, this is wonderful." Dorothea beamed, perking right up, her little-girl voice as chirpy as a baby bird's. "Now, Liv, if your brother..."

Olivia shook her head. "Oh, no, Chris won't."

"What won't I?"

He stood at the landing above, looking more handsome than ever. He wore a black dress shirt and black jeans. His ebony hair was swept off his forehead. Nikki's heart kicked and her throat dried. He resembled a grand matador, invincible and gloriously sexy, poised to face down a ferocious bull. And he was just the man who could do it. She knew the cruelty of his lips, the devastation of his kiss. Thank God she wouldn't be sucked into his sensuous clutches again.

Olivia gazed up at her brother with pure adoration and swallowed hard. "Nikki just agreed to play Theresa in our skit, until the actress arrives. Dorothea and I hoped you'd fill in for Tomas, the actor who'll be playing Uncle Luis. It's most likely only for a few rehearsals."

Chris's dark eyes landed on Nikki. His brows arched in surprise as if to say, "Have you lost your mind?" She lifted her chin and cast him a defiant smile.

"Will you, Christopher?" Olivia twisted her hands tighter. "For my sake."

Nikki knew she was wasting her time. He would pass. He was as determined as she to keep a distance between them.

He tilted his head and gazed at his sister. The hard expression he'd given Nikki and Dorothea softened. Despite the hurt he'd handed her, despite her ill feelings toward him, Nikki was touched by the love he had for his sister, by the respect and kindness he made readily available to Olivia.

How could a man who loved his sister like this be so insensitive to the feelings of other women?

Or was he? She recalled thinking Chris was controlling his emotions, corralling his feelings like a herd of unruly calves. Occasionally one or another broke free, giving a glimpse of the real man inside the attractive package, but always Chris captured the maverick emotion and roped it in. Why? It was almost as though his own emotions frightened him.

Nikki nearly laughed at the absurdity of her thoughts.

"Okay," Chris said. "I'll do it."

Nikki jerked toward him. Her eyes flared open, and she sucked in a sharp breath. What? What! Fury heated her cheeks and she struggled to keep from shouting at him.

"Thank you, Chris." Olivia hugged herself.

"Oh, this will be excellent." Dorothea chirped anew at Olivia. "We're going to have our success, Liv."

She spun toward Nikki and Chris. "We'll have to have some costume fittings. Just in case. There are two dress rehearsals. How about later tonight?"

Nikki was still choking over Chris's agreeing to play Luis. Somehow she managed to say, "Fine."

"Not me." Chris clambered down the remaining stairs. "I'll be out all night."

He brushed past Nikki, trailing mind-numbing aftershave in his wake as he hastened down the stairs and outside. Nikki excused herself and started up the stairs, carrying her laptop pressed to her thundering heart. From outside she caught the rumble of a powerful sports car engine. Through the library window she watched Chris depart in a Jaguar convertible as sleek as his hair. As black as his heart.

Fuming, Nikki returned to her room. She replaced the laptop on the desk and began shuffling through the papers in her file, thinking to occupy herself again with her book. A bright yellow sheet caught her eye. She pulled it free. The anonymous note.

"The answers you seek can be found in Wedding House."

Her throat tightened. She'd assumed this note was about her father, but now she doubted it had anything to do with him. Who had sent this? What answers had they meant for her to find? Something about Theresa?

She paced the length of the room. Yes. It had to be. Perhaps Diego Sands could solve this mystery. Perhaps he'd sent the note.

She decided it was past time they talked. He wasn't in his room. Or anywhere else in the house. Damn. Maybe she should search the grounds. She stalked to the front door. Then stopped cold. What if she ran into Jorge? Her stomach knotted. She retreated up the stairs. Somehow she'd waylay Diego at dinner and arrange for a private chat.

But it was not to be. Diego had apparently left after lunch to meet friends in town, Olivia informed her at dinner. He wasn't expected back until late. Just like Chris, Nikki thought, frustrated, her anger at Chris finding new life. No, she would not think about that infuriating man, would not wonder where he'd gone looking so determined to forget about her.

But when her mind wasn't on Chris, it was on the anonymous note, on the possible motives each of the diners might have had for wanting her to discover her relationship to Theresa.

By the end of the meal the only conclusion she'd reached was that she couldn't trust any of these people, or anything they said. She was the first to leave the table. She headed straight to the ballroom. Dorothea had gone home, but would be returning any minute for the fittings, and Nikki wanted some time alone to gather herself for the ordeal ahead.

She strolled through the open doorway and into the vast room. Despite the rack of clothes, the Chevalier mirror, the dressing screen, the desk and sewing machine hugging one corner, there was an abandoned feeling here that echoed the one in her heart. As she moved across the bare planking toward the floor-to-ceiling windows, the hollow click of her footsteps emphasized just how alone she was, not only in the world, but here in this mansion. She hadn't one true friend.

But what about enemies?

Nikki pressed her forehead against the cool glass, watching the sinking sun paint the sky in deep yellows, reds and purples. Her gaze skipped to the land mass across the glittering bay, a small private isle of rocks and trees. Protection Island. She had the unsettling sensation that she could use some protection herself. But from what? From whom? From whomever had attacked her with the chisel?

She turned her back to the glass. Was she in serious danger? Or had Dorothea tossed the chisel at her for what amounted to a publicity stunt? It had made such perfect sense when Chris suggested it. But on reflection, the idea seemed far-fetched. Ludicrous even. How could Dorothea have hoped the incident would lead to Jorge being taken away by the police?

But if not Dorothea, if not Jorge, then who? And why? Her blood flowed icy with denial. No, it had to be Dorothea. The publicity-hungry fool had probably stashed the flattened chisel in that desk. Nikki raced across the room, praying this assumption was correct. The alternatives were terrifying. She reached for the middle drawer.

"Oh." Dorothea swept into the ballroom in a blaze of yellow and red that might have been torn from the sunset, her lemon jumpsuit blinding. "There you are. I worried you'd changed your mind."

"No. I'll go through with it." Nikki yanked her hand back, her heart skidding sideways at nearly getting caught snooping. She drew a couple of slow breaths, regrouping, shifting mental gears. If she couldn't find what she wanted by searching this desk, then she'd have to use plan A and gain Dorothea's trust. Make her confess. She forced a smile. "I'm ready, if you are."

She glanced at the mug Dorothea held. It was steaming and appeared to hold coffee. The perky redhead nodded. "Ready and excited."

Striving to sound calm, Nikki said, "You know, I was wondering—"

"Are we late?" Marti strutted through the door, clutching her journal, a pen poked behind one ear. She was followed by Olivia and Lorah.

Nikki sighed to herself. So much for plans A and B. Her hands balled into fists as she bit down this newest frustration.

"We wanted to see, too." Olivia sniffed. "You don't mind, do you, Nikki?"

"No." Yes! Nikki wanted to shout. Instead, she gave Chris's sister a shrug.

Olivia's eyes were overly bright. "Good, good."

"Let's get started, then." Dorothea set her coffee on the desk atop a coaster, then strolled to the clothes rack and began shuffling through the hangers. "Theresa's character has three costume changes, but this is the pièce de résistance."

An "ah" resounded from everyone when she plucked a three-tiered white lace wedding gown from the rack.

"Holy Joe," Marti proclaimed. "Is that the original gown worn by Theresa?"

"The one in the portrait?" Inexplicably, Nikki was repelled by the possibility. She'd have thought she would find the dress appealing. Instead, she stepped away as though it were exuding some noxious odor. A clammy chill swept her flesh. Why had she agreed to standing in for the absent actor? It was insanity. "Is it Theresa's gown?"

"Heavens, no." Olivia twisted her hands. "That was never found."

Lorah grasped a handful of the delicate lace. Her eyes glazed as though she were watching a closed-circuit TV only she could see. "The original was destroyed."

"In the fire?" Marti asked, whipping her pen from her ear and flipping open her journal. She plopped down in Dorothea's desk chair.

"No." Lorah shook her head, her gaze still distant, unfocused. "Someone cut it to shreds. A man."

"Uncle Luis?" Olivia twitched as though her nerves had the hiccups.

"I'm not certain. I see a handsome, swarthy face etched in rage." Lorah waved a hand. "No, sorry, it's gone."

As if she'd witnessed the deranged act of destruction Lorah suggested, Nikki shivered. But a part of her was relieved not to be wearing Theresa's gown. Why?

Marti scrawled on a blank page, then asked Lorah, "Do you have any idea *why* Luis De Vega killed those three people? I mean, it was such a violent act…it seems to me the cause should have been something greater than a fit of jealousy."

Lorah smiled her secret, all-knowing smile, a slight uplifting of the corners of her full mouth. "I should think you of all people would know better than to underestimate the power of envy."

Nikki had supposed Lorah was referring to jealousy as a motive for murder, that Marti, being a mystery writer, would have researched every homicidal inducement known to humankind. But Marti paled, her hand tightening on the pen until her knuckles shone white. The edges of her ears reddened like someone choking down incredible rage.

Apparently the reference was to something personal, and it reminded Nikki that she knew little or nothing about any of these women. That she couldn't trust any of them.

Lorah snagged Dorothea with her perceptive gaze. "Maybe Luis was a secret drinker."

Now Dorothea blushed. She fingered the lip of her coffee cup, making no move to drink, though clearly she wanted to. Instead, she tucked the wedding gown back into its place on the rack and extracted a blue summer dress. She handed it to Nikki, gesturing toward the screen. "Try this one first."

The dress hung off the shoulders, a flounced border accentuating the bustline. Nikki wished the mirror were behind the screen with her, so she could see how she looked in this.

"Show us," Marti coaxed.

Nikki smiled to herself, recalling a favorite shopping trip with her mother, when Carmella had sounded as anxious as Marti about viewing the new purchases.

She stepped from behind the screen, catching a glimpse in the mirror, a vision of a tall blonde in a cloud of blue.

Olivia nodded her approval. "It's very demure. Floaty."

"I think it's sexy." Marti grinned.

"In a subtle way," Lorah concurred. "Very nice."

The psychic's compliment surprised Nikki after the verbal jabs she'd given the others.

Dorothea beamed with obvious pride. "Wait until Chris gets a load of you in this."

Nikki's face flamed. She didn't care what Chris Conrad thought of her in any of these clothes. *Don't you?* a tiny voiced asked. No! she shouted silently.

Dorothea fluttered around her like a butterfly with pins in its mouth. "You're thinner than Victoria, so I'm going to baste this here and here and here." She jabbed pins into the fabric as she spoke, pulling the dress tighter at the waist and the middle of her back. "Then I can let it out easily later."

The procedure was the same with the next outfit: a severe black dress with a high neckline, long sleeves and ankle-length hem. It so resembled what Olivia wore every day, Nikki wondered if it had been borrowed from her wardrobe. She felt decidedly uncomfortable in it, as though the dress were cutting off her oxygen. But from the approving response, she apparently didn't look as ugly in the dress as she felt.

Lastly Nikki donned the wedding gown. As she slid her arms into the lacy sleeves, she was surprised to feel a lump in her throat. She would never wear a gown like this. Would never marry. At least, not anytime soon. And when she did wed, her mother would not be there to witness her happiness. Would her father?

With her chest throbbing, she stepped from behind the screen. A collective gasp rang from the four women.

"Oh, I knew it," Dorothea cried. "You *are* Theresa."

"It's eerie," Olivia whispered on a sucked-in breath.

She stood to one side, her eyes wide, distressed, her hands kneading together.

Marti eyed Nikki up and down. "Are you sure you aren't related to the De Vegas?"

"Blood is thick in this house," Lorah pronounced. "Thicker than anyone suspects."

Nikki barely heard Lorah. She was caught by her own reflection in the cheval glass. She stood frozen, staring at the image, feeling as though she were peering at the portrait, as though it had leaped from the wall in the master suite and zipped into the reflecting glass. Her pulse jerked, and an icy cold spread through her, chilling her to the bone.

She couldn't get out of the dress fast enough. "Are we done? I've got some work to do."

"Well…sure, I guess." Dorothea plucked at the waistline of the gown. "But this fits you like it was made for you. I'm probably going to have to let it out for Victoria."

"I wonder if I left enough room in the seams?" Dorothea muttered as Nikki ducked behind the screen.

Nikki heard Lorah say, "You won't need to take out the seams."

That's what she thinks, Nikki swore to herself. *I'm not carrying this charade a second past proving Dorothea dropped the chisel on me.*

When she came out from behind the screen this time, dressed again in her T-shirt and jeans, only Olivia and Dorothea remained in the room.

Nikki handed the gown to Dorothea, then addressed Olivia. "I spoke with your brother about using the pool for my nightly laps. He said it would be okay."

"Of course, Nikki." Olivia seemed more anxious

than ever to please her, to affirm that they were great friends. "You'll need a key for the house and the pool gate. We keep them locked after 9:00 p.m. I'll leave them in your room."

"Thank you."

Dorothea stopped Nikki as she started toward the exit. "Must you leave so soon? I was hoping to go over the script with you, so you'd have some idea what to expect at the rehearsal in the morning."

Nikki hesitated. Rehearsal in the morning. With Chris. Every muscle in her body ached with the dread of facing him in the role of Theresa. But it might not be necessary, if she could find the flattened chisel. She glanced at the desk, deciding in that moment to return and search it after Dorothea had gone home for the evening.

A tiny pain tapped her temples, threatening a full-blown headache. What if the chisel wasn't there? A shiver climbed her spine. It *had* to be there. "Why don't I just take the script with me?"

NIKKI WAITED until nearly eleven to head downstairs. It was a balmy night, and the swim would ease her tensed muscles. But first she wanted a look inside Dorothea's desk. Wearing her short terry cloth robe, favorite one-piece swimsuit and sandals, she crept down the stairs, making her way as quietly as possible.

The doors to the ballroom were closed. No light shone from within. She glanced up and down the hall, peered over the railing. She seemed to be alone. Smiling to herself, she grasped the doorknob. It refused to turn. She tried the other.

Damn and double damn. It was locked. She groaned

softly, then had an idea. Maybe one of the keys Olivia had given her would work. She dug them from her robe pocket. The first didn't fit the lock. The second fit, but wouldn't engage. She heaved a sigh and stood staring at the doors as though they'd spring open if she wished it hard enough.

The house creaked. Nikki jumped and spun around. Was someone coming? With her pulse thrumming, and grumbling under her breath, she hastened downstairs and slipped outside. Wispy clouds, like strips of shredded nylon, veiled the moon, and crickets chirped louder than she'd ever heard, muffling the slap of her sandals on the redbrick as she hurried down the path to the pool.

She unlocked the gate and inhaled deeply. The night air was rife with brine and chlorine, a swimmer's favorite perfume. *Here, at least,* she thought, *is something familiar. A true and trusted friend.* Draping her robe and towel over the diving board, she sat on the edge of the pool and lowered herself into the heated water. She never dived while swimming alone, wouldn't risk knocking herself unconscious and drowning.

She'd swum half a dozen laps, her muscles beginning to ease up, when she felt it: that awful creeping up her neck like someone was watching her again.

She stopped and clung to the ladder, and glanced around, realizing how isolated she was. How vulnerable. She couldn't see anyone, but there was lots of cover for someone to hide behind. Apprehensive, she decided she'd had enough for the night, and climbed from the pool.

Headlights shone through the trees surrounding the top of the driveway, and she heard a car move as slowly as a cat down the drive. Hopefully whoever was coming would scare off her watcher. She donned her robe and sandals, her wet hair dripping on her shoulders. She locked the gate and started up the path just as the Jaguar convertible pulled onto the parking area and cut her off from the house.

Chris, his hair windswept, his expression unreadable, gazed at her as though he wanted to ask her something. But neither spoke, that undefinable link between them holding each prisoner to its whim. They stared at each other for a long moment.

A flash of light beyond his shoulder jerked her attention. She glanced up and gasped. Chris spun in the car seat to where she pointed. In the open doorway of the mansion stood a bride, a veil hiding her face. She seemed to flutter, as though made of gauze, a giant silken scarf caught on a breeze. Then she disappeared.

Chapter Eight

"What the hell was that?" Chris gaped at the entrance to his home, then back at Nikki. She watched him grab his keys, turn off the car and scramble out of it. The night grew suddenly still, the only sound, his feet hitting the bricks. Even the crickets had ceased chirping. "It looked like a ghost."

"Phooey!" Nikki stormed past him, her wet hair flicking droplets of water as she ran. "It's someone dressed like the bride in the portrait."

"Are you sure?" He caught up to her. "I mean, how...?"

"Yes, I'm sure—and I'll prove it." She reached the front door first, grabbed and twisted the knob, then stepped back, disgruntled. "Locked."

"Locked?"

"Oh, don't sound shocked." She couldn't see his face clearly. Someone had turned out the porch light, and the front stoop was nothing more than shadows. But she could read Chris just fine at the moment. "The ghost didn't walk through a locked door."

"Well, I didn't hear the door close or the latch engage, did you?"

"Couldn't hear anything over that sputtering car of

yours, or the clamor you made shutting it off and banging out of it.''

''Sputtering?'' he sputtered.

''Let's get inside.'' She dug into the pocket of her robe, her hand hitting the two strips of metal. ''I've got a key.''

''So do I.'' His met the lock first. The door sprang inward as though someone had wrenched it open from indoors. Chris blocked the entrance, protectively holding her back, his arm pressing against her breasts. She gasped and jerked back. Her heart slammed her rib cage, but she couldn't have said if it was his touch she feared or an attacker waiting just inside the door.

He glanced down at her, his dark eyes like black ponds in the hazy light. There seemed to be some sort of heat issuing from him, flowing straight from his gaze on a direct route to her belly. In that moment she knew he was more dangerous to her than any ''ghost.''

She twisted to move past Chris. ''Whoa,'' he murmured, holding her at bay. ''First let's make sure someone isn't lying in wait inside the door.''

''To do what—shout, 'Boo'?'' She ducked under his arm and rushed inside, then glanced over her shoulder at him.

He was staring at her legs as though the sight had him frozen in place. She tugged self-consciously on the hem of her short robe, anger heating her cheeks. She snapped in a loud whisper, ''Do you think you could admire my legs some other time?''

His gaze snapped to hers. ''What?''

''I need your help. Now.'' She shook her head. ''Come on.''

''Sure. Right behind you.''

The huskiness in his voice sent a sweet shiver

through her, one that licked her temper a notch higher. She would not let this man undermine her again. The hell with him and his male magnetism. She wasn't getting seduced by it anymore. She charged up the stairs.

As she climbed, Nikki's gaze scoured every corner of the second floor and the landing above. No one seemed to be stirring at this late hour. But she knew at least one person had to be. Maybe Olivia. Maybe Marti. Maybe Lorah. Maybe even Dorothea, who might have sneaked back to pull off this latest trick.

Behind her, she heard the soft jangle of metal against metal as Chris obviously looked for the proper key. He asked, "Why the ballroom?"

"You'll see."

To her surprise, the door *was* locked.

"Hurry," she told him, stepping to one side. But the second he opened the door, Nikki darted ahead of him, then stopped abruptly just inside the dark room.

Chris charged in, running smack into her backside. Reflexively he snaked his arms around her in an effort to keep them both upright. She pitched back against him, slender and curvy and feminine, and all of the images that had haunted his evening swept him anew. He closed his eyes, breathed in the enticing mix of shampoo and chlorine wafting from her damp hair, relished the feel of her body pressed to his, remembered her lips, so sweet and hungry. A sigh climbed his throat and cleared his mind. Her passion was the seed of his madness. His passion for her, the latchkey to a padded cell.

She tugged at his arms, and he released her as though he'd just realized she was dripping wet beneath her robe. Her muted voice seethed with fury and frustration. "Where are the lights?"

He reached for the switch from rote. A soft golden glow filled the room, illuminated her lovely face, her damp golden hair, the anger dancing in her aquamarine eyes. All held him a captivated audience of one.

"Over here," she breathed, flying to a rack of clothing. "You'll see. It'll be gone." She began rifling through the hangers, from the front to the back, halting with a sudden gasp. "Oh, my God, it *is* here. But…I…I don't understand. No one could have gotten into this room, taken off this gown, hung it back up, then escaped leaving the door locked behind them—all in the last few minutes."

Chris frowned, finally putting it together. "You think what we just saw was someone wearing this gown?"

"Well, obviously not *this* gown," she spat out. "So, there must be another one."

"Are you saying Dorothea is 'haunting' the mansion as another publicity stunt?"

Although Nikki had entertained that possibility, now she wondered. "Who would Dorothea hope to impress by doing that?"

The question brought his eyebrows down low. "How the hell should I know? Lorah. Mr. Sands. You."

"Why?"

He shrugged. "To justify the séance."

"I suppose it's possible." But it didn't add up. She frowned at Chris. "It doesn't explain that business with the actors."

"What are you talking about? What business? I thought they were just delayed."

"No." She blew out a loud breath and cinched the belt of her robe tighter, drawing his attention to her waist. "Didn't you hear? Someone claiming to be

Dorothea called the actors' agents and canceled this booking.''

"Dorothea wouldn't do that." He shook his head. "She and Liv have worked months on that skit."

"Exactly."

"Then who?" His handsome features twisted with disbelief. "Why?"

"I don't know." Nikki glanced toward the windows, having the sense that their two reflections were more real at this moment, in this unreal situation, than either Chris or herself. "It has to be someone with a reason we haven't considered."

"What kind of reason?"

"I'm not sure." A possibility had been flitting through her mind most of the afternoon. She grabbed hold of it now. "You said something the night I arrived about someone sabotaging your grand opening. Is there actually someone who wants you and your sister to fail with this bed and breakfast?"

Chris laughed as though he thought the idea absurd. "I know I said that, but—" He broke off. But what? He remembered the sensation that someone or something was causing all the mishaps, trying to sabotage the grand opening. But he had decided he was overreacting, letting his nerves about this risky new venture stir crazy ideas. Someone canceling the actors booked for Liv's skit wasn't his nerves. What the hell was going on? Did someone really want Olivia and him to fail? If so, why? And what might that do to Liv's recovery? Her stability?

"Is there someone?" Nikki asked again.

He shook his head, but like a whirlwind lifting rocks to release the slimy, slithery vermin beneath, his mind churned, considering one possibility, then another. No one hated Olivia enough to destroy her. Not even *his* enemies would be that vindictive. "We all step on a few toes in our lives, but I can't come up with one person in my past who'd be so incensed with either Liv or me that they'd sneak in here and screw with the plumbing and some of the wiring."

"Or play ghost." She had her hands on her hips, her sweet, lean hips.

He cleared his throat. "It suggests, an inside job, doesn't it?"

She nodded. "Maybe we won't know why until we find out who."

"Then who? Surely not Rameriz."

"No, he wouldn't have called the actors' agents."

He narrowed his eyes. "That eliminates Dorothea, too."

"It has to." Nikki concurred, accepting that fact. "She could have made a second wedding dress, and she might parade around the house as a ghost, but as you've pointed out, she wouldn't risk her skit. Especially since she had no reason to believe you or I would step forward and fill in if she terminated the actors."

"Damn straight." He nodded and blew out a hard breath. "I don't want anything to do with it. Don't know why in hell I agreed…"

Her anger and her pride twisted together in one big knot in her chest. She squared her shoulders. "The only reason *I* offered to help was because I thought *you'd* never agree to it."

His glance, warm and dark and richly brown, swept lazily over her, heating her from her toes to her cheeks and every intimate spot in between. Damn this man. She wrenched her gaze from his. "But mostly, I wanted to find out whether or not she dropped that damned chisel.''

She spun around and stared at the desk. Then attacked the drawers like a mad woman.

Chris watched her searching, but made no move to help. He couldn't trust himself near her. ''I know you said you prefer swimming at night, but why did you risk it tonight after the frights you've had today?''

''I told you before—I don't scare easily.'' She didn't look up, just kept digging through the drawers. She found sewing accessories, a couple of *People Weekly* magazines, and an opened bottle of vodka. But no chisel. She banged the drawer shut, glanced at him and made a face. ''It isn't here.''

He hadn't moved, still stood near the door. It struck her suddenly that he seemed to be keeping his distance on purpose. He said, ''She could have taken it home.''

''I don't think she dropped it.''

''Yeah, I agree.'' He shoved at a wayward lock of his hair, still uncombed since his ride in the convertible. The windblown look gave him a rakish appeal. He shifted his weight to his other foot. ''So, we've eliminated Rameriz and Dorothea Miller, and that leaves...?''

''The other household staff—'' she gathered a steadying breath ''—the guests, and us.''

''Us?'' He glared at her. ''Neither one of us just played ghost.''

He was right. They, too, were eliminated from suspicion. An awful thought sent a shiver through her. ''If neither Dorothea nor Jorge dropped that chisel on me, then someone else did. Someone who meant to hurt me. Perhaps kill me.''

At the thought, Nikki's knees buckled.

Chris did move then. He rushed to her and caught hold of her, gently gripping her arms, speaking low, with tenderness. "It's imperative we find out who's doing these things before there's another attempt to harm you. Have you a history with any of our suspects?"

"I didn't know any of you until I arrived here. But someone knew about me."

His face grew instantly dark. "Are you implying Liv—"

"Oh, no." She hastened to assure him. "I guess I have a confession to make."

He sat her down in Dorothea's chair, then hitched his hip onto the edge of the desk. "Confess away."

She glanced at her clenched hands, then up into his warm chocolate eyes that darkened to coffee as she told him about receiving the anonymous note. "The ironic thing is that it's what gave me the idea to do a book on bed and breakfasts."

He tipped his head, his gaze intense. "What 'answers' are you seeking here?"

She swallowed hard. "I'm trying to find my father. I've been trying for many years, and have visited lots of places looking for clues to his identity. I had no idea what I'd find here, if anything. But I had to try."

His eyes narrowed. "How would someone have known you were looking for your father?"

"It's not a secret." She crossed her legs, inadvertently hiking the robe higher on her bare thighs. She tugged the hem. The simple action snared his gaze, and he swallowed as though an orange were lodged against his Adam's apple. She felt a knot in her own throat. "I may have mentioned it in an interview or two."

Nikki had long held the belief that telling as many

people as possible about her search might bring her the right lead to identifying her dad.

Chris sighed. "But the note doesn't mention your father."

"I didn't think of that until after I was here." She licked her lips. "I guess someone who'd seen Theresa's portrait and a photograph of me sent the note."

He ran his hand over his hair, mussing it worse. "Why would anyone care about you looking like Theresa?"

"I don't know. Why would someone try to kill me? Like the ghost, I think we're going to have to find out who before we discover why."

THEY'D MADE A PACT—more like an uneasy partnership, if she were honest—to work together to unmask the culprit behind the note, the attempt on her life and the ghostly vision they'd seen. She could tell he hadn't liked the thought of the extra time this meant they'd have to spend with each other any better than she did. But at the moment, this devil of a man was the only one she halfway trusted at Wedding House.

He had locked the ballroom, then gone down and put the Jaguar away. She'd headed upstairs, dried her hair and dropped into bed. But sleep wouldn't come. Her nerves were still as tight as cornrow braids.

She'd listened to Chris in the shower, and resented the way the images of him climbed inside her mind, disrupting her attention to her goals, her resolve to find her family. She had no time for wasting romantic thoughts on a man who wanted to do nothing more than toy with her feelings and emotions.

Besides, she had bigger worries to contend with. Like someone wanting her dead.

Maybe they just wanted her to leave. She punched her pillow. A part of her feared her unknown nemesis enough to actually pack and go first thing in the morning. A larger part of her would be damned if someone was going to drive her away before she'd discovered the bride's secret and what it meant to her own heritage.

MORNING CAME TOO QUICKLY, and with it, a nasty thunderstorm. Nikki settled for coffee and a piece of toast, eating in the TV room as she downloaded her e-mail. Two messages were from sources she'd been expecting. Her heart raced as she opened the first and read with speed, then disappointment. Jellybean, the Internet name used by her contact Jill Beane, was out of town and would do what she could with the information Nikki had sent yesterday and get back to her as soon as there was anything to report.

The second, Zeus the Moose, had found families with the surname of Aznar in Southern California, South Texas and Northern Arizona. Theresa was a common first name for the women in the family. He needed something more to help him narrow the field.

She typed her responses, supplying both of her sources with a couple more details, then sent the messages, feeling encouraged, but still experiencing that edgy impatience.

As she ascended to the third floor, she heard Dorothea's voice in the foyer decrying the pouring rain. A flash of lightning lit the sky near the window over Nikki's head. She cringed. The day and the skit director had her wanting to retreat to her room and hide out. Hugging the wall so as not to be seen from the floor below, she sprinted upstairs and ducked into the library. She glanced at her watch. Dorothea would be in the ballroom within minutes. Then she could make it back to her room undetected.

Rain drove against the windows, clinking like a million tiny claws. She shook off the unpleasant image and wandered to the farthest wall. Standing with her laptop cradled in her arms, she absentmindedly scanned the bookshelf. Funny, she mused, the book spines facing her were mostly of the same width and height, as though someone had chosen them for that reason instead of for the contents of the books themselves. Luis De Vega's idea of the well-stocked library?

She braced her hand on the molding that ran vertically down the side of the bookshelf. The molding gave beneath her palm. Nikki jerked, but couldn't stop the piece of wood from moving. It slid to one side, revealing a narrow slot. Something was tucked inside the aperture. A thin book, the cover grayed as if from age. Gingerly she freed the book. Across the cover in faded gold lettering was the word "Diary."

With her pulse leaping in her throat, she closed the hiding place, set her laptop on one of the tables, sank into a reading chair and flipped the book open.

On the inside cover someone had scrawled the name Theresa Delores Maria Aznar De Vega. More information for Zeus. Nikki's heart kicked excitedly. And most important, she may have found the key to everything. She caught hold of the first page, the storm and her dread of Dorothea forgotten.

"Good morning, Ms. Navarro." Diego Sands appeared in the library doorway.

Nikki flinched. Her head jerked up as though he'd yanked her hair. She closed the book, crossed her arms over her lap, hiding the diary from view as if she were a teenage boy caught reading pornography. She smiled self-consciously. "Good morning."

He wore a soft gray suit that accentuated the silver at his temples and complemented his dark complexion, his jet black eyes. Although he wore no tie, the tiny red hankie in his breast pocket surprised Nikki. It said this man was not all business, as she'd assumed since meeting him.

Under other circumstances, she'd have been delighted at the chance to finally have Diego alone, to finally be able to question him. But why had he shown up just as she'd discovered Theresa's diary? And what had he been doing before he appeared in the doorway? She'd swear he hadn't come up the stairs, but down the hall from the direction of the master suite. Had he been looking at the portrait? Remembering an old friend?

Thunder rumbled nearby, raising goose bumps on her flesh.

"Am I interrupting your work?" he asked, hesitantly taking a step into the room.

"No." She slid the book across her thighs and down the inside of the chair, poking it deep under the cushion. "I'm contemplating what I want to say about this charming room. How to describe its unique appeal and not make it sound like every other library in every other old house."

"For your book?"

"Yes, but I'm not sure I'm including Wedding House in the book yet. It's the first bed and breakfast I've visited of twenty possibilities."

He lifted an eyebrow. "Oh, come now. You can't possibly not realize your resemblance to the portrait is a great gimmick for selling a book."

She smiled for real at this. "I'll admit it crossed my mind."

"Of course it has." He smiled broadly and moved closer.

She wiped her damp hands on her pant legs. The rain grew softer. "Actually, I was hoping to have a chance to speak to you."

"About?" His eyebrows lifted.

"About Theresa Aznar. How you knew her. Where you knew her."

He studied Nikki a long moment. "Are you inquiring as a family member or simply from curiosity?"

She wasn't sure how to answer. Or why he was being evasive. "I'm curious."

Her response seemed to disappoint him. He gathered a breath that lifted his chest as though some heavy weight pressed it. "I guess you could say we had a past."

A romantic past? Before Luis and Theresa? "Here or somewhere else?"

"Here, there, what does it matter?" His strong features locked, and pain passed through his dark eyes. She'd obviously touched a nerve. One he didn't want touched again. Why? After all, it had been twenty odd years, and *he'd* brought up the subject originally, not Nikki.

She decided on another tack. "What were you doing in the master suite just now?"

The question surprised him. She saw it in the slight lift of one brow, but he recovered with the ease of someone seldom caught off guard. "I was—"

He broke off and shifted toward the landing. Voices were rising from the staircase. Nikki followed his gaze, hearing first Lorah's jangling charm bracelet, tinkling like a metal wind chime, then glimpsing Marti's thick vanilla tresses and her signature purple outfit.

She was surprised to see Marti with the psychic, after the way Lorah had upset her last night. The two women quit conversing the moment they spotted Nikki and Diego. They all stared at one another like four leery big-city strangers boarding a late-night bus.

Marti clutched her mauve journal to her chest. She was the first to break the stilted silence. "Holy Joe, have we interrupted a serious tête-à-tête?"

"Don't be silly," Nikki protested, heat brushing her cheeks. She rose from the chair, shoving herself up by the armrests. She wanted nothing more than to snatch the diary from its hiding place and scurry off to her room to read it. She dared not even glance toward it. "I asked Mr. Sands whether he'd seen the books you donated to this library the other night. I was hoping to read one of them, but haven't been able to find a single lavender book cover on these shelves."

Nikki felt a zip of satisfaction at the color sprouting on the mystery writer's face. So, Marti *had* lied about donating the books. Why? When looking for something to read was a much more logical, believable excuse for being in the library late at night? What had she been doing that evening? Nikki's mouth dried. Had Marti been looking for Theresa's diary?

The desperation to snatch it from its hiding place twisted Nikki's stomach. She forced herself to keep a calm expression. She retrieved her laptop, hoping against hope that the diary would go undetected until she could return for it.

"No offense meant, Ms. Wolf," Diego said. "But I told Ms. Navarro that I don't read mysteries."

Nikki was grateful that he'd gone along with her lie,

but she'd known instinctively that he would. He hadn't liked her questioning him about Theresa; he would appreciate less the conversation being repeated, perhaps dissected.

Lorah clapped her hands, a short, sharp, attention-grabbing gesture, punctuated by the jangle of charms. Everyone glanced at her, which was obviously what she'd intended.

"Ms. Wolf and I were chatting about the ghost," Lorah stated haughtily, her translucent green eyes seeming to take them all in at once. "She was afoot last eve."

The reminder of her encounter with the "ghost" spiked Nikki's blood pressure. She gave a caustic laugh, striding past Diego to the two women. "Is that why you've come to the third floor—to try and rouse Theresa's spirit?"

Marti hid a smile behind her hand, but couldn't keep it from her shrewd hazel eyes. "Nope. We're going to scope out the master suite."

"I'd have thought by now you'd have 'scoped' it from top to bottom." Nikki stepped into the hall.

Olivia trudged to the landing, dressed as usual in black, her hair swept severely off her face. Her dark eyes gleamed and color stood out on her normally pasty cheeks. From the climb, or expectation? Nikki couldn't tell, but she detected an aura of anticipation issuing from Chris's sister.

Olivia's expression grew cautious as she absorbed the tension between her four guests. "Is everything all right?"

"It's wonderful," Lorah assured her, her bracelet clanging as though in protest to this lie.

Nikki glanced at the armload Olivia carried: a folded

white cloth and two shoe boxes full of white candles of various sizes. Olivia's dark eyes swept the group, coming to rest on Nikki. She smiled stiffly. "Dorothea asked that you come to the ballroom as soon as possible. For rehearsal."

The thought of facing Chris whipped Nikki's pulse like a top spinning at full speed. She hadn't bothered reading the script yet. Would rather be reading the diary. But before she could recover it, she had to get rid of all these onlookers.

Thunder cracked again, and her gaze fell to the candles in Olivia's arms. Nikki's stomach hit the floor. She wanted to get back on-line. E-mail Zeus Theresa's full name. But she wouldn't be e-mailing anyone if the storm impaired the phone lines. "Are you expecting a power outage?"

Olivia blinked, then shook her head. "Goodness, no. At least, I hope not."

"The candles are for the séance." Marti tapped a short fingernail against her journal.

"As is the cloth." Lorah lifted her chin, her pale, eerie eyes sending a shiver through Nikki. "We're holding the séance in the master suite this evening."

Chapter Nine

A séance for a ghost that doesn't exist. Nikki tamped down the urge to laugh at the foolishness of it all. Somehow she managed to hang on to her composure and make it to her room. She settled the laptop back on the desk, then returned to the door and tugged it open a crack. No one lingered near the library, but she couldn't retrieve the diary without being seen by the three women in the master suite. It would have to wait until later.

"Patience, patience," she whispered to herself, hating the anxious need for action that swirled through her stomach, her limbs. Hating the sense of being trapped.

Thunder banged overhead. Nikki jumped. Would the storm knock out the power? Her nerves tickled the underside of her skin like a million tingling electrodes. She glanced back at her laptop, biting down the urge to snatch it up and head to the TV room to e-mail Zeus. She couldn't risk being waylaid by Dorothea. She had yet to read the skit script, and according to Olivia, Dorothea was itching to get the rehearsal underway. She was likely pacing in front of the ballroom at this very moment.

Nikki glanced out into the hall again.

Diego was coming up the stairs carrying a ladder-back chair. She stared in disbelief at Chris, who was right behind the architect…also hefting a chair. How had he gotten talked into helping set up the séance he so opposed? Was he doing this because of their pact last night?

He glanced toward her, confirmation of this in his dark eyes. Her heart skipped. But she refused to admit her reaction to his warm gaze held any other meaning than that they were coconspirators.

She tore her gaze from him and shut the door softly. Crossing the room, she flipped open the laptop, activated it and composed an e-mail to Zeus. She'd send it at the first opportunity. The room lit with a flash of lightning, and Nikki started, her nerves still at the surface. She turned off the computer, found the script for the skit, stretched out on the bed and began reading.

The script wasn't half-bad, but the scenes Chris and she would be playing demanded more physical contact than she wanted to share with him. That, however, was easily remedied. They were stand-ins. No one expected their performances to be perfect. Or accurate. They were only feeding lines to the other actors, giving them a sense of how the scene would work.

She was not required to kiss Chris. Nor would she.

THE STORM SOUNDED WORSE than ever in the ballroom. Wind howled against the windows, stealing inside like invisible ice monsters. Dorothea, defying the dull day in her neon-orange jumpsuit, had positioned metal folding chairs in a circle in the center of the room. But as bright as her outfit was, she seemed subdued, as though the weather worried her, as though it would somehow ruin her skit.

Nikki squirmed in her metal chair, glancing surreptitiously at the two actors across from her. The woman who was playing the cook, a stocky, gray-haired matron-type, alternated between staring at the open script on her lap and closing her eyes as though memorizing her lines. The other, a younger woman playing the role of maid to Theresa, seemed bored.

"Where is my Luis?" Dorothea implored of them between sips from her coffee mug.

As though on cue Chris strode into the room, his boot heels clicking across the bare planking. The set of his shoulders and cocky toss of his head proclaimed he had better things to do. He barely acknowledged Nikki, showed no response to her appearance. In an effort to look as little like Theresa as possible she'd slicked her unruly hair off her face in a style as severe as Olivia's.

Nikki fingered the edge of her script, curling and uncurling it. It was obvious Chris didn't want to be there. Well, neither did she. She'd rather be reading the diary. She cursed to herself, hating that her old ability to temper her patience seemed to be slipping from her more and more every hour. Every minute.

Chris snatched up the script and slumped onto one of the folding chairs, crossing his long legs at the ankles. He read silently, his expression intense, his eyes narrowing. "What is this?"

He lurched straighter in the chair and poked at the paper.

"Which page?" Dorothea tensed, her tiny voice two notches higher than normal.

"This one. Where Luis gets 'physical' with Theresa."

Physical? Nikki's mouth dried. Was he talking about the fight scene, or the kissing scene?

"The page number is on the bottom." Dorothea swigged from her coffee mug.

"Page six," Chris growled. "Where Luis shoves Theresa into the wall."

"What about it?"

"It needs to be rewritten."

"What?" Dorothea bristled.

"I won't do it. I don't manhandle women."

"This isn't you." Her face glowed red, a shade lighter than her hair. "Dear boy, it's a character. You're 'acting' is all."

"It says here that I shove her into the wall."

"Well, yes, but not actually. The scene relies on Nikki. You just pretend to shove her, she merely falls backward as though you have."

She looked to Nikki for confirmation, as though Nikki did this kind of thing all the time. Nikki shook her head. "I have no idea how to do this. I guess you're going to have to show us."

Chris's eyebrows arched, and he looked as though he'd like to shoot Nikki for her suggestion. Her pulse tripped, and she glanced away.

"Then, come on, you two." Dorothea motioned to Chris and Nikki. "Stand up."

Chris made no effort to hide his reluctance. Nikki strove to cover her own. If Chris could be rude, she could be gracious. They rose and took a step toward each other. He wouldn't look at her. She couldn't look anywhere else. Her stomach twisted. Why did he have to be so obstinate, so ornery, so inordinately sexy? She stepped back, as though putting distance between them would sever the cord of attraction she felt.

"Oh, no you don't," Dorothea complained. She waved her hands like twin fans gesturing for them to move closer and closer together. When they were inches apart she finally seemed satisfied. "Okay. Now Chris, put your hands on Nikki's shoulders."

His Adam's apple bobbed. He hesitated, then gingerly placed his hands on her shoulders. His touch seemed to sear Nikki's skin through her sweater. Stifling a moan, she glanced sharply at Chris, only to find him staring at her. His brown eyes grew darker, as dark as the clouds crowding the sky.

"When I say 'action,'" Dorothea enthused, "then, Chris, you swear as though you're furious and give a gentle push to Nikki's shoulders. Nikki, at the first pressure of Chris's hands, you scream and lurch backward, arms flailing, as though you've been shoved."

A red hue climbed Chris's neck, and Nikki read anger in his eyes. Why? The weight of his hands on her lessened, as though he could barely tolerate touching her, and even though she knew she shouldn't, Nikki felt as though he'd stabbed her with a giant icicle.

A spear of lightning cracked though the sky, touching down somewhere on Protection Island. The sudden flash of light and the ensuing roll of thunder jolted Nikki, reminding her just how alone she really was. Just how unsafe. The protection, the love she longed for were not available to her through Chris Conrad. She could rely only on herself.

"Okay." Dorothea frowned, clutching her mug in both hands. "Action."

Chris mumbled his lines, but forgot or refused to deepen the pressure on her shoulders.

Dorothea yelled, "Now, now."

To no avail. Chris wouldn't push Nikki.

"I don't like this," he protested anew.

"Please, just try it." Dorothea plowed a hand through her hair. "This once?"

Chris nodded. Dorothea called "action" again. This time Chris gave Nikki a slight shove. Nikki overcompensated and lost her balance. Before she could hit the floor, Chris grabbed her.

Dorothea screamed, "No. No. Let her fall."

He settled Nikki firmly on her feet, then rounded on Dorothea. "Like hell I will."

With that, he released Nikki and stalked from the ballroom and clambered down the stairs. A second later the front door slammed. Heat raced through Nikki, fueled by outrage. How dare he run out on her? Leave her to face these gaping actors? Dorothea's questions?

She mumbled an apology and stormed from the room, following Chris's route. They were supposed to be working together. She slammed outside, then stood on the stoop for a moment, glaring out into the pouring rain. He knew damned well she didn't want to act in this skit. *His sister's skit.* The least he could do was cooperate. Where had he gone?

She started for the pool area, the rain soaking her clothing. It felt good against her hot cheeks. The gate to the pool hung open. She moved faster. She found Chris in the cabana. He was stacking boxes of fireworks into a corner, moving them from beneath the overhang outside.

"You coward," she spat.

Chris jerked. Nikki stood not ten feet from him, her eyes flashing like the lightning, her glorious face slick with rain, her sweater wet, clinging to her like a second skin, tight at her small waist, her full breasts. Her erect nipples nudged the fabric. He tried not to notice. He couldn't look away. His throat tightened, his control broke, and need rocked through him. He dare not acknowledge it, dare not give in to it. Or he'd be lost.

She narrowed her eyes. "What was that?"

He knew she referred to his behavior in the ballroom. "What was what?" he asked, being deliberately obtuse.

It seemed to enrage her more.

"Finally you start acting," she ground between clenched teeth. "Acting *dumb*."

"You ought to be grateful." He shoved the box aside and started toward the door for another.

"Grateful?" She raced at him. As fast as she came forward, Chris scrambled backward. The wall stopped him. Nothing stopped Nikki. Her wet shoes slipped, and she slid into Chris. Even that didn't slow her down. Her breath hot against his mouth, she railed, "Grateful that you find me so repulsive you can't even touch me?"

Repulsive? Good God, how could he be repulsed by a woman like her? When her ripe curves pressed the very length of him? He resisted the urge to pull her closer, fought the awareness spiking his veins, but he couldn't still his burgeoning erection. Didn't she realize one smile from her drove him wild? That thoughts of her haunted his sleep? His waking hours? "Repulsed?"

"Yes." She twisted against him, apparently unaware in her angry state of the effect she was having. "I saw the way you looked at me the last time you kissed me. Believe me, I know when a man doesn't want me."

Her provocative movements burned Chris's restraint like so much dried straw. "Lady, you don't know anything."

He grasped her head in both hands and brought his mouth down on hers so savagely fire seemed to leap from her lips into his blood. For a full five seconds, he did all the work. But then he felt that hunger she'd shown the other times he'd kissed her, that response of need to need. He swept her into his arms, pulled her so close he could feel her heartbeat against his chest.

Her arms circled his neck, her fingers laced into his hair as if she was taking possession of him, laying claim to him. And with her ownership came a calmness he'd never known, a rightness, as though letting go would leave him, oddly, more in control.

For the first time in his life, he wasn't afraid. Not of this woman. Not of this giving, this taking. Not in this moment. Every concern melted in the fire roused by their dancing tongues, in the searing sweet desire rippling through him. His hands feathered along her back, lower and lower, until he held her bottom cupped in both hands.

Nikki breathed in rapid-fire gasps. She couldn't believe the heat licking through her veins, the need to be with Chris, a need that she'd denied from the first moment she'd seen him. His urgent touch was as gentle as a butterfly wing, as solid and true as his soul. He broke the kiss, and she braced for another rejection, but it didn't come. The control usually visible in Chris's eyes was gone; smoldering passion darkened those thick-lashed orbs now. Passion for her.

She felt an odd sizzle in her chest, as though the eternal cold spot were shrinking. She didn't care whether this was right or wrong, whether this would lead to commitment or complication, she only knew she needed confirmation that she was desirable, needed it from this man who'd reinforced her sense of being unloved and unlovable. Somehow the need seemed deeper, but she could no more examine it at this moment than she could fly.

Her fingers found the buttons on his shirt. Eagerness

and anticipation made her clumsy; still, the forbidding garment was swiftly opened. She shoved her hands inside his shirt and wallowed in the feel of his warm, naked flesh, in the silken hair on his chest and stomach.

A honeyed sigh slipped from her as Chris lifted the hem of her sweater and moved his hands against her bare back. Then he was tugging the sweater up and off. The hook of her bra gave and he peeled the lacy undergarment down her arms. She watched as he gazed on her for the first time, and melted in the awe she saw reflected in his eyes, in his tender expression. No man had ever looked at her as though she were precious.

Chris felt like a man in a dream, with the woman of his dreams. She had the most glorious breasts he'd ever seen. Gingerly he reached to touch them, thumbed the taut nipples and then tasted them. She cried his name, a breathy whisper embraced by the aching need in his heart.

She undid the button on his jeans, then the zipper, and then she was pulling them down along with his shorts. He stood naked and vulnerable before her, but in that moment he wanted to believe Nikki would never hurt him. As he meant never to hurt her.

Nikki gasped at the size of him, at the sheer beauty of his whole body. Her throat constricted, and her words came out in a breathy whisper, "You're so perfectly proportioned—like a statue created with loving, gifted hands."

Matching her visual pleasure with tactile gratification, she swept her open hands over his shoulders, down his arms, up his arms, down his chest, to his flat stomach and lower, finally taking him in both hands and stroking gently up and down the taut, silken length of him.

Chris groaned. "Oh, Nikki."

A moment later she was also naked. Chris kissed her neck, her breasts, her stomach, his devilish fingers dipping inside her, finding her moist and eager and ready for him. He knelt and pulled her to him, his head pressed to her belly, then he kissed her between her legs, found the bud of her femininity and tortured it erotically with his tongue, bringing her to the edge of rapture.

Nikki dropped to her knees, cupping his head, reaching her lips to his, encouraging his mind-boggling kisses, and then, somehow they were on the floor, the brightly colored cushions beneath them. Outside the storm raged on. Neither noticed. The loud crescendos were a symphony, a backdrop to the sighs and moans of love they sang to each other.

She opened her legs and Chris thrust inside her, deep, then deeper and deeper until she was filled with him, expanding to take all of him. The candied friction of their joining aroused such bliss she immediately climaxed.

But before she could start down the mountain of ecstasy, she was carried up over the top again and again. Through this fog of euphoria, she felt Chris tense, heard him softly cry her name as liquid heat spilled into her. Seconds later he slumped against her, but made no move to disengage himself.

Tears slipped from the corners of Nikki's eyes. Her heart felt full to bursting, the cold spot undetectable as though it had gone forever. She'd never experienced anything close to this, never knew it was possible.

But too soon, he rolled off her, taking with him the warm cocoon in which he'd wrapped her. The chill that brushed her flesh felt bone deep, heartbreakingly foreboding. He lifted himself on one elbow and studied her long and hard, and as he did, she saw fear. That haunted look crept back into his eyes.

Chris hated the dread he saw on Nikki's face. She wouldn't hurt him, not on purpose. But she didn't understand that he might very well hurt her. The thought stole the afterglow of their lovemaking, sobering him as surely as an ice-cold bath. Dear God, he'd lost complete control. What was he capable of because of her? She'd made him forget himself. For both their sakes. It must never happen again.

"This was a mistake."

He knew his words would hurt, he intended them to. It was best. She'd thank him one day.

A nasty heat seared through Nikki as though her whole body had been slammed by a semi-trailer. She hadn't thought it possible to feel more vulnerable, more completely stripped of her dignity than she felt at this moment. Everything she'd gained from the lovemaking, she lost. She'd be damned if she'd ever let Chris Conrad close to her again. "Believe me, it won't happen again."

With her back to him, she grabbed her clothes and dressed in haste. She could hear him donning his own clothing, but neither spoke. They might be strangers who'd never met, never shared anything more intimate than the space of this room.

With her heart splitting in two, she bolted out of the cabana. The rain had stopped, but the roiling black clouds on the horizon indicated it was just a lull between storms. Humiliation shivered inside Nikki, the chilliest spot in the very center of her chest, her lifelong torment, no longer hiding, no longer pretending to be gone. She wanted to run, and keep on running until she collapsed. But the tide was in, the beach nonexistent.

She charged into the gardens, tears leaking from the corners of her eyes, her feet flying across the wet ground. Moist bushes and shrubs slapped her face, her hands, her clothing as though the plants were flogging her, punishing her for forgetting her promise to herself about Chris, for ignoring her resolve to keep her mind on finding her father, her family.

At length her limbs cried out in pain, and she pulled up short, a stabbing ache in her side, her breath thready. She bent over, holding her waist, panting, and sobbed until the tears were spent. Only then did she glance around. She'd run this way and that and now couldn't see the house through the overhang of trees and dense underbrush. She might be in a forest with predators behind every plant.

Trepidation threatened to swallow her. She spun right, then left. She could see no one. But the hair on her nape prickled and the sense of being watched hit her hard. Her gaze raked the shadows. A twig snapped. She whipped to her left. Jorge. She sucked in a sharp breath that lodged in her throat.

Terror swam in the groundskeeper's eyes. "I told you to leave me alone."

Nikki retreated a step. "I—"

She broke off as she realized with a jolt that Jorge's terrified gaze was locked, not on her, but on something past her left shoulder. She lurched around. Ten feet through the bushes, she spotted a wispy white shadow, shaped much like a woman. She yelped and reared back. The vision disappeared.

So had Jorge.

Nikki hightailed it to the spot where the vision had appeared. Nothing. No one. Only after she'd trampled the area looking for something tangible did she think to check the grass for footprints. If there had been any, she'd obliterated them. Damn. Raindrops splatted against the maple leaves and Nikki knew it was a matter of seconds before she'd be drenched again.

She hurried back to the mansion, moving up the stairs quickly. Chris was coming down. He hesitated as though he'd like to speak with her. She ignored him.

Chris stared after Nikki as she skirted past him, and watched her go up the steps. He knew she hated him now, but it was for the best. She didn't understand his need to control his emotions. Didn't realize his sanity and her safety relied on his doing exactly that.

But knowing he was doing the right thing didn't ease the self-reproach he felt for hurting her, or the ache he felt at the thought of not being able to be near her, to touch her, to hold her, to kiss her and make love to her for the rest of their lives.

NIKKI DECIDED she wouldn't even think about Chris, or their lovemaking. She thought of little else. She showered and changed into dry clothes, but still felt chilled. She climbed into bed and took a long nap, dreaming of Chris and all the joy he'd given her, and all the pain. The new series of storms woke her hours later. Night came early, thanks to the heavy cloud cover.

Her concern about a power outage revived, and she took the laptop to the TV room and e-mailed Zeus. On her way back upstairs, she realized no one else was on the third floor. She could get the diary. She slipped into the library and dug her hand down the side of the chair. Her pulse skipped. No. No. No. The diary was gone.

Hoping someone had moved it, she spent several minutes looking for it, under the chair, in the opposite chair, on the bookshelves. It was nowhere. She balled her hands into fists. Someone had taken it. Most likely Diego. Well, he wasn't going to get away with it. Later she would search his room.

She stalked to the hallway.

The same shadowy shape she'd encountered earlier in the garden appeared near the master suite. Nikki froze, gaping. The vision grew stronger and stronger until she recognized the familiar face—Theresa's face. Her face. It was a trick. But how? And who? Before she could figure it out, the "ghost" vanished.

Chris gained the landing. Nikki jerked back, startled, her dander rising. She wanted to see him even less than the "ghost." Her mind barreled. The moment he'd appeared, Theresa's image had disappeared. Was he in on this hocus-pocus?

He hesitated, studying her. "What's happened?"

She glared at him, suspicion fueling her ire. "I suppose you expect me to believe you didn't see it?"

"Didn't see what?"

She recounted her encounter with the "ghost" in the woods. And the one just now. "How'd you pull it off, Chris? Cameras? Mirrors?"

He stepped dangerously close to her. His breath hot on her face, his voice a growl. "I don't care what you believe. I'm not behind any 'ghostly' sightings. But don't be surprised if there's more such nonsense at the séance."

Chapter Ten

Thunder grumbled across the rooftop like a vexed creature on the attack. Wind followed in its wake, a vicious, howling consort. Nikki shivered as she stepped into the hall to join the others in the master suite. Chris came out of his room at the same time. Not wanting to walk with him, she started ahead, but he caught up to her and leaned down toward her, coconspirator again, nothing personal, as though everything between them hadn't shifted off-kilter, as though they'd never made love, as though the memory of his touch wasn't burned into her brain, seared on her senses.

Anger licked through her blood.

"If we sit across from each another," he whispered, "we should be able to detect any tricks Lorah has up her sleeve."

"The farther I sit from you, the better." Nikki hated the constriction in her throat, hated the thoughts of Chris's lovemaking that filled her mind and elicited unwanted shivers of pleasure through her. Damn it, she would *not* recall. Would not long for a repeat match. She stomped the memories. The only time she wanted to remember this afternoon was if she ever forgot how he'd hurt her. If she ever even considered allowing him to touch her again.

Stepping away from him, she glanced at the others coming up the stairs. Olivia, a specter in black, seemed thinner than usual, a paradox considering the huge meals she ate. Lorah looked as regal as royalty in her loden caftan with its wide bejeweled sleeves, her charm bracelet punctuating her every step. Diego, attired in designer slacks and sweater, appeared unusually edgy, his black eyes watchful, and Marti, a vision in purple cashmere and wool, had slicked her vanilla-blond hair back and tucked a pen behind one ear. Her mauve journal poked from the waist of her grape slacks.

The lights in the hall flickered. Marti sighed, "Holy Joe, we're going to lose the power. How perfect."

Perfect, indeed, Nikki thought, a perfect night for trickery, and perhaps for unveiling the person behind the attack on her. Cold jabbed her belly, a sudden sharp sensation that something bad was going to happen.

"Where's Dorothea?" she murmured to Chris. "This séance was her idea."

He glanced down at Nikki, something odd deep in his eyes. She braced her foolish heart. Whatever vulnerability she saw in Chris Conrad was a sham, as phony as the séance they were about to attend.

He said, "Lorah's probably enlisted her help for all the 'behind-the-scenes' antics she's set up for our entertainment."

"We'd be able to see her. Olivia has about a hundred candles—" Nikki broke off as she entered Theresa and Luis's former bedroom.

The cord across the entrance had been removed. An oval, dining-size table stood near the fireplace, surrounded by seven ladder-back chairs. Instead of the white cloth Chris's sister had brought up earlier, it looked as though a gypsy's shawl, red velvet with golden tassels, draped the table. Gone, too, were the myriad white candles. In their place a single brass candelabra with three tapers served as a centerpiece.

The air held a chill and the scent of rain, as though the patio door had only just been shut. Nikki glanced toward it, recalling her first encounter with Jorge Rameriz. Had he sneaked in here and disappeared outside? On this awful night? Why would he do that? No, she was letting her imagination get the best of her. She hugged herself and gazed at the portrait, then back at the patio doors. That old man was unpredictable. Likely unhinged. God knew where he'd pop up next. Or why.

The lights flickered again.

Hem sweeping the floor, Lorah moved ahead of the others, a lighter in hand, and touched the flame to the three candles. "Mr. Conrad, could you please turn off the hall lights."

Thunder shrieked overhead as raucous as the cries of a thousand disturbed souls. Or one restless apparition? Nikki swallowed hard and pulled her gaze from the portrait. She would not get sucked into the craziness going on here tonight.

Lorah's eerie eyes seemed more translucent than ever in the candle's glow. She gave a sharp clap of her hands, underscored by the tinkling of her charm bracelet. "Everyone, please, take a seat."

Chris chose the chair across from Nikki. But Lorah waved a hand at him, the bracelet jingling. "No, no. I want the skeptics together. Mr. Sands beside me please, Ms. Navarro, then Mr. Conrad, Ms. Wolf and Ms. Conrad."

"You like to orchestrate everything, don't you?" Chris stated, circling the table to Nikki's side.

Nikki's muscles tensed as he sat, and in the cloud of perfumes now girding the table, she detected his distinctive aftershave. She shifted toward Diego, holding her body away from Chris. This séance was getting more irritating by the moment.

Lorah took a gulp from the glass of water someone had placed beside her seat, then set it down and gazed at Chris. Her pale eyes glowed as if from some ghostly inner light. "You shall soon see that I have little to do with what occurs here. The spirits are in control, not I. I merely provide the medium so that we may understand their reasons for remaining between this world and the next."

"And how do we come to understand that?" Diego asked, suspicion curling the edges of his tone. "Do they speak through you?"

Marti lifted her pen from her journal, pausing in the notes she'd been taking.

Lorah tossed her head. "Through me, or through...one of you."

Olivia sat across from Nikki, twisting her hands. Her cheekbones seemed more pronounced than ever, the hollows deeper. Had she lost weight? Or was the candlelight creating shadows where there were none? Did she fear she'd be the one the ghost of Theresa chose to speak through? Poor woman. She was scaring herself for nothing.

"Sorry I'm late." Dorothea, dressed uncommonly in an ebony jumpsuit, her fiery red hair covered with a black silk turban, bustled in. The outfit suggested she *was* up to some deviltry. As she claimed the empty chair between Olivia and Lorah, enthusiasm gushed from her like rainwater through the downspouts. "This is so exciting."

Diego eyed the three eager women with hooded disdain. Chris seemed eager only to get the whole thing over. Nikki sensed his tension matched her own.

Lorah said, "I'll have to ask you to stop writing now, Ms. Wolf."

She waited until Marti closed the journal and laid the pen aside. Then she clapped her hands again. "Quiet. We must have absolute silence."

Even the storm obeyed this command, mysteriously ceasing its boisterous assault on the house. Lorah nodded in approval. "Join hands." There was a rustling movement as the attendees obliged. All except Nikki and Chris. Lorah lifted her perfectly shaped brows and gazed pointedly at them. "Everyone. Now, please."

Reluctantly Nikki offered her hand to Chris. Impossibly, he seemed more hesitant than she to take it, but when he did, there was something so warm and reassuring in his grip she almost forgot she hated him. Almost.

Lorah's glance encompassed her audience. "Under no circumstances must you break the connection."

"Not even to scratch an itch?" Marti asked on a chuckle.

Diego snickered softly. Nikki didn't find anything funny in this whole procedure. In spite of herself, she glanced sideways at Chris. He was gazing into the dark room beyond the table. Nikki couldn't make out anything that would hold his attention. Just a lot of indefinable shapes. Even the portrait appeared hazy.

"Silence!" Lorah insisted.

Quiet fell over the group. Despite her conviction that this séance was a sham, Nikki watched the medium with interest. Lorah closed her eyes, and she began to move her head from side to side. The swaying was hypnotic in a peaceful way, and Nikki began to relax.

The table jostled.

Nikki's heart leaped. Reflexively she squeezed both Diego's and Chris's hands. Both men squeezed her back as though reminding her that this was all theatrics, and she should hang on, the first act was only starting. She nodded to herself. Every nerve in her body tingled with anticipation.

A bump sounded across the room. Nikki gazed toward the bathroom, but spotted nothing in the pitch-darkness.

Lorah moaned softly, the noise echoed by the wind against the patio doors.

The candles flickered. A puff of cold sailed over Nikki, a draft of air as though through an open door. A low moan echoed from somewhere in the room. Nikki jerked around, trying to locate the source.

Lorah said, "Who is here?"

Another moan sounded in the darkness.

"Theresa De Vega, is that you?" Lorah asked. She still had her eyes closed, still swayed, the movements more intense than ever, her small shoulders tossing left, then right.

The low moaning grew louder, closer to the other side of the table. Nikki glanced at Marti, who seemed to be mentally recording the whole proceeding. Olivia seemed at once anxious and fascinated. Dorothea's eyes were closed, and she was rocking from side to side in a mimic of Lorah.

The psychic said, "If it's you Theresa, give us a sign."

Someone or something thumped the table near Dorothea.

The sudden noises kept jarring Nikki. *Calm down,* she counseled herself silently.

"Theresa," Lorah chanted. "Can you speak to us?"

The disembodied moaning sounded again, but this time it came from Dorothea.

"Speak to us, Theresa," Lorah urged in her sing-song tone.

The candelabra scooted across the table as if on wheels, spattering warm wax droplets in its wake. Nikki lurched back against the chair, cracking her spine.

Dorothea moaned harder and pitched from side to side. She bumped against Olivia. Olivia's lips were pressed together, but her eyes were as round as quarters. She looked ready to faint.

Lorah twitched. "Theresa, are you here?"

"Yes," Dorothea groaned in a voice so deep and throaty and unlike her own, Nikki couldn't figure out the trick.

"What do you want to tell us?" Lorah asked.

"Luis killed me."

"Yes, we know."

From somewhere behind Dorothea came a metallic clinking like lengths of chain striking together.

Dorothea moaned again.

Thunder cracked.

"Danger," Dorothea muttered in her stranger's voice. "Danger for the bride."

"Danger?" Lorah questioned.

"Death." The word was drawn out.

Despite her resolve to remain detached, Nikki felt a chill on her neck as though someone had placed a spectral hand on her. She gulped loudly. Jerked. Chris's grip tightened.

"Death?" Lorah pressed.

"Too much anger. Bad blood," the ghostly Dorothea murmured. "Blood to blood."

Nikki felt Chris stiffened.

"First me," Dorothea intoned. "Soon Nicole."

Nikki gasped.

The candles blew out, snuffed as if pinched by invisible fingers, all three at once, pitching the room into complete darkness. Smoke burned Nikki's nostrils.

"Stop this right now!" Chris yanked free of Nikki's death grip. He shoved out of his chair, stumbled across the room and groped for the wall switch. But when he found it, nothing happened. Furious, he hollered at Lorah, "Get that lighter of yours out and relight those candles. Now."

"Is the power off?" Olivia asked, her tone tremulous.

"Yes." Chris sounded livid.

Lorah flicked her lighter on. Dorothea wriggled in her seat like someone rousing from a nap. Chris grabbed the lighter from Lorah and lit the candles himself. Lorah reached for her glass of water and took another huge swig. She looked exhausted, showing all sixty plus of her years, her eyes underscored with dark bruising, as though she'd been punched.

Marti was scribbling in her journal. "I don't want to forget any of this."

Chris paced the room, seeming to search for whatever tricks Lorah had used to create the sounds of chains and moaning from beyond the table.

Nikki felt shell-shocked. She sat in stunned silence. Dorothea, prompted by herself or someone else, had just warned her of impending death. Logically she knew she was the victim of a nasty hoax. Emotionally she felt rattled to her toes. She struggled to regain her composure.

The storm was building again, rain battering the glass balcony doors, wind howling over the roof. A huge gust blew the French doors open with a bang. Everyone jumped. All jerked toward the gaping portal. Lightning flashed. Lorah screamed.

"No. No. No." Jorge Rameriz, dripping wet, tripped inside, a real live spook in the flickering candlelight. His gaze lashed wildly around the room before settling on Nikki. He pointed at her. "I must stop this evil!"

Chris launched himself at the groundskeeper. "Rameriz, what the hell were you doing out there?"

Jorge shook himself and ran from the room with Chris close on his heels.

Lorah gasped, clutched her throat, then groaned. She tried to speak, reached for Diego, then her eyes rolled back and she slumped unconscious in her chair.

"Oh, oh, oh." Dorothea lurched forward, overturning the glass of water.

Diego bounded up, getting to Lorah first. He grasped her wrist as the others found their feet.

Nikki held her breath. Olivia's hands were pressed to her chest, her eyes wide with horror. She stared alternately at Lorah and the liquid soaking into the red velvet table covering.

"Holy Joe," Marti exclaimed. "Does she need CPR?"

"No, she's breathing and she has a pulse." Diego glanced at them with panic in his black eyes. "I'm not certain, but I think she's having a heart attack. What she needs is an ambulance."

The next few minutes passed in a blur of activity.

Chris returned and he and Diego wrapped Lorah in a blanket. Olivia, showing more initiative and stamina than Nikki would have credited her with after watching her reaction to Lorah's collapse, retrieved her shoe boxes full of assorted candles. She directed the other women, and soon the candles were placed strategically throughout the downstairs foyer, up the staircase and in the master suite.

Under good circumstances Nikki would have found the shimmering candlelight pleasant, but this night the shadowed illumination underscored the dire situation, the nauseatingly sweet clash of aromas reminding her of Carmella's funeral. Her mother had not survived her heart attack. She prayed Lorah would.

The paramedics arrived with a clamor, attached Lorah to a heart monitor and strapped her to a stretcher. Promising a doctor would call, they carried her off as fast and efficiently as the night and the conditions allowed.

Nikki swore she heard the charm bracelet tinkle, then the door banged shut like a mausoleum slammed on disquieted souls. The silence roared in her ears. She had no idea what to say or do, other than to mouth reassuring words, the kind of meaningless platitudes she'd been offered when her mother collapsed that morning in church.

Shouldn't someone go with Lorah? Why hadn't anyone volunteered? Why hadn't she? "Maybe I should go to the hospital…"

"Why?" Diego Sands placed a hand on Nikki's shoulder, his solid touch as poignantly reassuring as that of a concerned parent. "There's nothing any of us can do at the moment. It's best we wait here for the doctor's report."

"He's right, Nikki." Olivia twisted her hands together, wringing them like tear-drenched hankies. Her complexion was as pale as the candlelight, her voice as quavery as the flames. "I've had Mrs. Grissom put out cold cuts and fresh coffee in the dining room for anyone needing sustenance after all the excitement."

Sustenance wasn't what Nikki needed, but she wasn't ready to face her empty room yet, either. She followed the others into the dining room. Settling for a mug of hot coffee to wrap her chilled hands around, she sat beside Diego.

Olivia stood to one side as her guests helped themselves. Marti and Dorothea conversed in hushed tones, the mystery writer apparently gathering more fodder for her work in progress. "Holy Joe, you really don't recall anything you said?"

"No." Dorothea squeaked. She shook her head, her turban bobbing. "A deep, sexy voice?"

"Honest." Marti nodded.

Nikki studied the two women. In the crisis over Lorah, she'd forgotten the weird voice issuing from Dorothea during the seance. Dorothea was an actress. Could she alter her voice to that extent?

Maybe she'd had help—some electrical device or other. Chris and Diego had been alone with Lorah for several minutes. Had either searched the master suite?

Chiding herself for accusing someone who'd just suffered a heart attack, Nikki couldn't forget the eerie warning. Was that also a ruse? Should she be even more on her guard? Her palms dampened. She prayed she was upset for nothing.

She glanced toward Chris, wishing she could talk this over with him, wishing for things that could never be, and her anger stirred anew. He sat at his usual place at the head of the table. His attention was riveted on Olivia, who was heaping food on her plate as though she hadn't eaten in days.

Chris frowned. "Didn't you have dinner, Liv?"

Olivia jerked as though he'd stabbed her. She pivoted, looking chagrined, a wishing-the-floor-would-open-and-swallow-her expression. A nervous laugh burst in her throat. "Are you monitoring my meals, Christopher?"

The reprimand held more hurt than ire, and Chris immediately hated himself for addressing her problem in front of their paying guests. Things were bad enough without his adding to it. No one had said it out loud, but he knew they were all blaming the Conrads for Lorah being scared into a heart attack, perhaps fatally so, by their groundskeeper.

Fury and fear coiled inside him. He wanted to smash his fist through a wall. Through Jorge Rameriz's face— even knowing he could injure the poor deluded soul. *God, I'm contemptible. Beneath contempt.* He derided Liv for handling stress by binging and purging, while he committed the worse sin of uncontrolled rage. He'd been livid at the "ghostly" threat against Nikki, his outburst rude beyond anything the situation merited.

Why?

Blood to blood. The words crashed into his mind like a premonition—fueled from childhood to the present time by his mother. Delmara Conrad never missed a chance to tell Chris how like Luis he was. How much he looked like him, acted like him, *thought* like him.

Blood to blood. His insane uncle's blood ran through his veins. Along with the same raging madness? His fear of going crazy spiked higher, and his appetite deserted him completely. He must never marry. Never risk that he would treat his bride as his uncle had treated his. Nor must he father children.

A horrid notion assailed him. Was it already too late? Had he and Nikki created a child this afternoon? Sick at the thought, he shoved his plate aside.

"I could use something stronger in this coffee." He trudged to the breakfront and withdrew a bottle of cognac. "Anyone else?"

Nikki, Diego, Marti and Dorothea all accepted his offer. Olivia shook her head, too busy stuffing food into her mouth to give him a verbal reply. How could she eat so damned much? Would she never conquer this illness? Ice twined his heart. Was he losing his sister as well as his mind?

Chapter Eleven

An hour later someone phoned from Jefferson General Hospital in Port Townsend. Lorah was still unconscious. Tests were being run to pinpoint the cause of her collapse.

Apprehensive, Nikki downed her second cup of cognac-laced coffee, then collected one of the candles in the foyer and retreated to her room.

She carried the candle to her bedside table and kicked off her shoes. The tiny room with the homely furniture was a welcome retreat. Her mind felt full to bursting. The cognac had made her sleepy, but she doubted her dreams would be peaceful. She yanked back the bedcovers. A piece of paper jumped at her like some fierce albino spider. She gasped, then gave a nervous laugh when she realized it was nothing more vicious than a page, like something from Marti's journal.

Her pulse kicked a beat higher. Could it be a page from Theresa's diary? With trembling hands, Nikki grasped the paper. It was yellowed, the handwriting elegant, the ink faded, but legible. She sank onto the bed. Dated October, twenty-five years ago, the entry read:

He came today. My own true love. And he feels the same, I could see it in his eyes. I tried to hide my excitement. Luis must not suspect—for his temper is vile. And I do not want ''him'' sent away. Oh, what my life would have been, if Papa hadn't sold me to Luis. Luis now owns my body, but he shall never own my heart, and he shall never know who does.

Nikki stared at the words, reading again and again. ''Papa'' had sold Theresa to Luis? Forced marriages in the seventies, an age of great enlightenment and free love, seemed impossible. In this case it had proven tragic for all parties. She knew what it meant to feel unloved, unlovable. Had Luis De Vega felt as she did? If so, she pitied him. But more, she pitied all the victims in his selfish life-drama.

Perhaps she hadn't been deprived by not knowing her father—if he were someone like ''Papa.''

A knock sounded on Nikki's door. Her heartbeat skipped. She hid the diary page beneath her pillow, then hastened across the room. ''Who is it?''

''Chris.''

With her breath hitching, she opened the door a crack. He held a candle under his chin as she'd done with buttercups in her childhood to see whether she'd find a true love of her own. The thought caused a catch in her throat. The passionate connection she'd shared with Chris this afternoon had been anything but love. He'd made certain she understood that. So, what was he doing here now? ''Is there more news of Lorah?''

''No.'' The candlelight cast shadows across his face, hiding his strong features, emphasizing his intense brown eyes that shone dark and sultry. ''But we need to talk.''

Now? In her room? In the half darkness? No way. Anger spiked through her. She began closing the door. "In the morning."

He caught the door and held it firm. "No."

"Why not?" Her ire twisted her nerves tighter. "What's this about?"

He glanced around surreptitiously, as though someone were listening nearby. "Let me in. It's important."

How dare he demand anything of her? Nikki clamped her jaw and ignored the pinching in her stomach. She didn't want to be alone with Chris. Didn't want to stand near him, smell him, touch him, need him. She hated that she couldn't forget this afternoon, couldn't wipe away the memories of how he'd pleasured her.

Or the way he'd hurt her.

She considered slamming the door in his face, but his foot was planted in its path. For a long moment they stared at each other like statues stationed on opposite sides of a walkway, so much alike, so lonely, yet with no way to reach out and touch, or talk, or connect. The cold spot inside Nikki spread cruel fingers of ice through her. She dug her nails into her palms. She had agreed to work with Chris. He'd said this was important. Had he learned something new?

Against her better judgment she opened the door wide enough to admit him, then spun away from him. "This had better be good."

Chris closed the door and leaned against it, watching Nikki move across the room to the desk. It was as far away as she could get from him, but she looked as though it weren't far enough. In the soft candlelight she seemed vulnerable, needy, as frightened as a small child awakened from a nightmare. But he sensed her nightmares were too real, and that tore at his resolve to stay his distance, to never touch her again; it fed the ache to pull her into his arms, to kiss the distress from her furrowed brow.

Desire fisted hard and hot in his belly. Maybe this was a bad idea. Maybe he should have waited until morning. Maybe he was worried about nothing. Or maybe he should drag her out of this room and haul her off to some safe haven far from Wedding House.

No, even to suggest that would make her think him mad. He had to act rationally. And not hurt her again. His hand tightened on the candle as if it were an anchor holding him in place, a solid hook restraining his hunger to stride to Nikki and claim her as he had this afternoon. He blew out a hard breath. The candle flame flickered. "I don't think we can dismiss the warning you received tonight."

Her eyebrows lifted, and her stance eased, but her smile was cold, dismissing his concerns. "Oh, that. Don't be silly. That was so much theater. Staged somehow between Dorothea and Lorah."

"That's just it." He took a step toward her, catching a whiff of her subtle perfume twined with the scent of vanilla from the candles. "How did they do it?"

"How should I know?" Nikki backed up, her bottom banging the desk. "Wires or something."

Chris came closer. "I found nothing in the master suite to explain the different pitch in Dorothea's voice."

Nikki gripped the edge of the desk. "The woman is an actress, trained to depict all kinds of personalities."

He rolled his eyes and moved another step toward her. "That range of tone would be impossible to affect by someone whose normal voice is two octaves higher than an electric drill."

She shrugged. "Then there has to be another explanation."

"Like?" Chris wanted to shake her. Why was she being so obtuse? He snapped his fingers. "Oh, I know, Lorah Halliard's hoard of talents includes ventriloquism."

The suggestion brought a grin to Nikki's lips, those luscious, torturing lips. God, she was gorgeous in this gentle light, shimmering hues twinkling off her golden hair. He took another step toward her, drawn by a force stronger than his very will.

Nikki tensed, her smile slipped into a sneer. "Don't you think it's more likely Dorothea had a tape recorder in one of her jumpsuit pockets?"

"Okay. I could buy that." Chris pressed his lips together, wishing he was pressing them to hers, but knowing full well he'd never experience that pleasure again. Nor did he deserve to. This afternoon should never have happened, and he prayed from the bottom of his soul that their moment of unprotected passion hadn't produced lifelong consequences. "What I don't understand is why Dorothea and Lorah would threaten you."

He was the one threatening her, silently, but surely. Why couldn't he stay by the door? Why did he have to stalk her like some giant cat, ready to pounce on her every vulnerability? Anger simmered inside her. "Maybe they picked on me because of my resemblance to Theresa. She was, after all, the 'spirit' they claimed to conjure."

He didn't seem convinced. She didn't want to dwell on the eerie warning. For all her denial to him, she hadn't been able to dismiss it as nothing. She shoved her hair away from her face and glanced at the bed as though the journal page were flashing neon from beneath her pillow. It was time she told him about the diary.

She described finding, hiding and losing it, then she showed him the page. "Someone left this on my pillow."

As she handed it to him, their fingers brushed. The contact seemed to distress him as much as it did her. He stepped away from her, raised his candle to the paper and read. When he gazed at her next, his eyes were wide with some private hell. "Do you think Luis was driven mad by her infidelity?"

The question surprised her. She'd expected him to ask *who* might have left the page on her pillow. She studied him a long moment. She'd swear her answer was important to him. Why? What was she missing? She ran her tongue across her dry lips. Did she really want to know? "Obviously Theresa loved someone other than your uncle."

She didn't say she also thought it possible Theresa and her mystery man had had an affair and that she was the child of that affair.

"Who?" Chris asked.

Nikki shrugged. She wasn't sure. "Maybe someone we don't know. Or maybe Diego Sands. He admits being close to Theresa at one time."

Chris stroked his chin, his long fingers brushing his jaw, reminding her of how those fingers had brushed her sensitive flesh, eliciting pleasure and heat on every inch of her. She swallowed back the aching need to feel that touch again. She'd be damned if she'd let herself feel anything for him.

He shook the page. "It would clear up a lot if we could find the diary."

"What I'd like to know is how someone got into my room to leave that page. My door was locked."

"Are you suggesting Liv…? Or *me*…?"

Even in the dim light she could see his hackles rising. Was he truly offended at the idea? Or trying to stay her suspicions? Yesterday, she'd actually trusted him. This afternoon he'd shattered that trust. Now, she wasn't certain what he was capable of. "If someone didn't get in here by using a key, then there must be another way in…like secret panels leading to secret passageways."

He laughed at this, shaking his head and glancing at the floor. "You watch too many old movies."

Nikki narrowed her eyes. If anyone knew the layout of this mansion it was Chris. His comment suggested her imagination was working overtime, but he hadn't denied the possibility of secret passageways. She gazed nervously at the walls, imagining all sorts of intruders appearing in her room at night, then at Chris. "I think Diego saw me hide the diary. Perhaps he has it in his room."

Chris frowned and stated pointedly, "I don't approve of entering guests' rooms without their permission, but I may make an exception." He examined the page again, then tapped it against the side of his hand. "You know, I think we're overlooking another possibility. Rameriz came to work here twenty-five years ago. In October, if I'm not mistaken."

"Jorge?" Nikki blanched at the thought that Jorge Rameriz might be her father. Diego Sands didn't thrill her much, either, but at least he seemed sane. "You think he got himself hired on as the groundskeeper to be near the woman he loved?"

"It's not impossible," Chris said.

Nikki prayed he was wrong. If Jorge were her father,

she'd likely never have a family. She had found him too late. "If Jorge was Theresa's mystery man, and her betrayal was the reason she died, then why didn't Luis kill Jorge as well?"

Chris's face paled. "How should I know?"

"Luis was your uncle. I thought *you* might—"

"Might what?" he barked. "Know that my uncle was a raving lunatic—unable to control a simple emotion like jealousy?"

The outburst startled Nikki. One would think she'd accused *him* of being insane. Why? Again, he shoved his hand through his thick hair, giving it a sex-tousled look, pulling unwanted images into her mind. She crushed the visions. "We need some answers. If not from your mother, then from Jorge."

He tossed his head, his nostrils flaring like a bull, and exhaled loudly. His control seemed to have returned in a flash. "If you think you can face Rameriz, then we'll do it in the morning, and this time I'll make him talk to us."

To Nikki's horror, he sounded as though he'd even use force to make Jorge talk. She wondered anew if Chris was a violent man—like his uncle? *Blood to blood.* Was that the meaning behind Dorothea's warning? Was Chris the one she should fear?

Or was she just so angry at him she couldn't acknowledge anything decent about him? She recalled his gentle treatment of his sister and knew, despite her wounded sensitivities, that there was goodness in this man. And if she were totally honest with herself, what occurred between them this afternoon was impetuous and spontaneous, without promise or obligation, ignited by her own passionate attack on him.

So why was she furious with Chris?

The question pricked her conscience, demanded she face some truths. Wasn't she actually angry with herself? Riled because she cared more for him than he cared for her? Because while they made love, she'd allowed herself to feel loved? And wanted? Had she really expected that feeling to endure? Expected him to feel the same? Contrition sifted through her, reproving Nikki. She wasn't a child. An inexperienced ingenue. But she'd been giving a good imitation of one.

She wouldn't apologize to Chris, but she would quit snapping at him. "Jorge may not tell us what we want to hear."

"No matter." Chris opened the door. "We have to try."

"True." Nikki watched him step into the hallway. "Let's make it early. I want to visit Lorah at the hospital."

She also intended to stop by the local library and look up old newspapers. More than ever, she wanted to find out whether or not a baby was mentioned in connection with Wedding House. And more than that, she wanted information on Luis De Vega, wanted to try and understand what was behind Chris's shifting moods. Maybe she could even lay her hands on a blueprint of Wedding House.

THE NEXT MORNING dawned clear and cool. In its wake, the storm left behind a nightmare of branches and debris, disturbing the usual polished appearance of the grounds, and vexing Jorge Rameriz into a clean-up frenzy. He ordered his yardmen about with the efficiency of a ship captain directing his crew. Chris also pitched in, after telling Nikki they'd corner Rameriz later.

Nikki checked her e-mail, but neither Zeus nor Jelly-bean had responded. She returned to her room, feeling at loose ends. It was too early for the library to be open, too early for visiting the hospital. She glanced around, wondering again about secret passageways. Knowing Chris was occupied outside, she tapped on the inside walls, listening for a change in sound.

Inching along, she knocked and listened, knocked and listened. Once, twice, ten times. Solid thuds each one. Disappointment, laced with relief, saw her to the wall beside her closet. On the one hand, she wanted to believe there was a secret way into her room, an expla-nation of how the diary page could have been left by someone without a key.

On the other hand, she didn't like the idea of some-one entering her room whenever they wanted. Didn't like thinking either of the Conrads would sneak in. Didn't like thinking Chris would do that. She raised her knuckles and rapped the panel beside the closet. A hol-low clunk. Nikki froze. Excitement billowing inside her, she tapped the wall again. The hollow sound echoed back to her.

Driven, she pushed, prodded and poked the length of wall from floor to ceiling and tried the same from inside the closet. After several minutes, she stood back and swore softly. If there was some way to open the panel from this side, she couldn't find it. She needed the blue-prints. Once she had those in hand, she'd present Chris with evidence he couldn't deny and demand he show her how to access the passageways.

Meanwhile she couldn't bear sitting here, watching the clock tick by. But she might get some answers—if City Hall were open. She called a cab and was soon heading down Hastings Avenue.

Wedding House sat on the shores near Cape George, almost directly across from the town of Port Townsend. Fifteen minutes later the cab slowed as it started along Water Street, the main drag through this charming seaport city.

Here, tourists congregated among the renovated and rejuvenated stretch of aged buildings that hugged Port Townsend Bay and that housed shops and restaurants geared to please with visual and culinary delights. The cab driver informed Nikki that the city was one of only three Victorian seaports on the National Historic Register, that it enjoyed an international reputation for its manufacturing of wooden sailing vessels and state-of-the-art motor yachts, and was famous for its many Victorian homes that had been converted to bed and breakfast inns, making it the B & B capital of the Pacific Northwest.

She already knew the latter. She directed the driver to the curb, thanked and paid him, then emerged near the Belmont Hotel. She intended to walk to her destination. Already the sidewalks were filling with families and shoppers of all ages. Nikki joined the throng heading toward Point Hudson.

As she walked, her gaze automatically scanned the eye-catching window displays. The morning was rapidly warming, but she felt a sudden chill on her neck. That odd sense of someone staring at her, following her. She stopped at a jewelry store and pretended to peer inside, stealing surreptitious glances back the way she'd come. No one seemed to be paying particular attention to her. Nor did she spot anyone pretending to be looking in a store window as she was doing.

Still, the sensation lingered. She ducked into the jewelry store and went to a window display that gave her a view of the sidewalk. She remained there for several minutes, but no one passed whom she recognized.

She started for the door when something in the display case caught her eye. A slew of tiny charms the size of those on Lorah Halliard's bracelet. She studied them a long moment, then saw the perfect one, a tiny crystal ball. Deciding it would make a much better get-well gift than flowers, she bought it.

As she paid, she asked directions to City Hall and decided to try the old one on Madison first, since it was closest. On the street, another wave of anxiety swept her. Her skin crawled. She picked up her pace. Was someone stalking her? Planning a fatal attack in this pleasant town, on this pleasant day? The tang of salt air and traffic fumes tangled with the acrid taste of fear coating her tongue.

She determined not to glance over her shoulder. Half a block later she did. But if someone were spying on her, or following her, she couldn't spot them.

Relief crashed through her as she sighted City Hall and hurried inside. She was breathing too hard and forced herself to calm down. She stood in a big empty lobby with a sign that stated the receptionist was upstairs. Council chambers took up the left half of the second floor, and various offices, the right. At the receptionist's desk, a woman was busily working on a computer. She glanced up as Nikki approached. "May I help you?"

The woman had a beautiful face and a disposition to match, if her face-lighting smile were any indication. Nikki asked where she might find the office where residential blueprints were archived.

The woman's brows lifted. "Oh, my. I'm afraid you've come to the wrong place. You'll be wanting to see the records manager in Archives. That's in a building on Washington and Jefferson behind the County Courthouse.''

The receptionist gave her directions, and Nikki realized she was nowhere near it at the moment. She'd need another taxi. Maybe she should try the library first. ''Where is the library?''

''Uptown. On Lawrence.''

''Is that within walking distance?''

''Both places are within walking distance, if you don't mind a real hike, some of it uphill.''

After all the climbing she'd been doing up and down the stairs at Wedding House, Nikki figured she could manage a little more. She thanked the woman and descended to the deserted lobby.

Her sense of danger loomed as fresh and black as a swarm of flies. It gripped her insides with terror. She wanted to run to the door and out into the sunshine and safety of the crowded street. No. She had to quit giving in to this unfounded fear. She forced herself to walk normally.

She heard the footsteps behind her a millisecond before the huge hand landed on her shoulder.

Chapter Twelve

Nikki's heart thudded. She spun around. Chris. Her breath wobbled from her. Dear God, was part of her actually glad to see him—in spite of the scowl on his appealing face? Anger at herself and at him bit her.

He said, "What are you doing at City Hall?"

"What am *I*—? You mean, supposing it were any of your business?" She struggled to stem her rising temper, to swallow the anxiety he'd roused. *Play the game, Nikki. Find out what he knows. Don't give anything away for free.* She forced a smile. "I took a wrong turn, found myself outside the building and wandered in."

He studied her hard. She suspected he knew she was lying but wasn't sure what he should or could do about it. Had he been the one she'd sensed following her? She asked sweetly, "What are *you* doing here?"

He made a face. "Trying to get a fireworks permit. But it seems I need the Permits Department over by Castle Hill Center."

Was *he* lying? Had he tailed her? They walked outside. The sun didn't warm her as she'd anticipated it would minutes earlier. Had Chris overheard her conversation with the woman in the reception area upstairs?

Did he know she wanted blueprints of Wedding House? Her mouth dried.

But why was she worried? Even if he'd eavesdropped, it didn't mean he knew she was trying to find out about the secret passageways. If he asked, she would say she wanted the blueprints for her book. She wouldn't tell him the truth until he started telling her the truth.

The annoying frustration she'd been experiencing the past few days sawed across her nerves. Her trip to the building department would have to be put off. She couldn't go there with Chris in tow.

"Still want to visit the library?" he asked, letting her know he'd overheard at least part of her conversation. "It should be open by now."

Without touching her, he held her close to his side, linked as acutely as though they shared a pair of handcuffs. What was it about this man that had climbed inside her from the moment they'd met? That demanded she notice him? That wouldn't let her walk away without a backward glance? Without regrets? Longings?

Was it his erratic behavior that both repelled and attracted her? His roller-coaster ups and downs of one minute flying wild on an emotional free-for-all, and the next clutching the speed lever with white knuckles— controlling himself and everything and everyone? Chris Conrad was one ride she wanted off.

But how, when the sun glinted across his ebony hair, painting it a vivid blue-black? When seeing him seared her heart with longing and the need to feel loved again, as she had felt yesterday in his arms?

The thought sobered Nikki. If discovering the secrets of the past weren't so important to her future, she'd return to Wedding House, pack and leave this very afternoon. She had enough information to write her book. But she was no closer to finding her father.

Chris pointed toward the Jaguar parked not ten feet from them. "I'll drive you."

She couldn't help but smile to herself. Chris was trying to control her even now—winding his invisible constraints around her. Why was she so susceptible to him? "Did you talk to Jorge?"

"No. Couldn't get him alone. Whatever else he is, he's very protective of the house and grounds. The clean-up was all he could think about."

Chris opened the car door for her, and, like a good hostage, Nikki sank into the low-slung seat. "Tomorrow, then?"

"Yes." He circled the rear of the car, waited for a break in traffic, then opened the driver's door and climbed inside the Jag. "The library's on Lawrence—in the same area as a lot of the bed and breakfast inns P.T. is famous for."

He drove a circuitous route, past James House and Starrett House, Rothschild House and Hill House. The wind, briny and fresh, brushed her face, tasting sweet in her nostrils. The sun rose higher. Her view from the convertible was unobstructed, and Nikki admired the different mansions, most of which were built in the late 1800s and early 1900s by the settlers of the seaport town. "They're wonderful."

"There are dozens more," Chris assured her with a chuckle.

His laugh filled her, melodic and resonating, stroking her senses like a master's bow on a Stradivarius. Unbidden images sprang to mind, roused a deep yearning, an ache for something stronger than physical gratification, a connection of soul to soul. Honesty. Trust. Friendship.

All the things she'd never had with anyone. All the things she'd felt within her grasp yesterday with Chris.

She swallowed against the lump in her throat. "You know the anonymous note is what gave me the idea for my book. So, Wedding House was always the only B & B in Port Townsend I even considered, and I suppose you realize that I will use it for my book."

"Yes," he said with a trace of bitterness. "Its history is irresistible."

"How that history affects me is the lure."

"Be careful what you wish for." He glanced toward her. His brown eyes exuded concern and a harsh glint of pained wisdom. "Sometimes a person is better off not knowing everything about their familial legacy."

His words tapped the cold spot inside her, made it feel twice its normal size. But even that wouldn't deter her. No matter what awful things her heritage held in store for her, she had to know.

"THE PORT TOWNSEND Public Library was once endowed by Andrew Carnegie," Chris said, as he maneuvered into a parking space. "Then there was a big restoration project done with city and privately raised funds in the late 1980s, early 1990s."

As they entered the library, Nikki was assailed with the smell of aged books and polished wood. She'd expected the inside of the building to be more modern, but the old-time feeling of it wrapped around her, welcoming her into an era she couldn't otherwise visit. The whole place seemed to declare books and readers had always been its primary treasures and would continue to be so as long as the structure stood.

The front door led into a hallway with a room for children to the right, the main library to the left and stairs straight ahead. "We'll be wanting old copies of the *Leader*," Chris said. "They're upstairs."

The upper level consisted of two rooms. Nikki followed Chris into the second, a thirty by thirty space that resembled an old-fashioned parlor with its brick fireplace, upright piano and dark-wood-paneled walls. An elderly couple sat reading the daily news on an antique divan, and a young man occupied one of two reading tables. The musty dry scent of aging paper was stronger here.

Nikki glanced toward the ten-foot-high ceilings. All four walls had windows starting five feet from the floor and shelves below. Magazines, arranged alphabetically, stood on end in cardboard holders of green, burgundy and tan. Back issues included everything from *Cosmopolitan* to *National Geographic*.

Chris headed straight to a back wall, knelt before some bound newspapers and plucked one from the group. He laid it out on a nearby table, the portable folding kind with metal legs and hardboard surfaces. "This is the year you want."

Nikki sat down. Chris took the chair next to her, looming tall and reassuring beside her, smelling too good for someone she'd declared off limits. Her pulse thrummed and her palms dampened. Because of Chris? Or what she might find in this folder of old newspapers?

Gingerly, she turned the seasoned pages of the *Leader*, hope and anticipation shivering through her. She found stories of a senator predicting the seventies recession, ferry news and scores of obituary notices. But birth announcements were few, only four that year, two girls and two boys, each accounted for by loving local families.

Disappointed, she tried the year before, then the year after. In a February issue she came across the first mention of Wedding House. It was the front-page story of the murders/suicide and the fire. It was obvious the reporter knew little of Luis De Vega, as the details were sketchy. He'd written more about the fire than the people who'd died.

All she learned was that the De Vegas had bought the ten acres near Cape George in the late 1800s, but had left it undeveloped until Luis inherited the property from his grandfather and had had Wedding House built the year before he married.

He and his bride had lived there for two years.

There was no mention of a baby or a child. In fact, the whole story was disappointingly lacking in detail.

Follow-ups included news that the case was closed, and that the mansion would be closed, as well, kept under the supervision of the groundskeeper and Luis's sister, Delmara Conrad.

Frustration threatened to swallow Nikki. It seemed her only hope of learning more about Theresa and the baby Jorge Rameriz had mentioned was either from Jorge himself, or through her e-mail sources.

"Next stop, the hospital," Chris announced, appearing not to share her interest, as though he couldn't wait to get away from the library, from the hateful news articles about his family history, while she ached to embrace any piece of news she could about her own family.

IN THE HOSPITAL PARKING lot, Chris got out and produced an armload of yellow roses from the trunk of the car. Nikki gaped. Given the price of roses, she was floored he bought so many. "Looks like you cleaned out a florist shop."

"Lorah's favorite flower."

"Oh?" How had he known that?

As though he'd read her mind, he answered, "Liv insisted."

Nikki thought about this, wondering whether or not the Conrads were trying to salve their consciences over Lorah's collapse, as if by employing Jorge they felt personally responsible.

She supposed they might very well be.

She fingered the tiny charm in her pocket, thinking its price rivaled that of the flowers. Why had she spent so much on someone she barely knew? Her heart was a stone, heavy in her chest. Because she couldn't forget the way Lorah had collapsed. Kept seeing her mother. Kept praying this would be different. She wanted desperately to celebrate a recovery. Needed it.

They made their way to the Coronary Care Unit and inquired at the nurses' station about Lorah Halliard. The nurse asked whether or not they were family, then directed them to speak to the woman in the waiting room. Lorah's daughter. She was a dark-haired woman in her thirties, weeping into a hankie. An older man was consoling her.

Chris said, "Miss Halliard?"

"It's Jacoby." The sniffling woman lifted eyes as eerily green as Lorah's. "Janice Jacoby. Halliard was my maiden name."

Chris and Nikki introduced themselves and asked after Lorah.

Janice Jacoby began to weep anew.

The man, wiry and middle-aged and dressed as

though he'd rushed there from the golf course, stepped forward. "Dr. Roland Wiggins. I've been Lorah's physician and friend for many years."

Nikki's stomach dropped. "Is she okay, Doctor?"

"No. Unfortunately…no." He choked on the last word.

"She's worse?" Chris paled.

Nikki held her breath.

Dr. Wiggins blinked. "I'm sorry to say she died before I arrived."

"Oh, no." Nikki's throat constricted. Just like Carmella. She curled her fingers around the crystal ball charm in her pocket. Her knees quaked, and she dropped onto the chair beside Janice Jacoby. "Oh, no."

Janice stopped sniffling. She wiped her spookily pale eyes with the mascara-stained hanky. A tinkle caught Nikki's ear, resounding with the intensity of a death knoll. Janice was clutching the charm bracelet as though holding a lifeline, as Nikki herself clutched the tiny charm she'd purchased for Lorah. Cold spread through Nikki.

The woman sniffed. "Mother's dead. Dead."

Nikki breathed hard. Just like her own mother. The ache in her chest grew. She knew exactly how Janice felt at this moment. Shocked, forsaken, alone, devastated. She reached a hand to her. Janice shrank back, as though she might collapse if touched.

The roses drooped in Chris's hand, the sweet scent now cloying and funereal in the compact room. His black brows dipped low over his narrowed eyes. "It was her heart, then?"

"That's what these quacks are saying." Janice's expression hardened. "But Mother's heart was as strong as a teenager's. The women in our family always live into their late nineties or early hundreds.''

Nikki couldn't take it in. She wondered for a split second about the females in her own family. Did the women all die young? She shook herself, concentrated on Janice Jacoby. "I'm so sorry."

"Why are you sorry?" Lorah's daughter asked, her mouth thinning, her gaze penetrating. Was she, also, psychic?

Nikki could barely breathe. "I lost my own mother to a heart attack last year."

Janice eyed her for a long moment, obviously taken down a notch by this news. "You have my sympathy. But you aren't listening to me. Mother could not have died from a heart attack."

"We don't know that yet, Janice," Dr. Wiggins said softly.

"I know it!" Janice insisted. "Complete misdiagnosis. If only Mother hadn't been unconscious—she'd have told those quacks what was causing her distress."

"We'll have our answers as soon as possible, Janice." Dr. Wiggins glanced at Nikki and Chris. "Soon as the autopsy is performed."

THE NEWS OF LORAH'S DEATH placed a pall on the mansion, and the rest of the day passed with everyone in a subdued mood. All retreated to their rooms early.

Nikki found the next morning held little improvement. The tension was so thick in the dining room, even Mrs. Grissom's wonderful array of breakfast dishes inspired few hearty appetites. Nikki settled for coffee and a bowl of fruit.

Marti seemed a wilted violet in her purple frock, her journal absent, her normal enthusiasm dimmed. Diego kept muttering what a tragedy it was that a fine woman had met death before her time. His black eyes held a faraway cast as though he were remembering a long-lost friend, not the recently deceased Lorah.

Chris and Olivia continuously exchanged worried glances, and Nikki suspected the autopsy had them on edge, the fear something would be found that would give Janice Jacoby reason to sue.

As though in defiance of the mourning exhibited by guests and staff alike, Dorothea wore an electric-blue jumpsuit and a cheerleader expression. She did her best to lift spirits, then finally on an exasperated sigh she chirped, "You know, I understand how distressed everyone is about poor Lorah. So am I, of course, but, well, the grand opening can't be canceled—what with reservations and all. And neither should the festivities."

Chris stayed his fork halfway to his mouth. His eyes narrowed as he waited for Dorothea to continue.

She gave him a nervous smile. "Don't you agree, that despite this tragic event, Wedding House deserves the best launch we can manage?"

"What's your point, Dot?" Chris snapped with impatience.

She flushed. "Well, I'm saying, of course, that the play must go on." She returned Chris's hard stare with a defiant one that included Nikki.

Nikki groaned inwardly. She'd all but forgotten the play, and now fervently wished she hadn't committed herself to it. Her only consolation was that Chris looked even less excited about it than she felt.

He finished his bite of pancake, then muttered, "Fine."

"Oh, good." Dorothea clapped her hands, then seemed to realize her triumph was inappropriate in the midst of the gloomy group. "Rehearsal begins after lunch. In the ballroom."

Nikki spent the morning on her book. Wanting to avoid another tense meal, she had lunch in her room. Chris came to her door just before the rehearsals were to begin. She closed her laptop and stepped into the hall with him.

They were alone on the third floor, but a buzz of activity rose from below, the melancholy of hours past lifting from the mansion like a departing fog—much as her lethargy seemed to rise and float away at the very nearness of Chris. She struggled against her susceptibility to him.

But for all the hurt and anger he'd caused her, something about the man made her blood sing, made the air taste fresher, gave her purpose and hope.

His handsome face was pinched, his expression rivaling the shadows in the hallway. She asked, "Is something wrong?"

He walked slowly beside her toward the stairs, keeping his voice low. "Diego left for a meeting in town, and I searched his room as we discussed."

Nikki's throat tightened. She gazed at him with her pulse licking a beat faster. "And?"

Chris's scowl deepened as though he were disgusted with himself, as though finding the diary wasn't important enough to set aside his ethics.

She wanted to remind him that her life might depend on their laying hands on that diary. "Did you find it?"

"If he has it, he's got it with him."

Long rays of sun poked through the stairwell windows, casting glittery beams across them as they descended. Nikki sighed, staving off her disappointment. She'd known finding the diary would be tricky. Perhaps impossible. But still she'd hoped for the easy fix. Did Diego have it? Or had someone else taken it?

Maybe Diego had nothing to do with any of this. She pressed her lips together, considering. No. He had known Theresa. But how well? She recalled how close-mouthed he'd become when she pushed him about that relationship. "I'm certain there was something romantic between Diego and Theresa."

Chris didn't look convinced. "If there was, I'd say he got over it fairly quickly. There's a photo on his bedside table of a dark-haired young woman about your age, who looks like she might be his daughter. She doesn't resemble Theresa."

That stopped Nikki. She stared up at Chris a long moment, considering the significance of this. Too bad she couldn't get a look at that photograph. But it was out of the question. She wouldn't ask him to breach his ethics a second time.

But what of the photograph? Did it mean she, Nikki, wasn't the baby who'd been at the mansion? "Perhaps Diego and Theresa had a child."

"That he raised?" Chris's brows shot up, his expression incredulous. "It's more likely Diego Sands has a nice wife and lots of kids tucked away somewhere."

"Oh, I suppose you're right." She shrugged, nodded and started toward the landing again. "But if he's married, why didn't he bring his wife here with him?"

"Hmm," Chris muttered thoughtfully as they reached the second floor.

In the ballroom, the sun was brilliant, raising dust motes across the wooden planking. Dorothea, as blue and red as a Brazilian parrot, Olivia, in her best Morticia Addams gear, and the other two actors in normal rehearsal casuals, all looked up as Chris and Nikki arrived.

"Right on schedule." Dorothea motioned them to the center of the room. "You know the scene. We'll just pick up where we left off last time. Do you need to see the script again?"

Chris and Nikki both asked for scripts. Nikki could see Chris growing more sullen as he read again the dialogue leading up to "the push."

Nikki's knees felt weak. Her palms felt damp. She stumbled over her lines, as clumsy as a child reading in front of a class for the first time. The real actors exchanged amused glances and she blushed.

Chris wasn't much better. His manner and dialogue were stilted, his movements as controlled as plays in a game of chess. Nikki's heart went out to him. It had to be awful to be that frightened of one's own emotions.

Of course, she was a fine one to talk, considering the state she'd been in, allowing her feelings to rule, to sway her this way and that like a windsock on a blustery day.

Dorothea called, "Action."

Chris read his lines with all the ardor of a plastic plant. He seemed to hate the words he was forced to say, wouldn't even look Nikki directly in the eye. But he did shove her. Too hard. It startled her. It startled him. She lost her balance.

Chris's eyes flew wide and, as he'd done two days ago, he caught her before she fell.

Dorothea groaned. "Not again."

"Perhaps this is not a good scene to work on." Nikki suggested, trying to ward off fresh outbursts from Chris and Dorothea.

"Oh, but we must get it right." Dorothea fluttered.

"Please, just once more. I promise it will be the last time, no matter what."

"Yes, it will be," Chris warned.

He and Nikki took their marks, the other two actors nearby. Nikki's stomach twisted like bent aluminum. But this time Chris spoke his lines as though they were his own. For some reason his confidence fed hers. She could hear the improvement.

Go with it, she coaxed herself.

And it worked.

If she didn't know better, she'd think she was having an actual confrontation with Chris. God knew, they'd had enough of them. He reached his hands to push her. Nikki readied to coordinate her backward lurch to his forward thrust.

"No." Chris dropped his hands and shook his head. "I can't."

Nikki sagged, relieved, yet let down.

"What is the matter now?" Dorothea looked crestfallen.

Chris kept shaking his head. "You have to rewrite this."

Dorothea blinked at him as though he'd lost his mind. "But it's history."

"Lookit, Dot." Chris pointed his finger at her, fire building deep in his brown eyes. "I don't hit women. And I won't parade my family's dirty laundry in public."

He pivoted toward his sister. "Liv, how did you ever approve this garbage?"

With that, he tossed the script at Olivia's feet and stormed from the room. Nikki stared after him in confusion. Despite appearances, he wasn't a spoiled child. Something about his uncle's violence caused his temper to arc out of control. She'd seen it more than once. What was behind his reaction?

Was Chris a violent man who didn't want anyone to know his secret? Or did he detest violence so much he couldn't even pretend it? As badly as she wanted an answer, after yesterday's fiasco, Nikki wasn't about to follow him.

But Olivia did.

Embarrassment painting her cheeks, she snatched up the script and chased after her brother. "Christopher, will you do the scene if we rewrite it?" Her voice echoed back to the ballroom

"I said I would," he growled.

"Promise?"

"Yes." The front door banged.

AFTER DINNER, with the revised script, which Dorothea and Olivia had worked on all afternoon and which none of the actors had yet seen, they retired to the parlor. Marti and Diego joined them.

Marti had her journal open, her purple pen poised. She'd announced at dinner that her newest mystery, based on the mansion, its ghost and other pertinent facts, was humming along at great speed. "All names changed to protect the innocent, of course."

Of course, Nikki thought. But who among them was innocent?

"Okay, Chris." Dorothea pointed to his mark, a pink, chalked X on the parlor carpet. "The new scene calls for you to kiss Nikki. And make it a good kiss. Then after a few moments, Nikki, you try breaking away and that's when you push so hard against Chris's chest when he releases you, you stumble backward."

Nikki's cheeks reddened. Heat climbed Chris's neck.

Everyone else waited with avid expressions. Ire swirled through Chris. But he had no one to rage at. He'd insisted on having the scene changed, and now that they'd accommodated him, he couldn't very well refuse or go back on his promise to Liv.

But kissing Nikki. Damn. He couldn't. But what choice did he have? It was either kiss her or admit to one and all that he feared he wouldn't stop kissing her once he'd started.

Trembling inside, he offered his open arms. Nikki stepped toward him with reluctance, then closer, until their breaths tangled. She lifted her face to him. He swallowed hard. Then, too aware of the audience and his heating blood, he brushed his lips across hers, tentatively at first, relishing the sweet, remembered taste of her. Then the flame that had ignited yesterday between them exploded anew, a flash fire of desire, and he whisked his arms around her and deepened the kiss until she moaned, until he wanted her so badly he'd have risked anything to have her.

Through the haze of desire enveloping Nikki, she heard someone shouting. Then again. At last she realized it was Dorothea. "Now, Nikki. Start struggling now."

The words struck with a sobering chill. How had she let this man sweep her up in his passion again? She fought his hold, felt his grip tighten, felt his body responding as it had yesterday, and she denied the corresponding need tingling her own flesh.

She thrust the heels of her palms against his chest. Unexpectedly he let go of her. She flew backward. The "audience" seemed to be holding its breath, but the silly grins on their faces left little doubt what they were thinking. Nikki's cheeks burned as brightly as the heat inside her.

Deliberately she tripped farther away from Chris. Her backside banged into the wall. Tiny shards of pain joined the humiliation spreading across her skin. She had but a millisecond to notice. For, like a hole opening in the earth, the solid panel supporting her vanished. And Nikki was falling.

Chapter Thirteen

Nikki screamed. With her arms flailing, she fell into the open space behind the panel. Dust and debris surged upward, lifted by her invasion. She dropped hard on her backside. Pain radiated from her tailbone toward each hip. The dusty cloud hovered above her for a split second, then rained down like dirty snow.

Coughing and batting at the gunk, she cowered against its onslaught. Hands caught her upper arms, and she heard Chris cursing. "Are you all right?"

Everyone seemed to speak at once, drowning out Chris, asking the same question. Was she okay?

Nikki stung with embarrassment, vaguely aware of some distant pain she couldn't pinpoint at the moment. She blinked through the flaky powder coating her lashes, her cheeks, her clothing and choked out, "I think so. What happened?"

But Chris was examining her chest, concern lowering his brows. She realized her blouse was torn, her right breast partially exposed. The heat in her cheeks intensified. She clutched at her blouse, felt something sticky squish against her fingertips, and realized she was bleeding. "I'm cut."

Chris told his sister to get the first-aid kit. He helped Nikki to her feet.

"I think you scraped against a nail," Diego said, his expression as concerned as Chris's, his probing gaze hitching her embarrassment another notch higher. "But the wound seems superficial enough."

"Have you had a tetanus shot?" Olivia asked.

But Nikki didn't hear her; she was trying to make sense of what had happened. She spun and gazed at the opening she'd fallen through, realizing as she did so, what it was that she was seeing.

Marti was peering into the black hole in the wall. "Holy Joe, what is this?"

"It's a passageway," Olivia stated, as though admitting some shameful secret.

Diego marched to Marti's side. "I knew this mansion had walls that didn't match the dimensions inside and outside." He glanced back at Chris. "Is there a network of passageways?"

Chris ignored him. "Liv, the first-aid kit."

"Where's a flashlight?" Diego stepped into the opening. "I've made quite a study of hidden corridors in houses all over the country. How exciting to add this mansion to the list."

"Where does it go?" Marti asked, following the architect through the portal. "Let's explore. I can use this for the book. Just think of all the transgressions my perpetrator could commit sneaking in and out of rooms undetected."

"Get out of there!" Chris roared. "I nailed that access shut. I don't know how it popped open, but I don't want anyone going in there."

"Why not?" Diego demanded, peering out at him.

Chris glared at the architect. "Because my insurance agent insisted."

Dorothea chirped, "Are you saying it isn't safe?"

"Bingo." He left Nikki's side and stood by the opening, motioning Diego and Marti back into the parlor. "It's off-limits. I'd appreciate it if everyone would respect that. Liv, where is that first-aid kit?"

Olivia shook herself, a sleepwalker waking. "Oh, my, yes, I'm sorry, Nikki."

She hurried from the room before Nikki could tell her not to bother. The wound didn't look worth the fuss Chris was making.

Marti brushed white dust from her lavender slacks and complained halfheartedly, "I won't say I'm not disappointed, Chris. But I've no desire to cause you or Olivia unnecessary grief, and I certainly have imagination enough to make these tunnels come alive on the page. This book just keeps getting better."

Chris rolled his eyes, obviously displeased with the whole idea of Marti's book.

"Don't worry about me, young man," Diego chimed in. He looked ready to concede to Chris's wishes, but something struck Nikki wrong. She couldn't put her finger on it, but would bet Diego had no intention of doing as requested.

Dorothea gazed uneasily toward the passageway, keeping her distance as though repelled by the opening in the wall. Why?

Olivia hustled in, a black cloud of billowing cloth and white solicitation, and Nikki forgot about Dorothea.

Chris settled her on the settee, then dug into the first-aid kit, took out disinfectant and bandages, and gently pushed Nikki's hands aside, positioning himself between the audience and her modesty. Still, her cheeks burned as the blouse fell apart like some enticing silken veil, revealing her lacy undergarment.

The bra was low cut, allowing him easy access to the wound on the high curve of her breast. His gaze seemed to burn into her, and heat feathered her cheeks as she recalled the awe in his eyes that first moment he'd seen her naked—the same look she saw now.

She forgot about the others, felt alone with Chris, trusted him not to hurt her. Her throat thickened with caring, caring she didn't want to acknowledge, didn't want to feel. But his breath was warm on her injured flesh, sweet in her nostrils, and she detected a slight tremor in his touch, a sensitive lover's touch, as he cleaned the wound.

"This might sting," he warned, daubing peroxide on the cut to remove the dust and dirt.

She winced and he winced with her, as though it hurt him to hurt her. Did it? Her pulse thrummed with the possibility. She stared at his hands, those wide wonderful hands, watched his tender ministrations and reveled in the caresslike brushes of his fingertips on her breast, her nipples growing hard and achy with honeyed desire.

He spread antibiotic salve into the cut, then smoothed the bandage down, his hand slipping lower, grazing her erect nipple. He drew in a sharp breath and swallowed hard. "Have you had a tetanus shot recently?"

She lifted her gaze to meet his. They might be alone in the room, alone in the world. Above the sharp tang of disinfectant, she caught the lure of him, the scent that was his alone, a mix of male and spice. She murmured, "Are you worried?"

He jerked as though she'd caught him with his emotions exposed. His features closed down. He stuffed the first-aid supplies back into the kit and banged the lid.

"If you haven't had a shot, get one. Right now the only thing I'm worried about is closing that hole in the wall."

With that he stalked from the room.

"Pent-up sexual frustration would be my guess," Marti whispered near Nikki's ear. "I'll bet after that kiss, you'd just love to help him blow off some of that head of steam he carries around."

Nikki, clutching her blouse to her chest, burned with embarrassment. She'd like to vent some anger of her own at the moment, would like to tell the smug mystery writer that if that was all that was bothering Chris, he'd have found a bit of release the other day. Instead she said, "No, thanks, but *you* may want to try."

"Oh, he's way too volatile for me." Marti grinned. "Diego, about that study you've done on secret passageways…I'd love to hear about it. I'll bet there's fresh coffee in the dining room."

"I'll see to it." Olivia bustled from the room ahead of Diego and Marti.

Dorothea was bidding the two actors good-night at the door as Nikki started up to her room. The insulating numbness following the impact of her fall was wearing off. Pain radiated from her tailbone. Likely bruised. She climbed gingerly.

"Oh, my." Dorothea sidled up to her. "Looks like that fall made your bum tender. Well, don't you worry. I've got some painkillers in my desk upstairs. I'll get you a couple."

"No, thank you. I don't like taking other people's medicine."

"Oh, I'm sure they're fine. We're about the same size. Besides, I gave one to Lorah the night of the séance. She had a bad toothache. Seemed to do the trick."

Dorothea swept into the ballroom. Nikki gaped after her, heard her rattling around in her desk. Had she forgotten Lorah was dead? Dead from something that appeared to be heart failure? Nikki clutched the torn halves of her blouse tighter. Could an overdose of a narcotic painkiller simulate a heart attack? She didn't know. Didn't know who to ask. But then Dorothea said she'd only given Lorah one tablet.

Surely one couldn't kill?

Just the same, maybe Chris would like to have one of these pills—in case he needed it—should Janice Jacoby decide to hold Olivia and him liable for her mother's death.

She poked her head into the ballroom. Dorothea was seated at her desk, drinking greedily from her mug. A near-full bottle of vodka reposed within easy reach. She lowered the mug, red-faced at being caught. "Helps me sleep."

Nikki pressed her lips together. "Hopefully not at the wheel on the drive home."

"Oh, no, no. I've only had a teeny bit." She stood, gathered her purse, stuck the bottle into a bottom drawer.

"Before you go, I've changed my mind. I will take one of those pain pills."

Dorothea shook her head. "Sorry. I can't find them. Been trying to figure out whether or not I took them home. But I guess I won't know until I get there and look. Good night, my dear. Sleep tight."

NIKKI WOKE WITH A START, sitting straight up in bed. Her heart banged her chest. Her skin felt clammy. What had she been dreaming that would startle her awake? She couldn't recall. Not even a wisp of a memory. She sat on the edge of the bed, breathing deep and long, felt her heartbeat calming. She glanced at the digital clock. Twelve-thirty.

Whatever she'd been dreaming, she wasn't anxious to return to it. She switched on the lamp and grabbed the book on her bedside table, a thriller she'd borrowed from the library. But after a few minutes the tension in the story had her pulse climbing again. She laid the book aside, visited the bathroom, washed her face and hands and returned to her room. No one else seemed to be stirring.

She envied them their nightmare-free sleep. But then none of them had been threatened or nearly killed during their stay here. Shrugging off the thought, Nikki scooted to the bed. Her foot struck something cold and hard. She yelped and leaped back, then froze as she spied the offending object. A chisel...with a blunted tip.

Her scalp prickled, and her heart pounded with fear. She spun around, expecting to see whoever had left the chisel standing there, taunting her. But she was alone. An awful thought swept her. Had someone been in her room earlier? Looming over her as she'd slept? Was that what had awakened her?

Her mouth dried. Or had someone sneaked in while she was in the bathroom? Were they here even now? Hiding under the bed? In the closet? Tremors raced over her clammy flesh. She gazed at the walls, her mind seeing through the plasterboard into the secret passageway.

For a full two seconds she couldn't move. Maybe she should get Chris...but what if he wasn't in his room? What if he'd been the one in here? The one who'd left the chisel? Ice wrapped her heart.

She had to do something. She couldn't just stand here, too frightened to move. First, she had to make certain she was alone. Nikki dropped down, grabbed the chisel and looked under the bed. Nothing. Her breath wobbled from her.

She pivoted toward the closet. Dear God, the door was ajar. She'd closed it firmly when she went to bed earlier. Her skin crawled, and an acrid taste spread across her tongue. Wielding the chisel before her, she tiptoed to the closet and tugged the door wide. Inside the clothes had been shoved to the left. The right wall hung open.

The passageway she'd been unable to expose the other night.

Her throat closed, and cool air, issuing from the black portal, brushed her fevered face. Despite Chris's warning that the passageways weren't safe, despite his dictum that everybody stay out of them, she *had* to examine this one. But not in her nightgown and robe.

Nikki slammed the closet door, flew into jeans, sweatshirt and tennis shoes, found the penlight she always carried in her purse, stuffed the chisel into her hip pocket and came back to the closet. The access to the passageway still gaped like the mouth of some carnival madhouse. Swallowing hard, she waved the light over the roughly framed side walls, illuminating a long dark corridor with a solid looking floor.

She stepped inside. Chill air, damp, musty, tinged with the aroma of rotted kelp and saltwater, assailed her. She moved gingerly, sliding her feet forward one step at a time. A flash of white caught her eye. She flinched, gulped, pressed her lips together, then pointed her penlight at it. Snagged on a nail near her shoulder was a piece of lace.

She snatched it from the nail and examined it. Yellowed, as if from age, it might have been torn from a wedding dress. Her pulse zipped higher. She poked the fabric into her front jeans pocket and took another few steps. From somewhere ahead, she heard a noise. She halted, debating the wisdom of continuing on alone.

Before she could retreat to her room, something tall and white raced toward her. Nikki reared back, and slammed her spine against a stud. Pain radiated the length of her torso. She swore, then blinked. Less than twenty feet from her stood a bride, her wedding gown floor length, flowing, the heavy veil concealing the bride's identity. *She* called, "Nicole, you must leave here...or die."

The disembodied voice echoed through the corridor, its message digging frigid fingers into Nikki's heart. Slicing her courage in two. She stood riveted a long moment, then she shook herself. *This was idiotic.* She started toward her taunter. "Who are you? Are you the one who sent the note about my father?"

The bride stiffened and backed away. Nikki picked up her step. The bride, obviously more familiar with the passageway than Nikki, turned and ran. Nikki followed, slower, less sure of her footing. A few seconds later, the corridor branched in two directions. She stopped. Which one had the bride taken? Her penlight beam poked, but didn't penetrate deep enough to offer a clue. Nikki stood perfectly still, straining to hear above her thundering pulse.

That one, she decided, setting out to her left at a cautious but steady pace. This corridor led to another Y. She listened again, caught the swish of lace and headed toward the sound. She soon concluded she was being led in circles—crisscrossing this corridor and that. Her penlight flickered and dimmed. Alarmed, she muttered, "No, no, no."

She shook the tiny flashlight. The beam flared brightly for a split second then dulled. Her heart sank. How long since she'd replaced the batteries? She didn't know. And she didn't want to get stuck within these walls. In the dark.

Making up her mind to return to her room and rouse Chris, she turned and hesitated. Which way had she come? She tried several of the corridors, and again had the feeling she was going in circles. The penlight beam fluttered. Panic grabbed her belly. She wanted to run before the battery died completely. She dare not.

She edged along as fast as possible. The air seemed to be getting colder, the smell of brine stronger. She took another step and nearly stumbled down a flight of stairs. She pulled back, her chest heaving. She leaned against the unfinished wall. Behind her the rustle of lace sounded. Nikki snatched the chisel from her pocket and shifted around. She was too slow. Something crashed down on her head. Pain exploded through her skull. She groaned and dropped the chisel. It clattered down the stairwell. The penlight blinked off.

Nikki fell to her knees, teetering on the edge of the top step. Her head swam. She felt hands on her shoulders, felt helpless to fight the inevitable shove, felt herself losing consciousness.

"Leave or die." It was the last thing she heard before the darkness engulfed her.

CHRIS CLIMBED THE STAIRS wearily. The beginnings of a headache grazed his temples. He suspected its source was the fury he'd struggled with since resealing the parlor access to the passageways. He would discuss what he'd discovered with Liv in the morning, positive she'd be even more distressed than he. He didn't know what the hell was going on, but he intended to get to the bottom of it.

He started up the third flight, his gaze shifting to Nikki's door. He'd like to discuss this with her now. Alert her to be on guard. But she'd be sleeping at this hour. Ah, hell, he was probably anxious for nothing. It could wait until tomorrow.

As he passed her room he noticed the light beneath her door. Surprise pulled him to a stop. What was she doing up? It was after 1:00 a.m. He thought of knocking, then hesitated, recalling with self-loathing his actions during the kiss they'd shared in the parlor. One touch of her sweet lips had stripped him of all restraint, turned him into a wild man who cared for nothing but the satisfaction of his own carnal needs. She'd actually had to fight him off in front of all the others.

Heat spiked his neck. God, he was a jerk. Abashed, he retreated to his own room. But sleep eluded him, chased off by the fierce headache now thumping his temples, and by memories of the silken feel of Nikki's flesh as he'd administered first aid. She'd trusted him implicitly, and yet, the moment he'd touched her breast, he was lost, carried off on a wave of desire.

He tossed off the cover, tugged on his jeans and went to the bathroom for aspirin. As he started back to his room, he noticed Nikki's light still burning. Was she working? Or restless, like he was—trying to figure out the mixed signals he'd been sending her? In that moment Chris had never felt more ashamed of himself. How dare he hurt this wonderful woman? He owed it to her to tell her the truth about himself so she'd leave Wedding House before he really hurt her.

He lifted his hand to knock, then hesitated, realizing that by telling her the truth, he'd be letting go of her forever. His heart ached at the thought. He'd come to care for Nikki more than he'd thought he would ever care for any woman. He understood now that part of him hadn't wanted her to know his secret fear. The part that was too like his uncle.

Determined, he lightly rapped on her door. She didn't answer. He called her name softly. Still, no answer. Had she fallen asleep with the light on? He considered. Perhaps he should go back to his room. Talk to her in the morning. But maybe then, he wouldn't be honest with her. He called her name again, then boldly tried the knob.

He frowned. Why hadn't she locked it? He slipped the door open. "Nikki?"

But she wasn't there. Nikki's laptop, writing bag and purse were at the desk, but the rest of the room looked as though the maid had just made it up in expectation of an arriving guest. The bed hadn't been slept in. Alarm shot through Chris.

He flung open the closet. The slacks she'd worn earlier were folded neatly over a hanger, the torn blouse discarded on the floor, her robe and nightie occupied the hook on the door. He fingered her silken nightgown, scowling. Minutes ago, he'd smelled her apple-scented soap lingering in the bathroom. By now he was familiar with her nighttime ritual and knew she used this fragrance only at bedtime.

So, she had prepared for bed, but what had prevented her from going to bed? Disquiet chattered through Chris. He glanced around the neat room again. Where in hell was Nikki? Surely, she hadn't risked swimming tonight with her wound? Not after the scare she'd had the other night? But maybe he'd better check.

Chapter Fourteen

Nikki awakened in pitch-darkness. Her head ached, pain spiraling out from a lump near her right temple. She took a quick mental inventory and decided, as far as she could tell, it was the only place she hurt. Wouldn't being shoved down a staircase produce more injuries? Even death? Hadn't she been pushed?

Gingerly she groped the floor around her in all directions. The unfinished wood was brutal with splinters, and several times she drew back tender fingers and plucked out slivers with her teeth. She couldn't find the staircase. Had she been moved? Pulled back from the stairs so she wouldn't tumble down them? It made no sense.

She lifted up on her arms and sat back, then winced from the tailbone bruise she'd gotten earlier in the evening. But besides her head and this bruise, she detected no other sore spots. She didn't understand. Why hadn't "the bride" killed her? She drew a ragged breath, taking in the cold, musty, sea-tinged air and considered what had occurred before she'd blacked out.

"Leave or die," the bride had said. A warning, Nikki realized. This whole escapade, the chase through the passageways, the different sightings of "the bride," the threat on the bathroom mirror—all meant to make her leave Wedding House before she discovered her connection to Theresa De Vega.

Why? What was "the bride" afraid Nikki would discover?

And if she didn't leave, would "the bride" carry out her threat?

She had to get out of here. Had to find Chris and tell him. Show him the piece of lace, try and find the chisel. He would know these passageways, would understand how to get to the staircase where she'd lost the chisel. She'd bet on it. But how did she get back to her room in the darkness? Or figure out how to open an access into one of the other rooms?

She struggled to her feet, swayed from light-headedness. She waited a moment, gradually regained her balance, then took a step forward. Her foot slipped on something hard and round. She squatted, groped the flooring close to her feet, and came up with her penlight. Hope bounced inside her, but when she thumbed the lever no light shone into the darkness.

Sighing, she pushed the penlight into her back pocket and began inching away from the cooler air. The roughened studs stabbed at her hands, and she tore through a spider's web, shuddering and blindly batting it away.

It seemed an hour or more before she came to a Y. She hesitated, uncertain which way would lead her in the correct direction. She chose the corridor to her right and warily strode on. A loud creak ripped away her courage. Nikki froze. Her stomach clenched. Her headache throbbed, and her breath came hard and fast. She listened. Was someone coming? Or was the house just groaning as old houses were wont?

After several minutes she decided she was still alone

and crept on. Her heart felt as heavy as her steps, weighed with apprehension and weariness. The farther she walked, the more she felt like a mouse in a maze.

Finally she slogged to a stop. This was getting her nowhere near an exit. In exasperation, she called, "Help! Someone help me!"

Her voice echoed down the corridor and resounded back to her. How well was this house insulated? Would anyone hear her? Or would she be stuck in this dark tunnel wandering in circles forever? Fear and frustration gathered into a hard knot in her chest. She hollered louder, "Help!"

Again her voice, a sad lonely wail, bounced off the walls, taunting her, punctuating her dire situation. Tears sprang to her eyes. No. She would not dissolve into a pool of self-pity. "Help!"

A noise. No. Footsteps. For a second she felt utter relief. But what if it were "the bride" coming back to act on her threat? In the distance a light bobbed dimly. Coming toward her. She cringed back.

"Nikki?" It was Chris's voice.

She blinked against the sudden light spilling through the corridor from his lantern and shuddered out a tautly held breath. "Here. I'm here, Chris."

He rushed to her. She stepped into his arms and collapsed.

CHRIS HAULED NIKKI from the passageway, using the access to the library, which he'd entered after hearing her cry for help. Fear licked through him as he hurried her to her room and laid her gently on the bed. Had she fainted? Or passed out from an injury he couldn't see? He stood back, taking stock. Her clothes were dirty, her lovely face smudged, her glorious hair laced with cobwebs, but she looked great to him.

"Nikki?" He sank to the bed beside her prone body. "Nikki?"

She sighed and opened her eyes. She seemed disoriented. Then her gaze focused on him, and her features softened. She reached up and touched his face as though seeing it for the first time, as though wanting confirmation that he was really there, as though she beheld a miracle. Her fingers were cool on his fevered skin, cool and calming. "The passageway."

"Yes, I know. I discovered earlier tonight that all the passageways I'd boarded up have been broached. I don't know what the hell is going on, but I intend to get to the bottom of it tomorrow."

Her eyes widened. She told him about waking suddenly, then finding the chisel near her bed and the open passageway in her closet. "I stepped inside to investigate, then was confronted by someone dressed like the portrait of Theresa—in a formal bridal gown."

Chris frowned. "The ghost?"

"This 'ghost' was purely human, and I can prove it. I found a scrap of lace snagged on a nail just inside the passageway. It's in my pocket." She reached for the cloth, digging deep. It wasn't there. It had to be. She tried the other side, then the back pockets. The only thing she found was her penlight. "It's gone. She must have taken it after she knocked me out."

"She knocked you out?"

"Yes. I don't know what she hit me with." Nikki flinched, a pained look crinkling the tiny lines at her eyes, as she brought his hand to a spot near her right temple. The lump was sizable. "But you can see her aim was good."

Fury flashed through Chris. "How dare—"

"I thought she was going to shove me down the stairs." Her gaze narrowed and she struggled to sit up. "But she didn't. She only wanted to scare me so I'd leave Wedding House. She said, 'Leave or die.'"

Chris's anger whipped higher. How dare anyone threaten Nikki? He wanted to find the culprit and throttle them. But who? "Do you have any idea who was masquerading as 'the bride'?"

"No, her veil was too heavy. That's not all, Chris. I dropped the chisel down the stairs."

"We'll find it tomorrow."

"Thank you, Chris." She reached up to touch his face again. Chris nuzzled her gentle fingers, then, giving into his need for her, he turned her hand and kissed her palm. Nikki pulled his head to her, lifted her lips, offered the sweetness he couldn't resist. He folded her to him, found her mouth with his, and he was lost, drowning in the passion only this woman roused in him, his control fleeing like seeds in the wind. Even his misgivings about getting involved slipped away, his misgivings about misleading Nikki.

But he cared about her too much to mislead her.

"No. No." Chris pulled back, breathing hard. Guilt and fear gathered his control, returned it to him.

"It's okay." Her lovely features grew stony. She blinked back unshed tears, wrapping pride around her like a cloak of armor. But not before he saw the look of self-loathing dart through her eyes, a look that said she was somehow at fault for his disrupting their kiss, that said she understood why he couldn't love her.

It tore his heart in two. "I don't mean to hurt you, Nikki."

"Then why are you?" She pressed her lips together as though she hadn't meant to ask.

"Because my uncle's blood runs through my veins. Because I have his maniacal temperament." The words rushed from him. The best thing she could do was take "the bride's" advice and leave. Run away from Wedding House and from him.

"Maniacal?" She sat up beside him. "Don't be silly. You're not mad."

"Maybe not. Yet." He heaved a heavy breath, his head down. "But I've been losing my grip the past few years. The last six months have tried my nerves the worst. I can never control my temper. First it cost me a couple of big jobs, then my closest friend and finally my business. I'm not Jack-of-all-trades at this mansion for the love of it—but because investing in Wedding House was the only option left to me.... And because it was Liv's chance of getting her life back on track."

"She has bulimia, doesn't she?"

"Yes." He was amazed that Nikki was so observant, and was touched at the sympathy he saw in her eyes. "Liv was getting better. I thought. But I'm wondering now if she'll survive this week and the grand opening she's worked so hard on."

"I think this week has been extraordinarily difficult on all three of us." She touched his hand. "Chris, give us a chance. Give yourself a chance. You aren't like your uncle."

"You don't know that." His mother's constant chant—about how like Luis he was—resounded in his head, reinforced year after year, his whole life long. "I don't know that. I may never know it."

He pushed his hand through his hair and seemed to have trouble swallowing. "And I won't condemn you to a life of waiting to find out which day will be the one when I slip over the edge. I won't risk your life by being selfish. I can't promise you a future. And I won't steal your present without that promise.''

In that instant Nikki saw raw love in his warm brown eyes, felt the emotion emanating from him like a beam of light that stroked her heart, her soul, felt the answering light within herself, and, to her surprise, realized she loved him, too, with the same rare energy. It was like nothing she'd ever felt for anyone before. All of her life she'd waited for this moment, and now that it was here, instead of filling her, healing her, instead of the cold spot in her heart shrinking, it stretched wider, burned icier.

THE NEXT MORNING Nikki rose late. She had no desire to dine with the others, no wish to face Chris in front of an audience. Her heart rivaled a dying weed, blackened and shriveling. Within minutes, she'd gained and lost the only man she would ever love. What she felt wasn't self-pity, but an odd mix of fear and determination. Somehow she had to prove to him that he wasn't like Luis De Vega. Or was he?

But that wasn't her only dilemma. *Leave or die.* During the fitful night, the warning had haunted her dreams. She had no delusions that to prolong her stay at Wedding House was to risk life and limb. And yet, how could she go, when she'd gotten nowhere in her quest to learn of her ancestry?

She decided she had to contact Jellybean and Zeus. See if she couldn't get them to treat this as a priority. On her way to the TV room with her laptop, she spied Marti snooping around the master suite. Nikki wondered what she was looking for, but didn't ask. They exchanged good-mornings, then Nikki checked her e-mail. Still nothing on Theresa from her two sources. She sent them urgent messages and signed off-line.

She trudged back up the stairs. Her muscles were tired from last night's ordeal. She could use a long swim, but doubted she'd risk another one here. As she gained the landing, a "swishing" sound in the library caught her attention. One of the bookshelves was swinging open. Marti emerged from behind it, and Nikki realized it must be the same access Chris had used to rescue her. "What are you doing?"

"Holy Joe." Marti jumped. Her cheeks flamed. Guilt oozed from her. She made a face and tapped her huge flashlight on the palm of her hand. "Well, since you've caught me in the act, I might as well confess. Chris told everyone at breakfast that someone had unblocked all the accesses to the secret passageways. He wanted to know which of us had done it. Laughable, actually— since no one would admit to it if they had."

"And you were exploring them now because...?"

"Well, obviously for the book. I suspected they were here all along. That's what I was really doing in the library the night we met. I took a quick walk through to make certain my descriptions are believable."

"You found your way from the master suite to the library without any trouble?"

"That's right. Helps to have a good flashlight."

Nikki hugged the laptop to her thudding heart. Was that a crack about how her own penlight had failed when she'd needed it most? Had Marti been the one posing as "the bride"? She seemed entirely too familiar with the passageways to be on a first exploration, awfully familiar with how to get from one room to the other, while Nikki had felt completely lost in the maze of corridors.

Nikki returned her laptop to her room. The maid had straightened it. The smoothed bed reminded her of how Chris said he'd found it last night, stressed how vulnerable she was in this room. Shivers raced over Nikki. She checked the closet, but to her relief she found the passageway hadn't been broached after Chris nailed it shut last night. It should have put her mind at ease.

It didn't.

What if there was another way into this room? What if Marti or "the bride" had been in there today?

She gave the room a quick search, but couldn't tell if anything was disturbed. The uneasy sensation grew, and she decided she didn't want to stay there waiting for something or someone to pounce on her. Maybe Chris had discovered something new.

She set out to find him and encountered Olivia in the foyer carrying a tray of sandwiches. "We're lunching poolside—in deference to this lovely day. I'm glad to see you're joining us."

"Actually, I'm looking for Chris. Have you seen him?"

"He and Jorge spent the morning moving the fireworks from the cabana into the boathouse, but by now I suspect Chris is at the pool with the others." Olivia grinned at her, then shoved the platter into Nikki's hands. "Would you take these down? Then I can get the pitchers of lemonade and iced tea."

She held the door open for Nikki. Chagrined, Nikki stepped outside, balancing the tray in both hands. The temperature hovered on the high side of eighty. She moved carefully across the brick cobblestones, then onto the pathway, heading toward the laughter and conversation that floated on the sultry breeze.

As she neared the wrought-iron fence, Jorge leaped from the bushes. She reared back, nearly dropping the platter. Her heart throttled into high gear at the gleaming pair of hedge clippers, the tips wickedly sharp, he held pointed at her. She gulped, fear rushing over her in tiny shivers.

His eyes narrowed. "Theresa…?"

Nikki's mouth dried. "No. I'm not Theresa."

"You look like Theresa. Why do you look like Theresa?"

She, also, wanted an answer to that question. And maybe he could clear up a few things for her, but she'd rather he weren't armed when they talked.

He took a step toward her, raising the clippers.

Nikki retreated.

"Rameriz, don't you have work to do?" Chris held open the gate for Nikki, gesturing for her to enter. But her feet refused to budge.

"*Sí,* Señor Conrad." Jorge shook himself, tipped his hat to her, and moved to the shrubs surrounding the fence. "I mean no harm."

"If you stand in the sun much longer," Chris said, his head tilted to one side, "those sandwiches won't be edible."

Nikki shifted her attention to him, and the quivering inside her intensified. He wore cutoffs and a tank top, his golden skin kissed by the sun, his ebony hair mussed, his brown eyes as warm as hot chocolate, yet guarded. She saw the reserve in their depths, the determination that he would not harm her in any way. Would not act on the love they shared, as though that would harm her worst of all.

The crack in her heart deepened. Somehow she managed to speak through the sorrow clogging her throat. "We need to talk."

Before she could suggest somewhere private, Olivia swept up to them. "Christopher, please take one of these before I drop them both." She thrust a crystal pitcher of iced tea at him.

They deposited the food and drinks on the bar beside an array of other dishes. Feeling more alone than she had her whole life, Nikki stood to one side, surveying the group. Everyone seemed to be present. Marti, in a purple one-piece, was floating on an air mattress, while Diego swam laps dipping his bronzed arms in long strokes. Nikki yearned to do the same.

Dorothea, stretched out on a lounge chair, wore a pea-green jumpsuit with rainbow epaulets at her shoulders and waist. Her red hair glinted golden in the sunlight. She was conversing with the two actors Nikki had rehearsed with the last couple of days and two newcomers, who she assumed were the actors scheduled to play Luis and Theresa. Thank goodness.

Glass-topped tables had been set up at the pool's edge, and Olivia, in an oddly joyous manner, seemed determined to convey a party atmosphere. "Come, come, everyone. Food's ready."

The squeal of tires on the brick cobblestones caught Nikki's ear. A car lurched to a stop in the parking area, and a woman emerged. She started toward the house, then apparently spotting the party at the pool, changed direction.

Janice Jacoby.

Nikki tensed. Lorah Halliard's daughter looked upset enough to spit nails as she charged through the gate. The charm bracelet wreathed her wrist and jangled as she moved, an ominous serenade. "One of you killed my mother!"

Everyone spun toward Janice. Her clothes were disheveled as though she'd slept in them. Her hair seemed uncombed, her makeup smudged. She glared at the group with eyes as cold as frosted jade.

Nikki saw Marti slip off the air mattress and duck behind it, as though hiding from Janice, and wondered if the woman might be dangerous.

Janice moved closer, spoke louder. "Traces of an opiate were found in Mother's system. She had no prescription for a narcotic."

Dorothea gasped.

Olivia reached for a sandwich and took a huge bite, chewing as though her life depended on it.

"Did she die from a narcotic overdose?" Chris asked, stress tight at his mouth.

Janice glowered at him, then at everyone again.

Dorothea seemed to shrink as the chilling gaze momentarily settled on her. Janice said, "I couldn't interest the police without solid evidence, but we'll have that soon enough. Dr. Wiggins is doing the autopsy personally. He's going to test for chemicals. And anything else he deems necessary. When we have our answers, one of you will be arrested and charged."

With that she left.

Marti popped up from behind the air mattress and shook her head. Her complexion rivaled the white of her hair. "Holy Joe, that woman is seriously delusional—suggesting one of us murdered Lorah. Can you imagine?" She gave a nervous laugh. "Oh, but if one of you has, what a great twist that would add for my book."

Nikki wanted to ask why Marti had been hiding from Janice, but her attention was riveted to Dorothea.

The pert redhead had gone as green as her jumpsuit. Nikki stepped to her side and said quietly, "Your pain-killers are opiates."

Dorothea lurched to her feet and strode to the bar. "A double vodka rocks, please, Chris."

She tossed the drink back like soda pop.

Nikki sidled up to her. "I'm sure you needn't worry. I can't imagine one pill would have killed her."

"Really, my dear, I don't know what you're talking about." She set her glass on the bar, seeming as terrified as someone about to be eaten by a bear. "Hit me again, Chris."

Chris frowned at Nikki, and she shrugged in answer, her fishing expedition netting her nothing more than a handful of new questions. None of which Dorothea would likely answer. Why was she lying? What had her so frightened? Had she given Lorah an overdose of painkillers?

"As soon as you've eaten, come up to the ballroom," Dorothea told the actors. "Costume fittings are going to take most of the day."

She left without eating. No one except Olivia had much appetite.

Nikki was the worst. Her emotions filled her stomach, keeping her edgy and heartsore. Twice she started to ask Chris to go for a walk along the beach, but both times she was interrupted by Olivia. Finally, she gave up and returned to her room to work on her book.

Evening had arrived by the time she heard Chris's familiar footsteps in the hall outside her room. Had he been avoiding her all day? Much as she'd avoided him? Two broken-hearted cowards. She'd decided to leave in the morning. There was no sense staying on. She had all the information she needed for her book and, it seemed, all she could discover here about her ancestry. If that changed in future, she could always return to Wedding House.

His rap on the door was gentle. She hesitated, then pulled it open. She'd have preferred a walk on the beach, or in the gardens, anywhere but a meeting in her room at bedtime. It seemed suddenly too small and intimate. And they were too sad. The air between them shimmered with repressed want.

It had seemed so urgent to tell him about Marti in the passageways earlier today, now the edge was gone, the urgency dulled. "Have you been busy?"

"I've been making myself busy—avoiding you." Chris winced as though the admission wounded him.

"Well, you won't need to do that much longer. I'm leaving tomorrow."

He nodded. But such pain filled his eyes it tore at her soul. She wiped her hands on her jeans. "Before I go, I thought you should know that Marti seems very familiar with the passageways."

She told him about her observation of the mystery writer's actions that morning. Chris frowned. "Do you think she was 'the bride'?"

"I don't know. I can't imagine why she'd want to scare me away from here. Or why she'd threaten to kill me. What motive could she have?"

"Then who do you suspect?" He held himself as tense as a soldier guarding a fortress.

He wouldn't want to hear what she really suspected. "Do you think Lorah was murdered?"

His dark brows lifted and his guard dropped. He

pulled out the desk chair and sat backward on it. "Why would someone murder her?"

Nikki sank onto her bed. "The night I tried on costumes in the ballroom, Lorah suggested, in a rather unpleasant manner, that Marti, Olivia and Dorothea each had secrets, secrets she knew they wouldn't want revealed. It was almost as if she were threatening them…like blackmail of some kind. Marti got absolutely livid."

"I can't imagine Liv taking such a threat well, either."

Olivia. Dare she broach the subject? She shoved her hair behind her ear. Since she was leaving in the morning, why not? "Chris, could your sister view me as a threat?"

"A threat?" He laughed, then sobered. "Because of my feelings for you?"

"No, because I might be Theresa's daughter. Could she fear I'd have a claim to Wedding House?"

He hesitated. "Theresa's family wanted nothing to do with Wedding House after my uncle murdered her. They gave it back to the De Vega family." Chris sighed heavily. "They didn't even want to sell it, they didn't want money with their daughter's blood on it."

Nikki could understand that. "Did they sign it over to your mother, or just tell her to keep it?"

"To keep it, why?" He eyed her suspiciously, the distance between them growing in that instant. "If you discover you are her daughter, will you lay claim to the estate?"

She blew out a breath. She couldn't answer him. She had no idea how she would feel if she discovered she was Theresa's daughter. She suggested another possibility. "I had time to do a lot of thinking today, and I was wondering if we'd miscast Diego Sands. Perhaps he was never Theresa's lover. Perhaps he's a relative of Theresa's. A brother or cousin or something.''

Before he could comment, a woman screamed. Chris and Nikki stared at each other for a split second, then scrambled up and out into the hall. It was deserted. They heard doors opening on the second floor. Voices rose from below. Nikki grasped the railing and scanned the lower levels.

At first she couldn't identify the mass of white lace heaped beside the overturned foyer table, the shattered Ming vase. Then she realized she was staring at a bridal ensemble.

She gasped. ''The ghost.''

''No.'' Chris moaned. ''Look.''

In the shadowed evening light, she spied a single foot poking from beneath the wedding gown. Even as she watched, a dark stain blossomed across the veil. Horror slammed through Nikki, pulling her stomach to her toes.

She gripped the railing so hard her knuckles ached. Chris's arms circled her. She fell back against him, grateful for the support. ''Dear God, Chris, who is it?''

Chapter Fifteen

"Who is it?" Nikki repeated, keeping a stranglehold on the third-floor railing. Shock and horror tangoed inside her; the only thing keeping her upright was Chris's grasp on her upper arms, her safety net in a world that had collapsed, leaving her free-falling into the nightmare of reality.

"Liv?" His grip tightened on Nikki, as though reassuring himself it was not she three stories down on the foyer floor, as though he needed her as much as she needed him, as though he was claiming her, tossing aside his fears of losing his sanity. And yet, there was apprehension in his hold. "Liv!"

"I'm here, Christopher." Olivia rushed to the second-floor landing. "Who screamed?"

Chris let out a hard breath that lifted Nikki's hair. He didn't answer his sister. He released Nikki. "Call 911."

He began running for the stairs. Nikki followed; the only phone she knew of was in the TV room.

"Who screamed?" Marti tumbled from her room in a flash of purple, her hair tangled from sleep.

"Look!" Olivia gasped, starting down the stairs. "Who is it?"

"No! Wait!" Chris caught his sister. "Get some towels."

"Of course." Olivia swallowed as though choking on something. "Who is it, Chris?"

"Just get the towels." He thundered down the stairs. "Quick."

As Nikki hurried toward the TV room, Diego emerged. He shouted, "I've called an ambulance."

Olivia returned with an armload of towels. Diego took them from her, suggested she stay put and scrambled down the stairs to help Chris.

Chris gave him a glum expression. "I'm afraid it's too late. She's dead."

"Holy Joe."

"Who?" Olivia's eyes were wide, her face white.

The three women stood at the second-floor railing, staring at the horror below. To Nikki, the air seemed sucked from the mansion, drawn in by the holding of their collective breaths.

Chris kneeling beside the body, his hand full of blood-soaked lace, gazed at his sister. "It's Dorothea Miller."

"What?" Olivia cried. "But it can't be. She left an hour ago."

"Did you see her leave?" Nikki asked, realizing even as she said it that it didn't matter whether Olivia had seen Dorothea leave, since she was here now. Dead.

"Well, I didn't walk her out..." Olivia held herself as stiff as a blade of burned grass, wringing her hands. Tears brimmed her dark eyes. "What happened, Chris?"

Diego shook his head. "To sustain these injuries she must have gone over the top railing—the one on the third floor."

Nikki felt sick to her stomach. "But what was she doing up there?"

"And why is she in that getup?" Marti asked.

"I don't know. I helped her hem that gown earlier tonight," Olivia sobbed. "I thought she'd gone home."

"Had she been drinking?" Nikki asked, recalling Dorothea's distress after Janice Jacoby's visit.

"Yes…a bit." Olivia twisted her hands tighter. "Lorah's daughter upset her something awful."

"Oh, that one." Marti blew a disgusted breath. "She's great for flinging accusations. Doesn't matter whether she's got proof. Or whom she hurts. Dorothea shouldn't have let that little twit upset her."

"But she did.…" Olivia burst into tears and fled for her room.

"Do you think she jumped from the third floor?" Nikki asked.

"Because of Janice?" Marti gave a startled laugh. "It's more likely someone pushed her."

Sirens sounded in the distance, and Nikki's gaze met Chris's. Her heart thundered and her throat was thick with fear. Had Dorothea fallen? Or jumped? *It's more likely someone pushed her.* Nikki shivered. Even though she realized Marti had made the suggestion in sarcasm, she couldn't dismiss the possibility. Couldn't help but wonder if a murderer once again stalked Wedding House.

Leave or die, "the bride" had warned. Would she be next? She wanted to run to Chris, wanted to cry out, "Chris, I'm frightened."

Wanted to hear him say, "I won't let anything happen to you, Nikki. I swear, I won't."

Instead, she stood, gripping the railing, watching him

hurry to answer the front door, and feeling as though nothing would ever be the same again.

THE NORMAL BED and breakfast tranquility had vanished from Wedding House, and with the invasion of EMTs, plain-clothes police officers and the medical examiner, it took on the surreal hustle of a busy hotel. Nikki couldn't wait to pack and leave in the morning.

Guests and household staff were questioned individually and at length. It neared midnight when Nikki's turn came. She entered the dining room and sat on the edge of the chair across from a detective in his early forties. His blond hair was clipped close to his head, reminding Nikki of boyhood chums who'd gotten crewcuts each summer, but this man's cut was even closer to the scalp. He had wise gray eyes and a nose that dominated his face.

"Ms. Navarro, is it?"

"Yes."

"I'm just asking everyone to tell us what they saw or heard prior to this tragedy."

Nikki gathered her breath. The shock that had insulated her earlier was dissipating into a somber melancholy. Dorothea Miller had been full of life, the kind of person who gave color and flair to the dullest day. Her neon light had been squelched too soon. By her hand? Or someone else's? "Did she fall?"

"We're not sure. Why don't you tell me what you know."

Nikki sighed. "I don't know anything. I was in my room on the third floor, talking to Chris, er, Mr. Conrad, when we heard a woman scream. We rushed into the hall and saw—"

She broke off as the horrible sight flashed into her mind.

"It's my understanding that Ms. Miller consumed quite a lot of alcohol today. Was she in the habit of drinking like that or did something unusual upset her?"

The question snapped Nikki's attention to the detective. He feinted an innocent expression, but she didn't buy it. This man was too smart to act dumb and carry it off. If he knew Dorothea had been drinking, he knew about Janice Jacoby's visit. So why was he fishing? She pushed her hair back from her cheek. "I assume others have told you about the visit Lorah Halliard's daughter paid us today, and her accusation that one of us had killed her mother with an overdose of narcotic. I suspect the traces of opiate found in Ms. Halliard's system were from pain pills. Dorothea told me she'd given Ms. Halliard one pill on the night she died."

He frowned and tapped the tablet he was writing in. "You mean she was upset because she gave this Halliard woman *one* pill?"

Nikki shrugged. "I didn't say it was logical. You had to know Dorothea Miller. She was dramatic. Perhaps there was more to it than we'll ever know."

"And she did drink?"

"She kept a vodka bottle in her desk drawer upstairs."

"Really?" He scratched his nose and stood. "Why don't you show me?"

Nikki led the way to the ballroom. Next to the sewing machine on Dorothea's desk, the vodka bottle stood like a glass tombstone. Sadness spiraled through her. "It's empty. It was three-quarters full just yesterday."

She glanced around. The clothes rack of costumes was pulled askew, the bridal ensemble missing. Her heart clenched, and again she struggled to hold the ugly memories at bay.

The detective sank onto the chair and began pulling open desk drawers, flicking through the contents, then through the magazines. Absently Nikki watched him. He sat straighter, pulled a couple of the magazines from the drawer and laid them open on the desk. "What do you suppose she was doing cutting letters out of these?"

Nikki's heart climbed into her throat. She couldn't swallow. Couldn't breathe. Couldn't answer. She shook her head, her mind racing to an awful conclusion. She had to get the note. Had to compare it. Had to be certain. A jag of ice cut through her, pulling the heat from her face, her body.

The detective scooped the magazines back into the drawer and slammed it, riveting Nikki's attention. He stood. "I think we'll find that Ms. Miller's death was an accident brought on by her own folly." He placed the vodka bottle in a plastic bag and sealed it. "But meanwhile, I'm asking all the guests to remain here until we're certain."

Nikki nodded woodenly, still trying to come to terms with what she'd just seen. She had to know. She followed the detective into the hallway. Chris sat on the bottom step. Nikki glanced at him, signaling with her eyes her need for him, then she rushed to her room and found the anonymous note. Chris was letting the detective out as she started downstairs again. She hastened to the ballroom.

He joined her there, moments later. "What are you doing?"

"Oh, Chris, look at this." She laid out several of the magazines on the desk, frantically flipping though them, seeking the pages with the cutouts. Her hand froze. She smoothed the note out beside the pages. "See?"

He came to her side, peered over her shoulder. She

poked the pages, then the note. "These are the letters used in this note. Look."

They could both see she was right. She lifted sad eyes to him. "Dorothea must have sent it to me." Her heart felt like a block of stone. "And now I'll never learn what she knew about my family."

"Your family?" Olivia had entered the ballroom without either Chris or Nikki noticing. Her eyes were narrowed. "She didn't know anything about your family."

Nikki jerked toward Olivia. "Then why did she send this mysterious note?"

Olivia blinked. "She sent you an anonymous note?"

Chris's ebony brows dipped low. "What do you know about this, Liv?"

Olivia Conrad seemed to have aged in the past few hours. "Oh, Chris, we meant no harm. Shortly after we started planning the grand opening, Dorothea was in the bookstore in Silverdale and she bought a coffee table book, your first book, Nikki. Your photo was on the inside back cover. We were both intrigued by your resemblance to the portrait.

"Dorothea got it into her head that you should be here for the grand opening. I wasn't sure you'd come. But she said she'd get you here. She had thought of a way."

Nikki blew out a taut breath, grappling with her disappointment. "Then she knew nothing of my past? My family? Neither of you did?"

"How could we? We didn't know you." Dots of color pinkened Olivia's ghostly cheeks. "I'm really sorry if we've upset you. That was never our intention."

Nikki felt like a complete fool. Dorothea had made up the message, hoping to hook her into coming to

Wedding House, and the bait had worked better than either Dorothea or Olivia had expected. She'd even based her newest project on that note. If it weren't so tragic, she'd laugh.

But her resemblance to Theresa couldn't be denied. *Had* she found a clue to her past?

Chris asked his sister, "Did you know about the pills?"

"Only that Dorothea took them for back pain."

"She wouldn't have mixed them with alcohol—would she?" He scrubbed his face with his hand. Weariness held his mouth tight.

"I don't know." Olivia shook her head. "But she said she couldn't find the bottle. She thought she'd left it here in her desk drawer."

Nikki closed the magazines, feeling like she was closing important pages in her life. All the possibilities, all that might have been, gone, lost forever to her now. "Dorothea told me she might have taken it home in another purse."

"No." Olivia twisted her hands together. "She looked and couldn't find it there, either."

Nikki moved away from the desk, hugging herself against an inner chill that seemed to grow by the minute. More than ever she needed Chris's reassuring embrace, the comfort of his silent support.

More than ever he withheld it. Chris sat in the desk chair and opened drawers, carefully emptying then replacing the contents of each. "If she had the prescription bottle here, it's not here now."

Silence fell over them, as heavy and separating as a blinding fog. The uneasiness Nikki had felt since morning gnawed at her with newer, sharper teeth. She wanted reassurance from these two that all would be well, that nothing bad would befall her as it had Lorah and Dorothea. She wanted a course of action, instead of this standing still waiting for disaster to strike afresh.

"Do you think she fell?" Olivia asked, at length. "Or jumped?"

"She wouldn't have killed herself because of Janice's threat, would she?" Nikki studied Chris's sister. "You knew her best of all."

"How well do we know anyone?" Olivia sighed.

"Just what does that mean, Liv?" Chris scowled at his sister. His usual tenderness was missing. Anger clouded his brown eyes, churning more and more at the surface—exactly as he'd warned Nikki.

"Oh, I don't know." Olivia stalked to the windows, then back. "Okay, I'll tell you."

"What?" Chris rose.

"I was in Lorah's room, packing her suitcase, when I heard the scream." She choked, cleared her throat and continued, "I'd just come across a day-planner. As I was putting it into the bag, this fell out of it."

She pulled an aged newspaper clipping from the pocket of her black dress and handed it to her brother. Chris read it, then gave it to Nikki to read.

She read with growing interest, then lifted her gaze to Chris. "I guess we should talk to Marti."

"And just what is it you all need to talk to me about?"

Nikki flinched, startled by Marti's sudden appearance in the doorway. What was she doing—eavesdropping? A worse notion flew through Nikki's head. Perhaps Marti was coming into the ballroom for some nefarious reason—like to return the missing Percodan bottle?

"Well, is someone going to tell me what's going on?" Marti moved into the room, shoving a hand into her robe pocket as though grasping on to something. A pill bottle?

No. Nikki shook herself. Why was she casting Marti in the role of murderer? How had the mystery writer gone from her favorite author to the top of her suspect list?

Chris perched his hip onto the desk. "Do you know Janice Jacoby?"

Marti's eyebrows shot upward. "Holy Joe, that little twit who stormed about with threats of imprisonment to us all?"

"Yes." He nodded.

Purple underscored Marti's hazel eyes, the color darker from the reflection off her robe. "We've never been introduced."

Olivia swept nearer. She nibbled at her nails as though they were hors d'oeuvres. "We have reason to believe otherwise."

Marti stiffened, eyeing each of them in turn. "What is this...an inquisition?"

"No. It's about this, Marti." Chris handed her the news clipping.

She read it and blanched as white as her hair. "Oh, all right. So, the twit sued me." Marti laughed bitterly. "For plagiarism, of all things. But the case was thrown out for lack of evidence."

Olivia frowned. "Why would Janice sue you—if it weren't true?"

"Oh, pul-leeze." Her hand dipped into her pocket again.

Nikki stared at the pocket, dark suspicions rising in her mind like oil on water. Was Marti fingering the pill bottle? Could she have somehow placed an overdose of

Percodan in the glass of water at the séance? No. The idea was ludicrous.

Shutting her eyes, she recalled the overturned glass, its contents spreading across the bloodred table cover, and Lorah gasping. But had she even been poisoned? They wouldn't know for a couple of weeks. "Why did Janice sue you?"

Marti sighed loudly. "She was, perhaps still is, an aspiring writer whose work I had volunteered to judge for a romantic suspense contest. Her entry stank. It was awful."

Nikki tilted her head. "She sued you because you gave her a bad score in a contest?"

"No, of course not. The dimwit got it into her head that I'd ripped off her idea. Used it in my next book. Believe me, it wasn't true. And after that experience I've never judged another contest. Nor will I."

Olivia gnawed harder on her nail. "It gave you a reason for wanting Lorah dead."

"So, you *do* think Lorah was murdered," Marti stated. It wasn't a question.

Olivia wrenched back. "No. I didn't say that."

Marti fingered whatever was in her pocket again. "I think it gave Lorah reason to hate me, but I had no reason to hold a grudge. The lawsuit didn't hurt my career or my reputation. In fact, it boosted sales."

"That's that, then." Chris stood.

"Yes." Marti smiled stiffly. "I'm going to bed. It's been a trying night."

CHRIS AND NIKKI WALKED Olivia to her room, then ascended to the third floor. He leaned toward her, speaking softly. "It *has* been a hell of a night. Are you all right?"

Nikki drew in the gentle scent of him and sighed inwardly, staving off the need that sprang through her. But she couldn't douse the memories of his arms on hers earlier this evening, or the sense of peering into what the future could hold—if only Chris and she… She let the thought trail away. "I'm not sure I'll ever be all right again."

"I'm sorry about what my sister and Dorothea did to you."

"Don't be sorry. If they hadn't done it, I might never have seen the portrait and found someplace to start looking for my family." *And I might never have met you.* She glanced into his arresting face, yearned to touch it, ached for him to touch her, to kiss her, to tell her that he no longer worried he was losing his mind.

But she could see the worry rode him still, an onus as real to him as responsibility to a single parent. The cold spot inside her widened into a gaping, gelid sinkhole. He lifted his hand as if to caress her, but pulled back at the last minute, swallowed hard and gestured toward her door. "I'll check your room, if you like."

"Please."

She stood in the doorway as he inspected the closet. "The passageway is still secure. Just lock your door and no one will bother you during the night."

"Thank you." She placed her hand on his chest. Felt his thundering heart beneath her fingertips. She gazed up at him. "Chris…"

He lowered his head. She lifted her lips and closed her eyes. He kissed her on the forehead. "Good night, Nikki."

She glanced at him with all the sorrow shredding her heart. *Goodbye, Chris.* Tears clogged her throat. She shut the door and twisted the lock, then stared at the bed. The bed she would never share with the man she loved.

Nikki expected sleep to elude her. Instead she dropped off immediately and woke late into the morning. She'd planned on leaving today, but now was forced by the police to stay—in a house where her very life had been threatened, where her heart had been devastated—one room away from the man she wanted and couldn't have.

Perhaps she should have told the detective someone was threatening her. At least earned permission to stay in a motel in Port Townsend. Somewhere away from Wedding House.

She growled and paced the room. Impatience and anger vied for control of her. She felt trapped. A puppet in a nightmare skit. Nikki had never allowed anyone else to control her life. She resented this new, uncomfortable position in which she'd been placed.

If only she knew who.

Knowledge was power, but at the moment she had little knowledge. She needed some answers to her questions, and she needed them now. She gathered her laptop and headed for the TV room.

"It's right through here," she heard Marti say as she passed the library. Peering in, Nikki saw the mystery writer and Diego stealing into the passageway. She shook her head. She supposed there was no stopping the curious. Let them face the consequences of their own actions. She'd had all the contact with the people in this house she wanted.

She settled down in the TV room, feeling more frantic than hopeful as she logged on-line. To her surprise, there was e-mail from both of her sources. Jellybean had narrowed her search and come up with an Aznar family in Texas who concurred that they had a relative named Theresa who had married one Luis De Vega in a seaport town in Washington State.

Zeus reported the same, but his research had netted news even more riveting. He'd discovered that Theresa had a younger sister named Carmella. The last anyone heard of Carmella was when she left Texas to visit her sister at Wedding House. She left Port Townsend before Luis De Vega's murderous rampage and was never seen nor heard from again.

My mother…Carmella? Nikki stared at the screen, trying to take it in. What did it mean? Where did *she*, Nikki, fit in? What secret had the two sisters shared? Feeling concussed, as though a bomb had landed near her, she returned to her room and deposited the laptop on the desk.

What had happened here? Was Theresa her birth mother? Compelled, her feet moving without her conscious will, she proceeded to the master suite, coming to rest only when she stood before the portrait. Again she experienced that elusive connection she'd felt the first time she'd laid eyes on this image that seemed to have been painted of her.

"Where do I fit in, Theresa? Am I the child of you and your secret lover? Did you give me to your sister to raise?"

She swore she heard Theresa answer, "Yes."

A calm settled over Nikki, as though the last puzzle piece had snapped into place and lifted a terrible tension from her body. She felt physically lighter.

Carmella, then, was her aunt. She'd raised her, and had refused to tell her anything about her father because of the tragedy that had befallen her real mother, Theresa.

The wall to the left of the fireplace slid open. Nikki lurched toward it, expecting to see Marti and Diego. The person standing there was a shadowy white figure. The bride. Nikki jolted, but this time she felt outrage, not fear. "Who are you?"

In her eerie voice, the bride said, "Leave...or die."

With that she turned and fled into the passageway, obviously certain Nikki wouldn't follow a second time.

"The bride" had misjudged her opponent.

Fury rushed through Nikki, propelling her forward and into the passageway. "Come back here!"

Chapter Sixteen

In the daylight, the passageways were gloomy, but not pitch-dark as they were at night. Nikki spotted the bridal gown ahead and raced after her tormentor. "Stop."

But the bride dashed on. She disappeared momentarily at the first Y, but today Nikki could see her charging through the corridor to the left. "Stop."

Nikki's anger climbed to rage and she quickened her pace. Right. Left. The clatter of their feet echoed in the passageway. The odor of sea water intensified, and suddenly the bride disappeared. Nikki rushed on, then skidded to a stop. The staircase. She heard the bride tripping down the steps. They were steep, the stairwell tight, the walls rough with splintered boards.

But the bride charged downward with such speed, with such familiarity that Nikki knew who she was. In that moment, she realized she'd always known—but she didn't understand why. She followed, descending with caution, her pulse at full gallop. She hit the landing and stopped. They were in another corridor. The bride was twenty feet ahead. The gown had snagged on a nail, stopping her. She was trying to tug it free.

Nikki bolted for her.

The lace rent, and the bride moved quickly, popping

open the access into the parlor. Nikki caught her just as she started through and pulled her back into the passageway. "It's over, Olivia."

Chris's sister seemed to collapse inside, growing smaller before Nikki's eyes. "Why couldn't you just leave here?"

Nikki grabbed the veil and yanked it upward. Olivia looked even more pale surrounded in white. "I meant you no harm. Truly I didn't."

"Meant me no harm? You nearly killed me with that chisel."

Contrition issued from her dark eyes. "I only wanted to scare you away."

"What about Lorah? Did you poison her? Did you shove Dorothea from the third floor?"

"No." Olivia blinked. "Why would you even think such a thing?"

"If you could try to kill me, you're capable of killing anyone."

"I didn't try to kill you. Just to frighten you."

"Why?"

"Because you must be related to Theresa. You'll take Wedding House from me. It's the only thing I've ever had of my own."

Nikki stepped back, trying to grasp what was real and what wasn't—the anger that had propelled her this far dissolving into pity for this woman. "How long have you suspected I was related to Theresa?"

"From the first time I saw you in person."

Nikki recalled how she'd blanched at their first meeting, and knew Olivia must have suffered as bad a shock seeing her as Nikki had seeing the portrait.

"I helped Dot get you here and I was never so sorry. I tried getting the skit canceled."

"You called the actors' agents?"

"Yes."

A shadow swept the light behind Olivia. Nikki glanced up. A shovel arced down toward Olivia's head. Alarm paralyzed Nikki. "Look out!"

Olivia shifted just in time. The shovel missed her skull, but clipped her cheek. Groaning, she dropped like a felled tree.

"I killed you last night!" Jorge yelled, standing over Olivia, the shovel raised for another strike. "Why you no die?"

"Jorge, no!" Nikki shouted.

He froze and jerked toward her voice, peering squint-eyed into the passageway. Then he spotted her. He reared back, fury flaring scarlet on his half-melted face. "Jorge? Jorge? You cry the name of your lover, Theresa? The pig who stole your honor from me? Stole your heart? I spit on his dead soul." He raised the shovel again. "No one makes a fool of Luis De Vega and lives."

She leaped back out of his reach, her mind scrambling to catch up. Luis? Was it possible? In that second she knew it was. It made sense of everything—providing Olivia knew her uncle wasn't dead. Fear shot through Nikki. Spread across her tongue. Filled her nostrils. Sickened her. She struggled for courage. Found none. She stumbled away from the madman and his shovel.

She shouted, "Help! Someone help!"

She turned to run, but the shovel came down on her head. The world spun, then went black.

NIKKI WOKE in a place that stank of creosote and sea-water. The boathouse? How had she gotten here? She struggled to sit up. Pain kept her down. Closed her eyes. Nausea climbed her throat.

She moaned, drawing in a breath full of smoke and heat.

Why was she so hot? She heard it then. A crackling sound. Then another odd noise. Hissing.

She forced her eyes open and glanced around. Horror brought her wrenching upright. The wall leading outside and to the passageway connecting to the house was in flames. The fire licked across the creosote, hungrily racing over the aged boards and gobbling into the boxes and boxes of fireworks.

A whistling Pete ignited, drowning out her scream.

Chapter Seventeen

Chris emerged from the dining room, his mind on Nikki and her departure. It had been staved off for a few days because of Dorothea Miller's death, but she would still be leaving too soon. And forever.

His heart was a block of ice, slowly evaporating in the heat of his distress, shrinking with every passing hour that edged closer to the time she walked out of his life. And he could do nothing to prevent it. Would do nothing.

A loud moan floated to him from somewhere on the lower level. He stopped and listened. It came again. Frowning, he hurried into the parlor, then pulled up short. The passage access he'd boarded up the night of Nikki's fall had been broached again. It stood wide open. He gaped at it, anger igniting in him like a gas torch.

Another groan lured him closer. A pile of lace was heaped on the floor of the passageway. His gut clenched as images of last night's horror flashed through his head, riveting his feet. Dread coated his tongue. Had someone else been killed?

"Ah, oh, oh." The moan lifted from the lacy pile.

Chris shook himself and rushed into the corridor.

"Dear God, Liv, what happened? What are you doing in here? Dressed like this?"

She tried answering him, but winced as he lifted her. Her cheek looked smashed. He swore. "You need a doctor."

"No. Not yet. Listen to me, Christopher."

He cradled her on his lap and felt a new fear grabbing his belly. Her eyes were feverish. He'd been so concerned about himself going insane, he hadn't been paying enough attention to his sister. "How did this happen?"

"Uncle Luis hit me."

"What? Are you telling me a ghost smashed your cheek?"

"He isn't dead."

"Yes, he is, Liv. For over twenty-five years."

"No. He's here. Pretending to be Jorge."

"What!" Had she lost it completely? "That's absurd."

"No, no." She clutched his shirtfront, pain slowing her speech, but clarity in her eyes. "One day, six months ago, I overheard Mama and him talking. He is Luis."

Chris could see she was serious. Not insane, but crazy with fear. His breath left him in a whoosh. He lifted her and carried her to the sofa, laying her down gently. "Why didn't you tell me?"

"Because I didn't want it to be true." Shame flashed into her eyes.

Chris, also, felt shame. Ashamed of his family. Horrified at his mother. Disappointed in his sister. "So, it was you posing as the ghost."

"Please don't hate me, Christopher. I didn't want Nikki to be Theresa's daughter, and I don't want her to claim Wedding House. I only wanted to scare her away.''

''Where is Luis?''

''He killed Dorothea. He's completely mad. He thought she was Theresa. He thought I was Theresa a moment ago. And now he has Nikki.''

''What!'' Chris jumped to his feet, swearing, fear stabbing his heart. ''Why didn't you tell me that immediately? Where did he take her?''

''Into the passageway.''

Terrified for Nikki, Chris darted into the corridor. ''Upstairs?''

''No.'' Olivia pointed in the opposite direction. ''Toward the outbuildings.''

Apprehension morphed into white-hot wrath as Chris ran for the boathouse calling Nikki's name. For the first time in his life he felt furious enough to kill. This was the day he had dreaded. The day he could no longer control the rabid blood that he'd inherited from his uncle. Rage flooded from the very depths of him, flowing into every limb, every pore, every nerve, every muscle until it consumed him. Drove him.

From the shadowy passage ahead, a familiar figure came rushing toward him, hefting a shovel. ''Luis.''

Luis De Vega froze. He glared at his nephew, his crazed eyes raking Chris from head to toe as though sizing up an opponent. ''Move aside and let me pass.''

''Where's Nikki?''

Confusion robbed Luis of his bluster. ''Nikki?''

Chris grasped Luis by the collar, all but choking him. ''Where is she?''

Sputtering, Luis struggled to free himself and managed to crack Chris on the shoulder with the shovel. Chris's rage shot higher. He wrenched the shovel from his uncle, knocking the older man to the floor. "Where is she?"

Luis gave a demented laugh. "Weep for your Theresa, Rameriz. For at long last, she is dead."

The words severed Chris's shriveled heart. In that moment he had never hated anyone as he hated this man. "I'll kill you."

Luis reared back in alarm. "No. I beg of you. Spare me."

Chris's stomach turned. How dare Luis beg for the very mercy he denied all of his victims? As though with a power beyond his control, Chris raised the shovel, the sharpest edge of the blade pointed directly at his uncle's vulnerable temple. One good swing and the man would be as dead as he should have been all these years.

Luis De Vega was every nightmare he'd ever had. How could his mother have adored and worshiped this monster? Protected him? Wanted Chris to emulate him? Convinced Chris he was the image of him? Sweat beaded his upper lip, flushed his body. He trembled, fighting the impulse to swing. But in the end, he couldn't stop himself. He rammed the shovel blade as hard as he could against the nearest stud. The solid wood cracked. Luis cried out as though the blade had found his head, instead of the wall.

He cowered, sobbing.

Chris tossed aside the shovel and raced down the corridor toward the boathouse. Something inside him burst free, like a bird fleeing a brass cage. He couldn't kill. Anger didn't control him. He controlled it.

He wasn't like Uncle Luis at all.

Oh, Lord, had he learned it too late for Nikki and him? "Oh, please, God, no! No! Nikki!"

The air should have tasted of seawater by now. Instead he caught an unfamiliar acrid stench. Smoke. His throat clogged with terror. "Nikki!"

He heard it then, the roar of fire, the explosion of fireworks, and the terrified cry of the woman he loved and couldn't reach.

Chapter Eighteen

Smoke fogged the inside of the boathouse, a smothering, blinding blanket. Nikki choked, coughed and ducked, covering her head with her hands as fireworks ignited and zipped unseen through the compact space. Sparks burst around her. Over her. Rained down on her. Singed her clothing. Her hair. Her flesh.

It was a war zone. The sounds, the smells, the throat-clogging fear.

The fire, fed by creosote, crackled as it devoured the old building with a speed she hadn't imagined possible. She had to get out before the roof collapsed. Before one of the Roman candles found her.

Killed her.

The only way was through the boat slips. She inched along the flooring, groping as she moved, recalling the first time she'd gazed into those bottomless black pits and thought that someone could die dropping into one of them. Now, she'd give all she had to find one and plunge into it. If she had to die, let it be swift.

Another burst of fireworks threatened to give her her wish. She darted ahead and found the edge of a slip. She cried out in relief. Water. Ice-cold water. The tide was in. She dove in headfirst, gasping as the cold engulfed her overheated body. She surfaced, pulled in air, but couldn't get a lungful. Too much smoke. She gulped and ducked below the surface.

A loud crack resounded overhead. The roof. She kicked out and away. She wouldn't be able to hold her breath her usual three minutes. Terror grabbed her belly. Could she make it past the collapsing boathouse and into safe waters?

Driven by panic and the will to live, she scissored her legs as hard as she could. Something heavy bumped her foot, threatened to drag her down. She felt a surge and was lifted, then dropped. She needed air. Now. She scanned the surface, gazing toward the light. Over her, the water was alive with burning timbers.

She turned left. Right. Left again. Which way was out? Nikki's lungs ached to bursting, but she couldn't find a safe place to surface. Something grabbed her from below. Horror shot through her. She kicked at it. Wanted to scream. Couldn't.

Then a face hovered near hers. Chris. She stopped struggling.

Seconds later he lifted her up and out of the water. Nikki gulped air. Glorious salty air. She hugged Chris, clung to him as he carried her onto the lawn. Black smoke blotted out the blue sky. Fire trucks, firefighters and fire hoses seemed everywhere, trying to contain the flames and what was left of the cabana. Police officers seemed to be in abundance, too.

She gazed at Chris and choked out, "Luis."

"I know." He nodded. "They're taking him away now."

"Olivia?"

"She's going to the hospital. And so are you."

THE CAR STARTED down the drive through the tunnel of maples, the last leg of the drive back from the hospital, and Nikki's stomach tightened with the same uneasy sensation she'd suffered the first night she'd traveled this lane. Although that journey had been a little over a week ago, it felt like a year.

Beside her, Olivia sat in stony silence. Her smashed cheekbone had been mended with what she called wizardry surgery, some wire and plastic, the incisions hardly visible. She would be as good as new in a matter of time.

The aftereffects of Nikki's concussion, headache and dizziness were lessening, her bruised ankle no longer swollen but still achy, and myriad burns, tender but healing.

The car emerged onto the flat, open area laid in brick, and Nikki had her first glance of the devastation. Her breath caught. Only the blues and greens and golds of the rolling hillside, sparkling bay and velvet sky were as she remembered.

The De Vega Mansion hadn't caught fire, but its white stucco, black wrought-iron trim and crimson roof tiles looked scorched, smudged and dirty—as though its true colors showed for the first time.

Wedding House.

She shivered. Had a mansion ever been more inappropriately named? This was not a house of romance and love. It was the site of betrayal and murder, thriving on lies and secrets, destroying the emotionally wounded.

But at last the veil had been stripped away, and now the healing could begin.

"Oh, Christopher." Olivia spoke for the first time since leaving the hospital. "It's awful."

"It's all repairable, Liv. Never weep for a building. People are what count." Chris smiled at his sister, then at Nikki, a warm lingering look full of promises they'd yet to make, a future they'd yet to discuss.

"I guess it does give a better view of the bay," Olivia conceded, climbing out of the car.

Chris helped Nikki into the house, even though she insisted she could maneuver on her own. In spite of her protests, she adored his attentiveness.

"Welcome." Diego Sands held the door open for them. His manner was more subdued than ever, resigned even, as though the events of the past days had somehow affected him as deeply as the trio he was greeting. "Mrs. Grissom has lunch prepared. It's just the four of us now. Ms. Wolf left yesterday—said she was anxious to get home and finish her book."

"Holy Joe," Chris groaned, but there was no anger in his eyes, just acceptance.

"She left this for you." Diego handed Chris a prescription bottle. It was Dorothea's missing painkillers. Chris raised his brows questioningly.

Diego said, "Ms. Wolf claims she found it in the hallway the night Dorothea died. In the confusion and shock, she picked it up and put it in her pocket, then later wasn't sure what to do about it. So she hung on to it, but now she thought you should have it."

The four retreated to the dining room and sat across from one another. "Before we eat, Nikki, Olivia and I have something to say to you."

"Please, Christopher, may I?" Olivia twisted her hands together. "I want to apologize to you again for my behavior, Nikki. I don't know if you can ever forgive me, but I hope someday you will find it in your heart. I am going into therapy for my bulimia. Meantime our plans to open a bed and breakfast are being disbanded. Chris and I are relinquishing all claims on Wedding House. As Theresa's daughter, it rightfully belongs to you.''

Nikki was overwhelmed. She hadn't expected this, didn't even want it. If she had her way, the mansion would be imploded, the property allowed to revert to its original wild condition.

Diego choked on his coffee. "Ms. Navarro is not Theresa's daughter."

"She's not?'' Chris gaped at the architect.

"I'm not?"

"No,'' Diego said. "Theresa had no children."

Nikki's throat dried. She'd been ready to claim the whole Aznar clan in Texas. Claim them, meet them, love them. She felt the foundations of her life slipping once more, the old coldness looming, pinching. "But…''

"How do you know?'' Olivia demanded, looking offended that her generous offer was about to be squelched.

"You once asked me how I knew Theresa Aznar.'' Diego scooted his chair back and faced her. "You do look so like her.''

Nikki clasped her hands on the table, trying to stop the quaking. "I asked how well you knew her.''

"And where I knew her.'' His eyes were not unkind, but his words were slicing away her life. "We grew up in the same tiny Texas town near the Mexican border. On opposite sides of the tracks. Theresa was the elder daughter of the wealthiest man in those parts. A daughter someone from the Sands family had no business even noticing.''

"But you and she…" Olivia encouraged as though sensing a real love story unfolding.

Diego glanced at Olivia, then back at Nikki. "She and her sister occasionally came into the ice-cream parlor where I worked. Theresa would make excuses to talk to me. She had a crush on me."

"And you on her?" Olivia sighed.

"Oh, no. No. Though until I came here looking for…until I came here, I didn't realize she thought I returned her feelings. When Theresa realized I hadn't come here for her, she began flirting with Jorge Rameriz, to make me jealous. But I wasn't the one driven insane with jealousy. Luis must have been aware Theresa had given her heart to another. I'm sure now that he thought the man was Jorge. From what I could glean from the diary, he must have suspected they were having an affair. I'd say that was why he killed them both."

"Then you're the one who found the diary after I stuffed it into the chair?" Nikki asked.

Diego nodded.

"Why did you leave that page in my room?"

"What page?"

"The diary page?"

"Ah, er, he didn't." Olivia's face was beet red. "I found the diary when I was cleaning Diego's room. I took it and left the page to spook you away from here, Nikki."

"Why did you come to see Theresa if you didn't love her?" Chris went to the sideboard, filled a cup with coffee and sat back down.

Diego sighed. "Ramon Aznar, Theresa's father, arranged for her to wed De Vega. After the wedding Theresa moved here, and her sister came to the ice-cream parlor alone. From the first, I had only had eyes for her.

I could never dare hope that she would love me in return. But she did. We both knew her papa would see me imprisoned if he discovered what we'd done. When she found out she was pregnant, I had to risk that. I went to Ramon. I begged for her hand in marriage.

"As we'd feared he would, he had me thrown in jail on trumped-up charges. To hide his shame, Ramon sent Carmella here to her sister. As soon as I was out of jail and had saved enough money, I came looking for Carmella and our child."

"My mother's name was Carmella." The breath jammed in Nikki's throat. Her pulse thrummed. "Are you telling me you're my father?"

He pulled a framed photograph from his pocket and passed it to her. "If this woman was your mother..."

"That's the photograph you had on your bedside table," Chris stated.

"Yes." Diego nodded.

Nikki took the frame in both of her shaking hands. The dark-haired beauty staring up at her was the woman who had raised her. Tears sprang into her eyes, fell freely down her cheeks and her heart thumped with joy. Carmella was her real mother. And, at long last, Nikki had found her father. She gazed at Diego Sands, seeing him in a whole new light.

Olivia said, "But you and Carmella both had brown eyes, and dark hair, how could you have a blue-eyed, blond-haired daughter?"

Diego shrugged. "It happens. A throwback. If you've any doubts, a simple DNA test will—"

"No." Nikki stopped him. "I don't have any doubts. But why didn't you come for us?"

"When Theresa found out I hadn't come here for *her,* she refused to tell me anything. And since Carmella had changed her name, I had no way of finding you. But you must know, I've never stopped looking. Hoping.''

He reached across the table, and for the first time in her life, Nikki took her father's hands in hers. Heat spread through her fingers, up her arms and straight into her heart, scattering the teeny chips of ice that had lingered from the cold spot.

"But why didn't she ever try to contact you?" Olivia sounded outraged.

"I can only guess. Ramon must have told Carmella her baby would be given away the moment it was born. My Carmella would never have given our child away. I now suspect she probably never told Theresa where she was going. Any contact with anyone from the past would have brought Ramon and his vengeance down on her.''

"Why did you take the diary, Diego?" Chris asked, in a tone that suggested he would keep on protecting Nikki whether she'd found her father or not.

Diego made a face. "I'd hoped there might be something in it that would tell me where to find Carmella or Nikki. There wasn't.''

"Well, I am happy for you, Nikki. And you, too, Diego. This is wonderful news." Olivia sank back in her chair, the look of expectation that had been in her eyes flattened. "And it still means Wedding House is yours, Nikki.''

"I don't want it," Nikki said. "As far as I'm concerned, it belongs to you and Chris, and I'll sign any legal agreement to that effect.''

"Are you sure?" Chris studied her intently. "It's worth a lot of money. You could sell—''

"I don't want a penny from this place," Nikki interrupted him. "It has brought my family nothing but unhappiness."

"Mine, too." He caught his sister's hand, his expression glum. "We'll have to deal with it, Liv, along with Mother and Uncle Luis."

The silence in the room expanded. Nikki sighed. "Did anyone ever figure out how Lorah managed to make all those things happen during the séance?"

Again, Olivia's cheeks went crimson. "Dorothea and I helped Lorah. We sneaked her assistant into and out of the master suite via the passageways. When everyone was downstairs after the ambulance left, he removed his equipment."

"You knew it was a sham all along?" Chris scowled.

"It seemed so important at the time."

"How did you manage the shadowy images I saw of Theresa? Holograms or something?"

Olivia looked completely confused. "I don't know what you're talking about. There was never a shadowy image."

Nikki's breath snagged in her throat. Olivia had no more reason to lie. Then who? What?

Theresa?

Had the bride actually haunted this house all these years, waiting for her secret to be revealed? Nikki felt suddenly certain of it, and she prayed Theresa had finally found peace and the power to move on, now that her killer no longer stalked Wedding House.

NIKKI AND HER FATHER sat alone in the library, discussing everything from favorite colors to Carmella. She learned he'd never married, never given up hope of finding his beloved and their child. They made plans to visit Texas, to introduce her to all the relatives on both sides of her extensive family. Nikki couldn't wait. She e-mailed her editor for an extension on her book deadline.

On the way back to her room she found Chris standing in the master suite, staring at the portrait. He looked so handsome and so lost, she yearned to comfort him. The days ahead would be tough on him and his sister, perhaps some of the toughest they'd ever faced, and God knew, they'd had their share of difficulties. She sidled up to him.

He lurched around. "I thought yours was the only secret she was keeping."

Nikki looped her arm through his, feeling a protective instinct of her own. "Are you avoiding me?"

He glanced down at her. His black hair was mussed, as though he'd been digging his hand through it. His gaze warmed as it reached out to her, and her pulse fluttered. "I didn't want to intrude on you and your dad."

"'My dad.' Doesn't that sound great?"

"Yes." He pulled her close. "You'd have liked *my* dad. He'd have liked you. I wish he were here today."

He didn't say it, but she guessed he was thinking if his father hadn't died when he was young, his mother might never have gone along with Luis. Might not be in such dire trouble now.

"We make our own destinies, Chris. You can't change the course your mother chose."

"She's facing prosecution as an accessory to murder—Theresa's, Jorge's, the maid and cook's, and for harboring a criminal, Luis, which led to Dorothea's death, perhaps Lorah Halliard's." He sounded bitter and deeply sad. "Despite the garbage she thrust on Liv and me, hell, despite everything, I can't desert her."

"I didn't expect you to. And I won't ask you to."

"But I want to. At this moment I want nothing more than to walk away with you and never look back. I want to spend the rest of my life making you happy." He kissed her long and hard, but looked even sadder as he pulled back. "But right now I'm not sure I can make anyone happy."

"You're not doing too badly…"

His smile was melancholy. "I've been weighing my options, Nikki. Liv isn't the only one who needs counseling. I've spent so many years suppressing my emotions, I feel like a dam splitting its seams. I don't like the feeling. I need to find a balance, to understand and accept myself."

Sorrow raked her soul. Once again she was losing this man she loved with such desperation. But as much as it broke her heart, she knew they couldn't be together until they were both whole. They were mending, but they needed to face their feelings for each other when they could do it honestly and openly, to see if his passion was based on more than rage. To see if hers was based on more than need. "And I have to get to know my father, my family in Texas."

It would have been too easy to fall into bed, to make love and pretend the rest didn't matter. But neither wanted that. Chris held her throughout the night.

As THEY SAID GOODBYE the next morning, Nikki hugged Chris tightly. "I'll call the minute I know where we're staying."

"You'd better," Chris whispered in her ear. "Because as soon as this is over, I'm coming for you."

"I'm holding you to that." A sob welled inside her.

"I'm not sure I'll be able to stand being parted from you. I love you so much it's breaking my heart."

"No, no. Don't be sad. You *are* my future. I won't let you down." He cupped her face in his hands. "I love you, Nikki, with every ounce of my being. We'll talk every day. Twice a day."

She laughed, then they kissed to seal their loving pledge, and she climbed inside the car next to her father. As the taxi edged away, Nikki glanced back at Chris through the rear window, wondering if she would see him again, if they really had a future. She made a silent promise, to Chris and to herself. "If you don't come for me, Chris Conrad, I *will* be back for you."

Epilogue

Eighteen months later

Nikki stared at Chris's image in her cheval mirror. He was breathtakingly handsome in his gray suit, but she would never get ready for the grand opening of Olivia's new establishment if she kept admiring him. She hurried into her dress, pleased that it accommodated her wondrous secret. "Could you zip me, darling?"

Chris came and stood behind her, kissing her neck as he worked the zipper. She nuzzled him. "At times like this I can't believe I walked away from you thinking we might never have a chance together."

Chris laughed, their gazes locking in the reflective glass. "Or that I thought I could find my center without you—when you are my center."

"Good thing we came to our senses within the month." Nikki grew serious, caressing his clean-shaven cheek. "I wasn't whole until you came for me. Until we married."

"Nor I, my love." He turned her in his arms and kissed her, roused her. The passion she'd worried would be lost had never burned stronger, deeper. He hugged her to his side, gazed at her adoringly. "I couldn't have made it through the trial without you."

His mother had been convicted of harboring a criminal and as an accessory in Dorothea Miller's murder, and was now serving her sentence in a state correctional facility. His uncle was in a mental institution for the criminally insane. Lorah Halliard's death had been attributed to natural causes. Her doctor discovered she'd had an undetected heart condition and had very likely overtaxed herself conducting the séance.

"Your dad and Liv are waiting downstairs." Chris looked at her approvingly. "Are you ready?"

"Yes."

In the living room of their new penthouse in downtown Seattle, Chris poured champagne into four glasses and handed one to Nikki, his father-in-law and his sister.

Olivia Conrad had blossomed. Her raven hair was clipped to her chin and flowed free around her face. No longer pale, but tanned and glowing, she'd given up black completely for a rainbow hue of pastel colors.

Diego beamed at his daughter and son-in-law. "Here's to the continued and prosperous success of Conrad-Sands Unlimited, Inc. May we soon be designing and building more structures like this one."

No one seemed to notice Nikki setting her drink on the coffee table next to her latest book and Marti McAllister Wolf's new bestselling mystery, *The Ghost Talks*.

Chris lifted his glass and turned to his sister. "Here's to the success of the Conrad Clinic. May all your patients overcome their eating disorders under your skilled and generous guidance, Liv."

Olivia Conrad blushed. Wedding House had been

sold to a wealthy Arab. Chris and Nikki hadn't wanted any of the money and had given their portion to Dorothea's family. Olivia was using hers to open an inpatient clinic to help women like herself.

Nikki left the champagne on the table. She linked her arm with her husband's. "This is a great day for the Conrad family. We're on our way to repairing the damage of the older generation."

"Long live the new generation." Diego raised his glass.

"I'll drink to that," Chris said.

"So would I." Nikki sighed. "But I think you'd better make mine sparkling cider."

Chris's eyes rounded questioningly. "Don't you feel well?"

"I feel grand, but I've been keeping a little secret from you all." She grinned at Liv, then her dad and finally at the man she loved more than life. "The first of the new generation will be here in about six months. And I want him as whole and healthy as his father."

HARLEQUIN®
INTRIGUE®

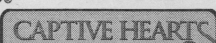

From Hostages to Prisoners of Passion—
Held at gunpoint in a mysterious crime,
three women are soon bound by desire
to the men sworn to protect them
at all costs....

Look for this heart-pounding new series coming
to you only from Harlequin Intrigue!

July 1999
#521 FATHER, LOVER, BODYGUARD
by Cassie Miles

August 1999
#526 HIS TO PROTECT
by Patricia Werner,

September 1999
#529 THE SAFE HOSTAGE
by Cassie Miles

**In twenty-four hours,
their lives change forever....**

Don't miss

CAPTIVE HEARTS!

Available wherever Harlequin books are sold.

HARLEQUIN®

I N T R I G U E®

COMING NEXT MONTH

#525 AFTER DARK by Rebecca York and Caroline Burnes
43 Light Street and Fear Familiar—a special 2-in-1 Intrigue!
Two couples must hide from the day...and anything can happen after dark....
Counterfeit Wife by Rebecca York—When a madman comes after her, Marianne pretends to be Tony's wife—and can no longer deny the desire burning between them....
Familiar Stranger by Caroline Burnes—When Molly's son is kidnapped, she has no choice but to find her mystery lover—and tell him of their son's existence....

#526 HIS TO PROTECT by Patricia Werner
Captive Hearts
In twenty-four hours, three women's lives were forever changed in a hostage crisis. Now Tracy Meyer must put back the pieces and fight to keep her stepdaughter, while sexy cop Matt Forrest moves in to protect them from the hostage taker's revenge....

#527 ONE TEXAS NIGHT by Sylvie Kurtz
A Memory Away...
In the heat of a Texas night Melinda Amery found herself staring into the double-barreled blue eyes of Lieutenant Grady Sloan. And he wanted answers about the murder of her neighbor. Only, she didn't have them—didn't have any. She had amnesia. But Grady was the type of man who wouldn't let go until he got what he wanted. And that included Melinda....

#528 MY LOVER'S SECRET by Jean Barrett
Only one man could protect Gillian Randolph from the madman who stalked her: private investigator Cleveland McBride. Their sultry past aside, Gillian trusted Cleve with her heart, but could she trust him with her secret child...?

Look us up on-line at: http://www.romance.net